RESTING IN MY SOUL

Tracing Threads of Myth and Memory

Frank Fitzpatrick

Resting in My Soul

by

Frank Fitzpatrick

This is a work of fiction. While it may reference real events, places, and public figures, it remains a fictional interpretation. Any depictions, dialogue, or perspectives expressed are the author's own creation and should not be regarded as factual representations. Any resemblance to actual persons, living or dead, outside of those explicitly mentioned is purely coincidental.

Dedicated to the memory of my grandfather, Captain Michael Smyth, an IRA Volunteer active during the 1916 Rebellion, the Irish War of Independence, and the Irish Civil War.

ACKNOWLEDGEMENTS

I would like to express my gratitude to the Bobby Sands Trust for their kind permission to reproduce an excerpt from Bobby Sands' poem *The Rhythm of Time*.

Additionally, I would like to acknowledge the reproduction of numerous excerpts from the works of W. B. Yeats, Padraig Pearse, Friedrich Nietzsche, William Shakespeare, George Bernard Shaw, Charles O'Neill, James Joyce, Margaret Fuller, Lady Jane Wilde, John M. Synge, Seán Mac Diarmada, Padraic Colum, John K. Ingram, William Kenealy, Dante Alighieri, Edgar Allan Poe, Diogenes Laertius, Lord Byron, and Immanuel Kant. Their works have deeply shaped the ideas and themes explored throughout my book, *Resting in My Soul*.

CONTENTS

PART ONE

CHAPTER 1

"Would you ever sit down, Ma?" Mammy said as Granny came in from the cold scullery holding two plates.

I paid little attention to her, taken by flames dancing in the blazing hearth, leaping and jigging on the black tops of searing red coals, throwing flickers of light and shadow across the tired wallpaper. It was a warm and happy room, but I knew the rest of the house hadn't seen a fire for a long time. Granny placed one of the plates in front of her empty chair and, with an unsteady hand, extended the other one towards me, over the salt and pepper, past the butter dish, and safely landed it between my knife and fork.

There were two sausages, two slices of fried bread, and a dollop of baked beans that was perilously close to overflowing. Granda looked at my plate, winked, and gave me one of his rashers. "That's the one to make your hair curly."

I blushed. "Thanks, Granda."

The table was pulled out from the wall to

accommodate Mammy and me, and there was "hardly enough room to swing a cat." That's what Granda used to say, and I always thought it was funny. Sometimes, I imagined him trying to swing a cat by the tail. Thankfully, they didn't have a cat, only a dog, a black cocker spaniel called Soot. He was old and cranky and spent most of his time curled in Granny's armchair, which was usually by the fireplace but this evening was shoved into the alcove beside the chimney breast. In the other alcove, Granda's armchair was pressed against his bookcase, which was stuffed with Yeats, and Pearse, and Tone, and Marx, and Russian names I couldn't pronounce. On top of the bookcase was his old box radio which had pride of place, especially if he was listening to it.

One time, I came bursting into the room to be greeted by a stern look and a snappy shush from Granny. Granda was softly singing along to the radio, John McCormack's "*Ireland Mother Ireland*," and I stopped dead in my tracks, not knowing what to do, until he reached out and pulled me closer. I remember his voice grew a little stronger, as though he wanted me to understand the words;

"If you sigh, we hear you
If you weep, we weep
In your hours of gladness
How our pulses leap
Ireland, Mother Ireland!
Let what may befall
Ever shall we hold you
Dearest—best of all
Ever shall we hold you
Dearest—best of all."

On finishing the song, he smiled and jostled my belly.

"Ever shall we hold you, Ireland," he said, holding me playfully. "Ever shall we hold you."

I laughed when his jostle became a tiddle, but not too much because I knew he wanted me to hold Ireland in my heart, to love Ireland like I loved Mammy. He didn't have to worry; I really did love Ireland. I even knew the national anthem by heart, and at family hoolies, I always sang "*Kevin Barry*." My Auntie Eibhlin used to say, "Aren't you the great little rebel?" I always felt proud when she said that.

Back at the table, I started on Granda's rasher, but sitting closest to the fire, I was half-roasted in my big Aran jumper that my other granny knit for me. I had two grannies and one granda; my other granda died before Mammy and Daddy got married, and my other granny was my favourite. She used to mind me when I was a baby and Daddy always said, "You're me mother's pet, that's for sure." I was her "Bubbles;" that's what she called me. She thought I looked like a little boy called Bubbles who was on a soap advertisement when she was young. I liked that she had a special name for me, but when my friends on the road found out, they started jeering. I didn't mind too much because I knew Bubbles was a funny name for a boy.

Then, Dermo Doherty, who lived around the corner, started jeering Granny for calling me Bubbles, so I kicked the shins off him. He was older than me, and I lost the fight, but he stopped jeering Granny. I think he knew I'd keep fighting him if he kept jeering her.

"Will you take that big yoke off you," Mammy said, still annoyed because I hadn't wanted to visit Granny and Granda that day. I was playing Cowboys and Indians with the street gang when she called me away.

A bead of sweat trickled down my spine, and I wondered if I was starting to melt. But, even if I was, I didn't want to take my jumper off because Granny knit it for me. Instead, I wolfed down the food. "Can I go outside? I'm finished."

Granda's eyes glinted. "That's a fine jumper, alright. Off you go."

Outside, my breath crystallised in the chilled evening air, and I huffed all the warm oxygen from my lungs, creating magical clouds, until I grew lightheaded.

The moon was gleaming on the frosted roofs of the huddled terraced houses that ran along the opposite side of the narrow lane at the back of Granny and Granda's small yard. On top of the glistening white slates stood a neat line of darkened chimney pots, each with a trail of smoke snaking into a breathless sky, and the imagery made me think about Santy.

I tried to calculate how many weeks it was to Christmas. I couldn't. So, I looked around the yard for an alternative diversion, even though I knew there was nothing else of interest except for the outside toilet with the big gaps above and below its door. I wondered about doing a number two on such a cold night, outside, in the dark. I considered the big bolt on the inside of the door, which was big enough to stop a full-on Indian attack, but I still didn't fancy doing my number two there, in the dark. Maybe I would if I was dying to go and there was nowhere else, and if they had proper toilet paper, not the cut-up newspapers that Granny and Granda used. I thought about the poor people in Africa who didn't even have an outside toilet or anything to wipe their bum with. I wondered how that worked, and what about cowboys? What did they use? Maybe they had some newspapers, but what about the Indians?

The yard was boring, and, for no particular reason,

I decided to stand completely still with outstretched arms and legs, like a starfish. It wasn't long before the icy darkness closed my pores, and the clammy cauldron between my skin and Granny's jumper quickly turned cold, driving me back inside to the blazing heat with the crisp evening air clinging to my clothes.

The plates had been cleared, and the tablecloth wiped clean. There was a cup of tea, the *Evening Press*, and an ashtray in front of Granda. Mammy was standing with Granny by the curtainless sash window in a plume of bluish smoke, talking under their breath about Uncle Joe's drinking.

"He was here last night, legless," Granny whispered. "Your Da was goin to put him out."

"And why wouldn't you put him out?" Mammy said.

"He has his troubles with that wan; God knows he has."

"He married her, Ma. He's a man now with a family. I know he's the white-haired boy, but he can't be upsetting Da, not now."

"Sure, don't I know."

Their lit cigarettes peered from their reflections in the black glass, and I imagined there were demons in the yard, pretending to be Granny and Mammy. I watched them mimic every move until the burning eyes stared right at me and scared me into sitting beside Granda. He took a sip of his tea, smiled, and lifted the newspaper. "I'll just see what's going on in the world." Then he shook his head in disbelief and looked towards Mammy and Granny. "They shot Che Guevara." Mammy and Granny weren't listening. "Do you see that fella, Con?" The newspaper showed a photograph of a bearded man wearing a black beret. "That's Che Guevara. His people came from Galway. Lynch."

"Why did they shoot him?" I asked.

He thought for a moment. "I suppose they didn't like what he stood for."

"What did he stand for?"

"You're a great man for the questions. Eh, he stood for the people. He stood against repression."

My heart began to race because I knew this was my chance to let him know that I knew. Unlike his other grandchildren, I knew. I knew who he used to be. "Was 1916 important Granda?" The words escaped before I decided to say them.

Mammy and Granny must have heard me because they fell silent, turning their heads to see his response. He looked at Granny, and she gave a near imperceptible nod before he beckoned me closer. "Would you like me to tell you about it?"

"Yes, Granda." I moved and stood at his knee.

Granny and Mammy eyed each other as if to say, well, now, we weren't expecting that. But I ignored them and gave Granda my undivided attention.

He placed the milk jug in the middle of the bright plaid oilskin tablecloth. "This is the GPO—Headquarters.". He moved the sugar bowl, thought again, and repositioned it. "This is Jacob's, this is where I was, on the roof." The saucer became Mount Street Bridge. The cup, Boland's Mills. The Evening Press was the Liffey, and so on. After conscripting his cigarette packet, a box of matches, Granny's glasses, and other bits and pieces, he explained the day-to-day actions of the Easter Week Rebellion. I was enthralled, and he was delighted to regale me with his exploits until he began explaining their surrender. Then I could see his mind was no longer in the kitchen but marching forlornly along the quays with his comrades, to prison or execution.

I put my hand on his hand, the same way my other Granny did with me when my dog died, and a smile creased his sad, resolute face. "There's not much else I can tell you about 1916."

I wanted to say something big, something comforting, but I didn't know how. Instead, I squeezed his finger. He patted my small hand and, looking into the middle distance, spoke to someone only visible to him. "We marched out Easter Monday, sixteen hundred part-time volunteers against sixteen thousand heavily armed British soldiers. I had a rifle and a handful of bullets. A blood sacrifice, Pearse said."

"Wasn't Ma pregnant with Bridget?" Mammy said.

"She was, but..."

I interrupted. "What's a blood sacrifice, Granda?"

He shifted his focus from Mammy to the invisible person. "It was a message in blood to the English King." His voice was steely. "It said, this is not your country. We are not your people. Get out of our country."

My arms got goosebumps.

Mammy's brow was furrowed. "But Da," she said, "did you...?" Granny's eyes pooled, and she touched Mammy's arm, halting any further questions.

He looked at me, although he was talking to someone else, maybe himself. "We didn't know then that we'd win an independent Ireland. How could we? But we had to let them know that we were right and they were wrong."

"You had to send the message." The words spilled from my young lips with a strange inner sense of certainty. "You had to tell him," I said, feeling every inch a little Rebel, ready to join the fight.

"He's getting that from Eibhlin," Mammy said to Granny. "She's teaching him rebel songs and poems I never even heard of."

With tightened lips, Granda took my two hands in his. "That's right, we had to tell him." His hands were warm and unexpectedly soft, and he appeared to be looking for something in my face, searching my eyes. "We got our courage to fight the greatest military power in the world from our ancient spirit. That's what cracked their Empire, our ancient Irish spirit."

"Eibhlin is teaching him songs, Da."

"Is she now?"

I nodded.

"Will you sing one for me? I'd love to hear a song."

"It's not a song, it's a poem."

"Better still. Stand out there in the middle of the floor. Head up, shoulders back, and make Ireland proud."

I moved to the only bit of clear space in the room. "It's called *Before the Battle,* I think. I'm learning it for the Christmas hoolie."

"Aunty Eibhlin won't mind," Mammy said, "if you give us a practice run. I think your Granda will like it."

"I will, for sure. I'm dying to hear it."

"Stand up straight," Mammy said, looking delighted for me and for Granda.

I stood to attention and saluted the way Aunty Eibhlin told me. All three of them smiled and Mammy put her hand to her mouth.

"Stand ye now for Erin's glory. Stand ye now for Erin's cause.

Long ye've groaned beneath the rigour of England's savage laws.

They have razed our proudest castles—spoiled the Temples of the Lord.

Burned to dust the sacred relics—put the Peaceful

to the sword.

Desecrated all things holy—as they soon may do again,

If their power to-day we smite not—if to-day we be not men.

God of heaven, bless our banner—nerve our sinews for the strife.

Fight we now for all that's holy—for our ancient spirit, land and life.

Men of Erin! Men of Erin! Grasp the battle-axe and spear!

Chase these foreign wolves before you like a herd of frightened deer.

Burst their ranks, like bolts from heaven, down on the heathen crew,

For the glory of our slain, and Erin's glory too!"

Granda was looking at me with eyes of admiration and pride. "*Maith an buachaill!* That's a powerful recitation: come here to me till I shake your hand. If we had the likes of you in 1916, we'd have finished them in jig time." I floated over to him, and as he took my hand, he produced a shilling from his waistcoat pocket. "That's for you, son; well done. *Maith an buachaill.* You're a great little Rebel."

"You better tell Eibhlin," Granny said to Mammy. "He's only ten. Let her teach him a few prayers for her sins."

Mammy said something back, laughing, but I was too focused on Granda to hear it. He took me by the two shoulders and, drawing me close, spoke in a hushed tone, "I'll tell you a secret about the time before my first battle." His lips were now beside my ear, and he whispered, ever so seriously, ever so resolutely, "I stood in a room without a flame, something rustled on the floor, someone called me by my name. It was my ancient spirit's call to war."

My body shivered as if someone passed through me called my name. I was trembling inside, but my heart gushed with belief—in what, I can't be sure. He sat back in his chair, put his hand on my head, and uttered the last words I remember him saying. "You have the ancient spirit in you. I can see it. It's a precious thing. Never lose it. Promise me that Con."

"I promise, Granda," I said, with all the integrity a ten-year-old boy could muster.

* * *

I'm not sure when Mammy said Granda was sick, but it wasn't too long after our visit and shortly after that, he was dead. I cried when Daddy told me, and I remember he took my face in his big, strong hands before wiping my tears with his two thumbs. "Big boys cry, too," he said.

"I didn't want him to... die, Dad. I wanted to say my poem for him at the Christmas hoolie."

"I know. But it was his time to go. He was sick, and it's better that he went when he did. Didn't you say your poem for him when you were last down? Mammy said he was delighted and so proud of you."

"Aunty Eibhlin says he'll never be dead while I'm alive."

"Your Aunty Eibhlin says a lot, but you wouldn't want to take all she says to heart. She lives in her own little world—you know that sort of way?"

"Yeah. But is it OK to say the poems and songs she taught me?"

"Yes, it's OK."

"Is it OK to love Ireland?"

"Yes, that too," he smiled, a tight-lipped smile with loving eyes. "But you can't forget your sums, spellings, and geography."

"I know, Dad."

Mammy, Granny, and me were sitting in the mourners' car outside Saint Peter's church when Dev, the President of Ireland, leaned in the window. I'd seen him before, on the telly, but I was still surprised at how old and frail he looked. "I'm sorry for your troubles, Katie," he said to Granny. "Mick was a good man."

Granny had a frosty face on her from the minute he put his elbow on the car roof. Her narrow shoulders squared and she threw her head back in an uncompromising air before nodding acceptance of his condolences, showing no deference to his Presidential office. He lingered, presumably thinking she was going to thank him for coming to the funeral. "In the end," she said, with a look that would slice steel, "he knew he shouldn't have gone with you. You let him down."

"I'm truly sorry to hear that," the President said before inhaling a long, slow breath. Mammy and me stopped breathing, waiting for him to exhale. "When he came up to the Aras a few years ago, on his retirement, we talked about old times. We had words, alright, about Collins and the split. But I thought he understood."

"He understood enough," Granny said, clipping her words, "to come home and take your picture off the wall."

The president looked wounded. "Well, sure," he said, "that's the way of it. I don't think history will be too kind to me." Granny said nothing, and he looked at Mammy with an uncomfortable smile. She returned a polite, nervous grin. He straightened to his full height and was about to walk away when he wavered and bent back down to the window, extending his hand inside. "Sinead sends her condolences." I watched with bated breath as his long, sinewy hand invaded our space, and I couldn't tell if Granny was going to shake it. She did, without hesitation, and a growing caustic knot of anxiety subsided in my belly.

After the burial, all the adults went to the Brian Boru pub for drinks and sandwiches. Dad couldn't go because he had to be back in work, so he got the job of dropping me home.

"Are you alright?" Dad said before turning the car's ignition with an exaggerated, worried expression. We had an old Ford Prefect that didn't always start the first time or second time, and I waited for him to do his usual pleading. But the engine purred on the first turn, and he looked at me with pretend surprise. "New battery!" he said.

I liked it when he joked, and for a moment, my heart smiled. "I'll really miss Granda."

"I know." He put his hand on my knee with a little squeeze, and we were off, his right hand on the steering wheel, his other on my knee.

"Do you think he knew I loved him?"

"Oh, he knew alright. Weren't you his little Rebel?"

"Why does Granny not like Dev? Aunty Eibhlin says he's not the president of Ireland?"

"He's the president of the twenty-six counties. Most of Ireland. She thinks he wasn't nice to your granda."

"How does he know Granda?"

"In the old days, they fought the English together."

"Who's Sinead?"

"Dev's wife. She liked your granda."

"How was Dev not nice to Granda?"

"Eh, when Granda retired, they got into a big row over why he sent Collins to England."

"Who's Collins?"

He navigated a corner, turning the steering wheel with the heel of his hand. "Eh, he was the leader of the Irish army, fighting the English. Your granda had a lot of time for him."

"Aunty Eibhlin said that Dev told Granda why he sent Collins?"

"Aunty Eibhlin would say Mass. Whatever he told your granda, it wasn't what he wanted to hear."

"How do you know?"

"I don't really—he never said. But he came home, took Dev's picture off the wall, and never spoke about him again."

"Do you think Granda told Granny, and that's why she doesn't like Dev?"

"Something like that. She blames him for leading Granda into the Civil War."

"Why did Granda leave all his books to me?"

"Probably because he knew you were a smart little rebel."

"I started reading the one about... eh... his name is Wolf."

"Wolfe Tone?"

"Yeah, him. But it has some very big words that I don't know."

"I didn't think you started reading them already."

He paused and pursed his lips. "What about if you get a big Oxford English Dictionary for Christmas?"

"Instead of new football boots!?"

He laughed, his full-bellied laugh. "No, of course not. The boots are from Santy, the dictionary can be from me and Mam."

"Yeah. Thanks, Dad. Will you help me with the dictionary?"

"I will. But it won't be long before you're way ahead of me."

"Granda told me he was in a room without a flame, and something rustled on the floor. Someone called him by his name."

"Did he? I think it's from a poem by W. B. Yeats. He met him once."

"I keep hearing him saying it, really low. Then the words go whispering around in my head."

He patted my leg. "Try thinking about other things, about going to the pictures or the next match in Croke Park."

I didn't tell him I had a dream about the room without a flame. Everything was pitch dark—black—but I could hear the words creeping, rustling, whispering on the black floor.

Then someone from far away called my name in Irish. *"Conchobhar, Conchobhar Mac Cárthaigh."*

"Who do you think will win on Sunday?" I asked,

trying to think of other things.

"I'd say Kilkenny have it?"

"Were you a good hurler?" I knew he was.

"I was handy enough."

The traffic was heavy, and he was about to put his hand back on the steering wheel when I took it in mine and held on to it. "Tell me about the time you played with Mucky Meagher in Croke Park?" I had heard the story before, many times, but I liked watching him tell it. He continued steering with one hand, and we chatted about his hurling days.

"Are you going to school tomorrow?" he asked. "You can stay out for another day if you want. But I'd say Mr Flynn will be disappointed if you're not togging out against St Vincents." Mr Flynn was our new school teacher and hurling coach.

"I'll go in, Dad. We have to beat them because they made a show of us the last time."

He chuckled. "Is that what Mr Flynn said?"

"A holy show."

"You better go in so. And it'll take your mind off things."

* * *

We won the match by a point, and I cleared the ball from the goal mouth in the last few seconds of the game. It was coming in high; there was just me and their big, lanky, full forward in the box. I knew he'd pull on it as it came in, so I turned my arse to him, blocked his swing, and took a fierce clatter. My arse was stinging like mad, but I scooped the ball from the ground and whacked it down the field. Mr Flynn clapped his hands and shouted. "Good man, McCarthy! Good man. *Maith an buachaill.*"

The clatter left me limping for a week, and when I showed Mammy the bruising, she said, "Think of poor James Connolly, executed and him not even able to stand." It's what she always said if I got hurt, and it's what I always did. But that day on the pitch, I didn't need James Connolly. I offered up the pain for my granda.

The following week was our annual school trip, and I didn't know if I should go or not. "I'll have none of that," Mammy said. "Of course, you're going. Your granda wouldn't want you moping about. He'd want you to go and enjoy yourself. Isn't Finn going?"

"Yeah." Finn lived two doors away from me; we were best friends. Mammy always said that herself and Mrs Mulcahy used to put our two prams together, and "ye hit it off from day one." She knew we were best friends, but she didn't know we were blood brothers. We got the idea from watching *Lassie*, the television program. The two boys in the show took an oath after cutting their hands with a knife and sharing their blood. We decided to do the same. "I swear to be true and faithful," I said, "to my blood brother, Finn Mulcahy." He repeated the same oath for me."

St Aidan's was a working-class all-boys school, and

in previous years, some of the poorer children couldn't afford to go on the trip. But that year, Mr Flynn made sure every boy in the class was going.

We assembled at 8 a.m. outside the school gates, all buzzing with excitement, everyone jostling and slagging. The tour was to the ancient tomb of Poulnabrone in County Clare, but we didn't care where we were going—being free of school on a school day was more than enough.

Mulligan, one of the boys, raised his arm and shouted at Mr Flynn. "Sir, Sir!"

"Yes, Mulligan. I'm not deaf," Mr Flynn said, shaking his head. He was much younger than our last teacher, and that day, he looked even younger without his tweed jacket and matching tie. But I thought his jumper around his shoulders and his pink nylon shirt with drainpipe jeans were a bit too trendy for a teacher from St Aidan's.

"What did one wall say to the other wall?" Mulligan asked.

"I don't know," Mr Flynn replied, distracted. He was trying to count the boys getting on the bus.

"I'll meet you at the corner!" Mulligan hollered.

All the boys laughed. Mr Flynn smiled, shook his head again and threw his eyes to heaven.

"Sir, Sir!" another boy shouted. I couldn't see who it was.

"One more," Mr Flynn snapped, having lost his

count, "and then it's *bígí ciúin.* I'll count ye on the bus."

"Sir, why was the math book sad?"

"I don't know." He feigned a long, weary sigh and looked to Miss Clarke, the student teacher who was already onboard. "This is going to be a long day."

"It had too many problems, Sir."

Mr Flynn laughed in spite of himself. "Right, so, enough now. Form a single line." His tone had turned stern and we all knew to stop messing. "Any boy not in single file is not coming."

With all the boys onboard and seated, Mr Flynn counted each of our thirty-eight heads twice, and Miss Clarke handed each pupil a packet of Perry crisps and a small chocolate macaroon bar.

"Testing. *A haon, a do, a tri.*" Mr Flynn said into a crackly microphone. "*Ciúnas.* That's your mid-morning snack; it should keep you going till we have lunch at a hotel in Athlone. Try not to eat it now."

Finn was sitting beside me, and he pulled a long face. "Hotel!"

"Swanky," I said, sticking my nose in the air.

The bus started to pull away, and we all rushed to the side nearest the school, waving enthusiastically, "Bye. Bye. Bye, bye, bye." And then, without prompting or orchestration, we all burst into song.

"So long, it's been good to know you.

So long, it's been good to know you.

So long, it's been good to know you."

"That's it!" Mr Flynn boomed, standing in the aisle without the microphone. "Back in your seats. Now!"

We all settled into our seats and myself and Finn proceeded to demolish our mid-morning snack. After a while, Sherlock, who was sitting behind us, stuck his head between the seats and said, "I'm bored. Let's play a joke."

I didn't know him very well because he only joined our class the previous year. Unusually, he came from town and always wore Wellington boots, even when it was sunny. I knew he wasn't afraid of getting into trouble, and his joke could be anything from letting a fart to setting fire to the bus.

"What sort of joke?" Finn said, reading my mind.

"I'll spill Healy's lemonade on the floor and say someone did a piss." Healy was a timid boy who kept to himself and just happened to be sitting beside Sherlock.

Finn and me were in unspoken agreement that this was an acceptable level of misbehaviour. "OK," I said.

A moment passed, and then a growing puddle appeared under our feet. "Miss! Miss!" Sherlock shouted, in disgust. "Someone did their wee." There was no response from either teacher. I think Mr Flynn was asleep. "Miss! Miss!" Sherlock demanded. "The wee is goin' down your way." This was followed by an eruption of activity from the teachers' seats as Miss Clarke hurried to pull her bag from the floor.

Mr Flynn stood in the middle of the aisle, holding the seats on either side for balance—the bus was flat out. "If anyone even thinks of doing a wee on the bus, it will be the last wee they ever do." He started to move along the aisle, seat by seat, and it didn't take him long to discover that the pee trail began under our seat. Glowering, he stopped beside us, "Did either of you boys do a wee?"

Finn stayed silent.

"No, Sir," I said.

"Then where did it come from?"

"I don't know, Sir." I wasn't going to tell on Sherlock.

"Sir, maybe someone spilt somethin'," Sherlock piped up.

"Ah, Sherlock," Mr Flynn said, with a puzzle-solving face, "maybe someone spilt something."

"Yes, Sir."

"I don't think we need your namesake to solve this one, do we? I suspect I've found the source of the flood. Have I not, Mr Sherlock? Mr McCarthy? Mr Mulcahy?"

I thought Sherlock was a goner because I knew he wasn't the sort to let us all hang for his joke. Anyway, I was fairly sure Healy was going to squeal.

"It was me, Sir," Healy said. "The cap came off my bottle of lemonade."

"Healy." Mr Flynn sighed. "For God's sake, would you be more careful?" He then looked from Sherlock to me to Finn. "I'm watching ye, *bígí cúramach.*" Turning swiftly to address the bus, he bellowed. *"Lámha suas,* anybody who needs to do a wee?" A plethora of hands went up, and Mr Flynn asked the driver to pull in for a wee break.

About ten of us were stood on a ditch beside the bus, looking and peeing into a field. "Healy," one of the boys jeered, "did you do your pee pee on the floor?"

"Leave him alone," Sherlock rounded, "or I'll give ya a kick in the mickey."

I blurted with laughter, and if I wasn't already doing a wee, I think I would have wet my trousers. Mickey was a word I only ever heard the big boys saying.

"Buachaillí," Mr Flynn shouted from the bus door, "let's get the show back on the road. *Anois! Go tapaidh!*"

When we started to board the bus, my laughter subsided to a giggle. *"Ciúnas,"* Finn said, with a serious face, "or you might get a kick in the mickey." We both took a fit of laughing until Mr Flynn caught our eye and wagged a very pointed finger. *"Buachaillí!"* It was enough to quell our giddiness, but we were still laughing inside.

Not much else happened on the bus that I can remember. We had our not-so-swanky lunch in a not-so-swanky hotel and were back on the road in no time, growing increasingly tired of our long incarceration. "Only another hour," Miss Clarke said over the crackly microphone.

It was a long hour in our stuffy and increasingly smelly mobile prison.

Eventually, we arrived at Poulnabrone, in the middle of nowhere. Mr Flynn stood at the top of the bus in front of thirty-eight wilting ten-year-olds and winked at Miss Clarke before pontificating. "Boys!" he said. "We have arrived at the Poulnabrone Dolmen, an ancient tomb that some believe is a secret gate to the other world of fairies and the souls of the undead. Both of whom come out at night to haunt the land and play havoc with the living. Now, out you go. Fly my pretties."

Miss Clarke laughed, and at the same time there was a rush of boys to get off the bus, pushing and shoving. "Wooo, Drackla," someone said.

Outside, we were welcomed by a bright, breezy day, and as the sun slanted through a white, cloudy sky, we set off squelching along a mucky track towards the tomb, which we could see on top of a small rocky hill. Miss Clarke read aloud from her jotter, but I don't think anyone was listening: "Poulnabrone Dolmen," she said, "is a primary example of an ancient Irish tomb. Built 6,000 years ago...6,000 years, jeepers, that's a long time, boys. It is an open-ended portal tomb, constructed with two large slab-stones on either side and a huge capstone on top, sloping from seven feet at the front to four feet at the rear."

I thought it looked holy, standing all alone. Not like Jesus, Mary, and Joseph holy, but like a place where you should whisper its name. I whispered, "P-o-u-l-n-a-b-r-o-n-e."

"What?" Finn said.

"P-o-u-l-n-a-b-r-o-n-e," I repeated in a deep, spooky tone.

"P-o-u-l-n-a-b-r-o-n-e," he responded with a witchy cackle.

Hickey, who was right behind us, stretched out his arms like a mummy and gave a monotone rendition. "P-o-u-l-n-a-b-r-o-n-e."

His was the best, and a group of us became mummies simultaneously. "P-o-u-l-n-a-b-r-o-n-e. P-o-u-l-n-a-b-r-o-n-e. P-o-u-l-n-a..."

Suddenly, Finn got his foot stuck in the mud and nearly fell over. We all laughed.

"No horseplay back there," Mr Flynn shouted without even looking around.

On reaching the tomb, Mr Flynn waited for the stragglers to catch up. They had been dawdling with Miss Clarke, playing goody-two-shoes. "There are certain days," he said, using his serious-teacher voice, "and this happens to be one of those days that if you stand inside this ancient magical place, you might see a fairy or the undead souls. But," he lowered his voice and gathered close his captive audience, "if they see you, you'll be trapped in their world, forever, in their cold, dark, wormy beds." He pulled his sweater over his head like a scarf, hunched his back, and moved about like an actor on a stage.

"My fairy lord, this must be done with haste,

For night's swift dragons cut the clouds full fast,

And yonder shines St Aidan's harbinger,

At whose approach ghosts, wandering here and there,

Troop home to churchyards. Dammed spirits all,

That in crossways and floods have burial,

Already to their wormy beds are gone."

Miss Clarke smiled affectionately and applauded discreetly. "Shakespeare! Wonderful."

Mr Flynn winked at her, proud as a peacock. "You're not dealing with muck here." They both laughed. "Now," he looked at the class with a devilish grin, "we'll separate the men from the boys. Who's brave enough to stand inside?"

No one volunteered.

"Well, what if I say the first three who volunteer will get off homework next week."

Mulligan shot his hand up. "I will, Sir." And no sooner than the words were out of his mouth, he turned to Jonesy, his faithful sidekick. "Come on, ya chicken. No sums!"

"Me too, Sir," Jonesy said half-heartedly.

"Why am I not surprised?" Mr Flynn said to Miss Clarke, throwing his eyes to heaven again.

Mulligan was a funny fella who saw everything as an opportunity for a laugh. He was also captain of the school hurlers, and to top it all, he knew every curse word in the book. I liked him, and on the spur of the moment, I raised my hand. "Me too, Sir."

"McCarthy," Mr Flynn said with faux surprise. "You might be missed more than these two clowns here." Everyone laughed. "Mulligan, you're up first." Mulligan moved forward, and Mr Flynn shook his hand as if he was an adult about to do something tremendously brave. "Now, remember," his voice was earnest, "if you think the fairies and undead can see you run like hell. Don't look back, and don't"—he gripped Mulligan's wrist while glancing nervously into the tomb—"this is serious, don't let them grab you by the legs." Mr Flynn squinted his eyes, Hollywood villain style, then steered Mulligan to the front of the structure. "If you don't come back, I'll say goodbye to your mother for you."

Miss Clarke tried in vain to conceal a giggle. "You're awful, Jack."

Finn pulled a smirky face and mouthed, "Jack!"

"Kissy, kissy, Jack," I whispered, and a few of the boys laughed.

"Now," Mr Flynn continued, unaware of the information leak, "once you're inside, I'll count to ten, and when I reach ten, get out as quick as you can if you can. But not before I say ten, or else, the fairies might put a curse on you. Alright now, are you ready?"

Mulligan nodded, completely focused on the challenge in front of him.

"Off you go so."

The boys looked at each other anxiously, and Mulligan stepped inside the tomb with a grave absence of his usual levity.

"A haon, a dó," Mr Flynn began counting slowly. *"a trí, a ceathair, a cúig, eh, a sé,"* Mulligan stood motionless, with his back to us. "*A seacht, a hocht, eh, a hocht.* No, no, that's wrong; what comes after *uimhir a hocht?"*

"A naoi!" the class shouted in unison.

"Oh, that's right, *a naoi.* Should I start again?"

"No!"

"A deich!"

Mulligan turned around and, with a skip and a hop, leapt from the tomb, landing perfectly balanced on his hunkers like an Olympian gymnast. He then sprang to his feet and, with outstretched hands, shuffled stiff-legged among the boys: "Wooooo!"

Everybody laughed, including Mr Flynn. Miss Clarke even screeched as he approached her.

Next up was Jonesy. I didn't dislike him, but he wasn't one of my favourite classmates. Unlike

Mulligan, he wasn't an open-hearted messer. His messing was usually at someone else's expense. One time, he made up a big joke about Decky Kelly being poor and doing a gick in his trousers. He kept calling him Smelly Kelly, and that sort of became his nickname. I got into a pushing match with Jonesy over it, but Mulligan broke us up before a fight started. I always called him Decky Kelly. Another time, he made Little Doyler cry, jeering him about his bunny ears, which I have to say were very big and floppy. But I didn't think the jeering was fair because Little Doyler was too little to fight back. When Mulligan saw Little Doyler crying, he told Jonesy to leave him alone.

Mr Flynn shook Jonesy's hand and gave him an abridged warning about the woes of the tomb, minus his show-off Shakespeare speech. Jonesy was hesitant about entering the tomb and Mr Flynn gently nudged him inside before repeating the arduously slow count. The class engaged with more gusto than the first time because they now knew their pantomime role.

On the count of ten, Jonesy turned and walked out, visibly shaken. His head was down, and there was none of Mulligan's theatrics. He looked scared. "Are you alright, Jones?" Mr Flynn asked casually.

Miss Clarke raised her eyebrows to communicate silent misgivings.

"Yes, Sir," he said. His head remained bowed, and his bottom lip was quivering.

"Did you see any fairies or undead?"

"No, Sir."

"Good. Mulligan probably frightened them away." We all laughed. "Now, McCarthy, let's see if they might take a shine to you."

Miss Clarke questioned Mr Flynn with a cautious look.

"Do you still want to do it?" Mr Flynn asked me.

"Yes, Sir." I knew he only asked for Miss Clarke's sake. The whole point of the game was to frighten us. Anyway, I was glad Jonesy looked scared because that left it open for me to do as good as Mulligan.

"Good man yourself." He shook my hand, gave me the abridged version of what might happen, and guided me to the front of the tomb. "Last chance to back out. You're sure?"

"Yes, Sir." The butterflies fluttered in my stomach and I wanted to do it before I lost my nerve.

"Sure, who am I askin'? It's the fairies should be afraid. Didn't you take a mighty whack for St Aidan's last week?"

I was chuffed with his praise.

"Off you go. But come back, we'll need you against St Killians."

Miss Clarke seemed more confident about me going into the tomb and winked her approval.

"Good luck now," Mr Flynn said.

I took a deep breath and stepped inside.

Immediately, it was cooler than outside and calm, really calm. It reminded me of floating in the sea with my ears under the water. I could hear my breathing, quietly cavernous and particular to me. The tomb's inside was bigger and somehow smaller than I expected. But the most striking thing was the silence, not a sound, just my breathing, until that too stopped. There was perfect silence. I felt I was drifting, falling deeper into the silence as the world ebbed further and further away. It was a nice feeling. I liked the distant timelessness of the place.

For some reason I felt a bit sorry for the tomb, and I stroked one of its standing stones with the outside of my fingers. The same way I stroked Granda's cheek when he was laid out in his coffin. I heard myself repeating what I said to Granda. "Don't be sad." The words came from deep inside my breathless chest, and I could see my curved fingers once again touching his smooth, waxen cheek as though I was at the funeral.

Something moved in the corner of my eye, a small swirl of darkness. I became aware of a presence behind my right shoulder in the tomb. I felt it was watching me, and my heart began beating as though its rhythm was being regulated from outside of my existence. It wasn't fast or slow but, somehow, just right. I mustered my courage and swivelled on my heels, hoping to catch sight of I didn't know what. A fairy? The undead? My ancient spirit?

Amazed, I saw a dim grey light, about the size of a

football. At its centre was a smaller, more intense, shiny silver-white light. The inside light was fluid, a mercurial substance. It extended a finger that touched my lips and opened my mouth, reminding me to breathe. I gasped, taking a huge breath and becoming intensely aware of my reawakened breathing. The air travelled up my nostrils, down my throat, and into my lungs, where it lived for a couple of heartbeats before reversing its flow.

The dark swirl was separate from the light and circled my head three times before disappearing abruptly. Only then did the light fade to transparency, growing lighter and lighter until it became a translucent shimmer and eventually vanished completely, leaving me immersed in hushed benevolence.

I wondered if Mr Flynn had reached the count of ten, and I turned only to find the whole class shouting and cheering: *Deich! Deich! Deich!* It was obvious they hadn't seen the light, but I still felt a need to conceal the experience as something that was special to me. So, I created a distraction, and putting my shoulder to one of the large standing stones, pretended to push with all my might, like Samson in the temple.

"Alright now," Mr Flynn said, "out you come. We don't want St Aidan's to be known as the school that knocked down Poulnabrone!"

Mulligan shouted, "Go on, Macker, push."

The class began to call out, "Macker! Macker!

Macker!"

Their words echoed about the tomb, and I felt my name reverberate deep into Ireland's ancient past.

Mr Flynn shouted, "McCarthy! Out. Now."

The class continued to chant, "Macker! Macker!" and I danced out with fists in the air like a victorious prize fighter.

My new-found kudos lasted well into secondary school and sometimes even into adulthood. Occasionally, after bumping into an old classmate and reminiscing about school days, they'd say, "Do you remember the day you wouldn't come out of the Dolmen?" Or, "What about the time you tried to push over Poulnabrone?"

On one occasion, I met Mulligan outside Croke Park after a lacklustre Dublin performance in a League game against Meath. "How's it goin', head?" I heard someone say, and there was Mulligan, with his usual big smile.

"Long time no see," I said, delighted with the chance encounter.

"Yeah, sure is. How's things?"

"Grand."

"Brutal fuckin' game." Then he added with a smirk. "They could do with you in their back line."

"Yeah, right." I grinned. "Still taking the piss."

"No messin'." His smirk grew to a chuckle. "You

were always good at getin' your arse in the way. If you couldn't get the ball, you took the man."

"And I have the scars to prove it," I said with a laugh.

"That's what the Dubs need, a bit of fuckin heart."

"It was a brutal game, alright."

"What are you at these days?" he asked.

"I'm in college."

"Fair play. You were always the one with the brains."

"What are you at yourself?"

"I'm just out of me time. I'm an electrician with the ESB."

"So, you're raking it in?"

He guffawed and rubbed his hands. "At last, a few bob."

"Do you ever see anyone from the class?"

"Naw, not really. You?"

"I'm still in touch with Finn. He moved to the States."

"Ah, yeah, I remember you were great mates. Did you hear about Jonesy?"

"No. What?"

"He's dead. He committed suicide. Well, that's what his brother told me."

"No. Jesus."

"He wasn't doin' well for a while. He wasn't well upstairs."

"Did you stay friends, keep in touch like?"

"Not really. He was a bit of a loner. I used to bump into his brother every now and then, and he'd tell me how he was doin'."

"Jesus, that's tough."

"I often wondered did you know."

I felt he meant more than just asking did I know about Jonesy's death. "How do you mean?"

"Do you remember when the three of us went into the tomb at Poulnabrone?"

"Yeah."

"Well, he thought he was possessed by a demon from the tomb. Years after, he told me he had seen a little dark shadow when he was inside, and he couldn't breathe until it disappeared down his throat. Fuckin mad stuff."

"Jesus. I don't know what to say. That's awful, sad, and a bit scary. Did you see anything in the tomb?"

"No," he said without hesitation. "Did you?"

"Eh, no. Nothing like that."

"Danny, his brother, told me Jonesy lived like a hermit on Tory Island, up in Donegal. One night, when there was a huge storm, the locals saw him go down to the sea. He was standing on rocks, starkers, shoutin' and roarin' at the ocean. A huge wave crashed over his head and swept him out to sea."

"Jesus Christ. That's sad. Possessed?"

"Yeah. It was weeks before his body washed ashore. Danny said fish had eaten his face and innards. He had to identify him."

"Oh, Jesus Christ!"

"Seeing as it was just the three of us that went in, I thought I should tell you. You know... I'm not saying... eh... you know."

"Yeah, sure. I know what you're saying." I didn't tell him about a dream I had where Jonesy was leering at me from the far side of an empty coffin. It didn't feel appropriate for a brief, casual meeting.

"Are you right, Tony?" A good-looking girl shouted from about twenty feet away.

"That's the moth and her sister," he said, pleased I got to see his girlfriend. "She has me on a short lead."

"I doubt that." I waved at the two girls, and they waved back, looking none too pleased with Tony.

"I best be off. Good to see you again. And good to know everything is, you know, good with you."

"Yeah. You too."

I hadn't paid much attention to my Jonesy dream because I had always dreamt, especially since my Poulnabrone experience. I loved their ethereal freedom and unpredictability. In my dream world, I had laughed with Celtic kings, ran with great warriors, danced with mythical gods, and cried with starving children. Most times, however, I couldn't remember them beyond the following morning, although Jonesy's leer did stick in my head.

CHAPTER 2

Being an Irish Republican remained hugely important to me, especially after 1969, when Catholics in the North were burned out of their homes by Loyalist gangs. Finn wasn't from a Republican family, but after the Bloody Sunday massacre in 1972, it didn't take much to persuade him that we should join the IRA.

We went to Aunty Eibhlin and asked her advice. "Tom Prendergast," she said with a knowing nod, "he's the man to ask. Tell him I sent you. He lives at 50 Nore Avenue. Leave it till after 6 o'clock. Your Granda would be very proud of you, both of you."

I knocked on the door.

"You do the talkin'," Finn said quickly after hearing movement in the hall.

A genial man with a pot belly, balding head, and round spectacles opened the door. He was holding an open newspaper and peered at us from above his glasses.

"Yes?" he said, giving us the once over.

"Hello," I said. "Are you Mr. Prendergast?"

He glanced about the street before his eyes settled

on me. "Yes."

"Eibhlin O'Brien is my aunty and she said we should tell you that we want to join the IRA."

He didn't blink or take his gaze off me. "That would make you Mick O'Brien's grandson?"

"Yes."

"Are you the little fella at his funeral that was holding your Granny's hand?"

"Yes. I think so."

"And you?" His eyes shifted to Finn.

"I'm his blood brother."

He smiled. "Do your parents know what you're askin' me?"

"No," I said.

"How old are you?"

"Fourteen."

"Your Aunty Eibhlin should have more sense."

"We want to fight the English," Finn said—just in case Prendergast had any doubts. "For what they did in Derry. His Aunty Eibhlin said you'd help us."

"We want to follow my Granda," I said in support of Finn's clarity, "and send a message to the English Queen."

"A message?" His brow furrowed with curiosity.

"Yes. He said that in 1916, they sent the King a

message: 'We are not your people, this is not your country. Get out of our country.'"

"They certainly did that."

"He'd want me to send a message," I said loyally, "after they murdered the innocent people on Bloody Sunday."

"I'm sure he would, but not at fourteen. Ireland needs good young Republicans like yourselves to grow into active older Republicans. Now, I'm in the middle of me tea. So off you go and have a think about that."

* * *

By the time we were old enough to join the IRA, it had embarked on a bombing campaign, and I wasn't able to justify the indiscriminate blood sacrifice of innocent people. Finn, however, was somewhat less circumspect.

"When the Americans are bombing the shit out of Vietnam," he argued, as we listened to Jimmy Hendrix in the safety of his bedroom, "and innocent people are killed, the Brits call it collateral damage. Or when the Brits dropped thousands of bombs and turned Dresden into a furnace of the innocent, they called it part of the war effort."

"I know what you're saying," I said, "but I couldn't plant a bomb."

"I'm not saying we should plant bombs. I'm just saying—war is war."

"I understand. And I'll understand whatever you decide to do. But I can't join up."

"You're some fucker. You turn me into a Provo, and then tell me I shouldn't join the IRA."

"I didn't say you shouldn't join. I said I couldn't join."

"Same difference. I'm hardly going to join without you."

The war in the North quickly became too harsh, too real, for my mythical sense of Irishness. My allegiances became deeply conflicted between the free Irishness of the South, with its Gaelic heroes, music, and legends, and the imprisoned Irishness of the North, with its blood, mayhem, and sorrow. Finn's militancy also ebbed as the North slipped into a depressing mix of rebellious despondency and normalised oppression.

By the time the 1980s began, I was studying history at Trinity while Finn was at Maynooth University studying economics. Like much of Southern Ireland, we had become acclimatised to the unrelenting darkness and conflict in the North. But everything changed on May 5, 1981, when Bobby Sands became the first of ten hunger strikers to die. My heart nearly broke. He was an exceptional Republican—a poet, philosopher, soldier, and MP—cut from the same cloth as Tone, Emmet, and Pearse.

I had no involvement with the Republican movement, but in my soul, I felt an affinity with the strikers. They were of Ireland, and like my Granda, they were sending a message to the English Queen. Their self-sacrifice screamed, *"You can imprison our bodies, but you cannot imprison our Irish spirit. We defy you. We choose the freedom of death."*

During the strikes, there were huge protests throughout Ireland, and it was the only time I felt the Irish people, as a whole, might be dragged into the Northern conflict, ceasing to stand idly by. At the end of one protest, outside Dáil Éireann, the mood of defiance had shifted to gloom as the crowd dispersed, with some people crying. A group of distraught women, desperate to save their loved ones, had their faces pressed through the Victorian railings of Dáil Éireann and were frantically shouting, "Don't let them die! Don't let them die! Don't abandon us again!" My heart was impaled by their anguish because I knew this was the same Dáil Éireann that had abandoned their parents, leaving them trapped in the sectarian statelet of Northern Ireland only 60 years earlier.

A man turned to me. "Are ye from Dublin yourself?" His accent was soft, Donegal, maybe Derry.

"Yeah," I said, shifting my stance to get a better look at him. He was a little older than my 23 years, over six feet tall and had a strong athletic build. I imagined there was probably a whiff of gunpowder about him, metaphorically, if not literally.

"Where might I get something to eat that's not too far?" His collarless shirt and green combat jacket fused with his facial stubble and rusty long hair, which was tied back in a ponytail. It was a ubiquitous fashionable rebel look, Che Guvara meets Yassar Arafat, and not dissimilar to my own: recent beard, jeans, black t-shirt and army-surplus combat jacket. Except, I suspected he was the real deal.

"You'll get a pint and a sandwich in most of the pubs around here but not much else at this time." If he was IRA, he was my first face-to-face encounter with an actual Volunteer.

"No, I'm not drinking. I have to be somewhere tomorrow."

I was surprised by his openness and considered his sentence for a second; it sounded portentous. "There's a McDonald's on Grafton Street?"

He paused before responding, as if calculating my suggestion. "That'll do. Could you point me in the right direction?"

"I'm going that way," I said, trying to hide my enthusiasm. "I'll show you."

"Great, thanks." He looked at me hard. "Are you involved, yourself?"

I wasn't expecting such a direct question, and I wondered—should I ask him to clarify, involved in what? But I guessed he meant the IRA. In my Walter Mitty world, I wanted us to be fellow souls on a righteous journey, and I toyed with the idea of saying yes. Then we'd look at each other, knowingly, two active Volunteers stoically recognising our dedication to Ireland's cause.

"No," I said and blushed at the exposure of my armchair republicanism.

His mouth curved slowly to a smile that accentuated his square chin and he turned his face right then left, in a pronounced light-hearted manner. "Which way?"

I regained my composure and answered in what I hoped was a self-assured tone. "My left, your right." But inside, I was kicking myself for blushing.

McDonald's was no more than a few minutes' walk, and although he didn't know the way, he set off at a brisk pace. I hurried to take the lead.

There was an aura of camaraderie about him, but we barely spoke on the short journey, which was stop-start given the size of the dispersing crowd. At the corner of Molesworth Street and Dawson Street, a blind man was sitting on the damp pavement with an outstretched hand, begging. I'd seen him before, usually on O'Connell Bridge, and I guessed he was taking advantage of the large crowd, as he might with a football match or pop concert. It made me think of how personal our troubles are, and before I could decide whether to part with some loose change, my companion was on his hunkers, folding the beggar's hand around a pound note.

"How's it goin'? Are you keeping well?" he asked.

"Not too bad at all," the beggar said with a brightened face. "Still pullin' the divil by the tail."

The might-be IRA man continued to hold his hand.

"Ah, sure, now you have it." He stood and laughed. "Keep a good grip, though."

"I will, no fear of that," the beggar said. "Take care of yourself now."

"You too."

"Do you know him?" I asked, after we moved away.

"No. But the few words are often worth more than the few bob."

As we turned onto Grafton Street, I wondered if a person could have such easy compassion for his fellow man and also shoot someone for Ireland's cause. There was no time, however, to conclude my musings because we had reached our destination.

"McDonald's, as promised," I said jovially.

He surveyed the busy street and briefly scanned the passersby before his eyes landed on me. "Can I get you a hamburger?"

Calling a McDonald's burger a "hamburger" sounded weird. I thought it must be a Northern thing. "Eh, no thanks. But I'll have a Coke, keep you company."

The place was busy with afternoon shoppers, oblivious to the anguish of the protesters only a few hundred meters away, and we were lucky to find a small table by the window.

"You hold the table," he said, "and I'll get the grub."

It was a nice sunny spot, very much at odds with

the earlier republican gloom. "Sorry, it's taken," I said authoritatively, a number of times, conscious that I was holding a table for a possible—probable—IRA Volunteer. "You managed to keep it." There was a cheeky half grin on his face as he sat down.

"I did," I said, "but it was touch and go there for a minute."

"What's your name?" he asked, pausing the unwrapping of his burger as though remembering his manners.

Our faces were less than a couple of feet apart, and his piercing blue eyes struck me almost to the point of distraction. "Conor."

"I'm *Aodh Mag Uidhir*, Hugh Maguire. They call me Red Hugh. What's your family name?" His eyes were overtly curious yet friendly.

"Red Hugh?" I gave an understated chuckle, emphasising the historic significance of his name. "You have big shoes to fill."

"Aye, it's a catchy name. There's a lot of Maguires in the North West we need different handles." He bent forward, picked up his burger, and, about to bite, looked at me from under his fiery eyebrows. "Did you know they were allies? Maguire and O'Donnell."

I took a wild guess that he was talking about the Nine Years War, the actual period I was studying at college. "Yes," I said casually, hoping to impress him with my knowledge of Irish history. "Maguire played a major part in the war, including Clontibret and

Yellow Ford, a great cavalry commander." His mouth was full of burger and he couldn't respond other than giving a glinty wink of approval. "My family name is McCarthy. I'm studying history at Trinity."

He swallowed. "Ah, that makes sense. For a minute there, I thought you knew him."

I gave another little chuckle. "I wish."

Smiling, he offered his hand. It was a strong, honest handshake. *"Conchobhar Mac Cárthaigh,"* he said, pronouncing my name in beautiful Irish. "It's a proud Gaelic name – you come from noble lineage. Kings of Desmond. Our Gaelic names are important to who we are; they're the pathway to our heritage."

I looked at him with an intentionally concerned expression. "When they took our language, they took part of our soul."

"Tír gan teanga, tír gan anam" he said. "Pearse knew the truth of it."

"Did you know Pearse only had two cases when he practised law? Both defending the rights of small businesses to use their Gaelic family names?"

He shook his head with amused interest. "I didn't know that."

"Actually, the Irish were the first in Europe to use surnames. *O'Cléirigh*, Clery, is the oldest, dating back to the tenth century."

It was his turn to chuckle. "I knew that one."

"OK. Did you know, for ten points, that Gaelic is the oldest written European language, after Greek and Latin?"

He was about to answer but we were distracted by a commotion outside the window. The shoppers on Grafton Street were giving way to a mock funeral of a hunger striker. It was led by a man in full IRA combat uniform holding a flagpole with an unfurled Tricolour. Behind him were six pallbearers carrying a coffin draped in another Tricolour, they were wearing black paramilitary uniforms and on the draped Tricolour was a black beret and leather gloves. The principal mourners followed the coffin, escorted on either side by six men slow-marching in full IRA combat uniform.

A young mourner, about twelve years old, caught my eye. Her face was tortured with blind loyalty, and I imagined she was the daughter of a hunger striker, attending a chilling rehearsal of her Daddy's funeral.

My emotions were overwhelmed by the scene, and we sat in silence until the procession passed. The young girl's face lingered in my thoughts and I was reminded of a Famine-poem Mr Flynn taught us in St. Aidan's. I recited the lines silently.

Little child, tears are strange upon your infant face.

God meant you but to smile within your mother's soft embrace.

Oh! I know not what is smiling, and I know not what is dying;

He's hungry, very hungry, and I cannot stop my

crying.

“I hear Patsy O’Hara is very weak,” I said, swallowing a lump in my throat.

“Aye, he hasn’t got long, nor McCreesh.” His words were slow and solemn. “It’s a brutal way for a man to die.” We both stared at the table, and I felt ashamed of my earlier nonsensical conversation. “There’s an awful, terrible sorrow hanging over the country.”

“O’Hara, or McCreesh, will be the third,” I said, unintentionally stating the obvious. “I can’t believe Thatcher is letting them die. But she’s a mad bitch, and I can’t see her moving. What do you think will happen?”

“I don’t know about Thatcher, but the strikers have the spirit in them, and it’s of no mind to bow down.”

I thought of Granda. “Do you mean the ancient Irish spirit?”

He took me with a solid look and scanned my face for a good number of seconds. “I mean, more men of Ireland are going to die a brutal death.” His tenor was reproachful but not of me. “What do you know of the ancient spirit?”

I told him all about Granda, him seeing the ancient spirit in me, and my promise not to lose it. I even told him about my dreams of Celtic Kings and ancient gods. When I finished, he said, “Thank you, *Conchobhar Mac Cárthaigh,* for sharing your story with me. I wondered what I saw in your face, and now I know.”

"But dreams of Celtic gods and ancient spirits," I said, "are meaningless to O'Hara or McCreesh."

"Maybe." He joined his hands at their fingertips. "Or maybe they mean everything."

His words hung in the air, and I wasn't sure how to respond. "I often think it's pathetic of me to revere my grandfather and all the great rebels that went before him while I sit on my arse, with men and women dying just a hundred miles up the road."

He inclined his head like a wolf, and I could see him watching me speak—so much so that I became self-conscious about me watching him watching me.

"I thought about getting involved," I said, "so many times. It's that constant row in my head between my reason and my heart until I'm paralysed by indecision."

"Joining the Army is a big decision, for sure. It's not for every Republican."

I sensed a tone of self-justification in his words that was inadvertently disparaging of my position, and I instinctively defended my thinking. "I couldn't plant a bomb," I said. "It's too indiscriminate."

He nodded slowly, knowingly, as though recognising a dilemma he had wrestled before. "Do you out-monster the monster or be quietly devoured?"

I didn't know what to say. I wasn't expecting such a philosophical response. "Eh, that's a big question."

"Aye, it is." There was a loneliness in his voice, and as if trying to subdue it, he interlinked his fingers so tightly that his knuckles turned white.

"I'm sorry," I said, for something he hadn't articulated, my heart heavy with his.

"I know. We're all sorry." Silence descended, and we remained still for a couple of minutes.

"What's going to happen? I don't just mean the hunger strike. I mean to Ireland. Can we ever win?"

The question sparked his resolve, dissipating the lonely aura that had surrounded us. "The IRA can bring the British Army to a standstill. Collins did it. But it can't beat a million loyalists. They're too tightly woven into the fabric of Ireland.

"Does the fighting go on forever?"

"The English must be run out of our country." His eyes were alive again, fiery. "Only then do we have any chance of peace. She is the never-failing source of all our evils."

"And what about the Protestants, the loyalists?" I asked, lost in the conversation.

"We build a new Ireland. An Ireland of accommodation and mutual respect. Without the English Crown. We have to remove the cancer before we can heal the wound."

"Do you think that can happen?"

"It's what we're fighting for—to unite Protestant,

Catholic, and Dissenter as Irish men and women. Tone's words are as true today as they were in 1798."

I was more comfortable talking about the romantic republicanism of Tone and Pearse than the idea of out-monstering the monster. But I couldn't miss the opportunity of getting an IRA man to answer questions that had been in my head for years.

"Do you ever think the IRA regret what they've done?" I asked. "What they're doing? Is there another way?"

His eyes were steadfast, and they reminded me of Granda. "I've never met one who didn't regret the taking of life, who didn't regret the atrocities of war, who didn't regret that there wasn't another way. You have to understand the IRA are not the instigators of the violence. They are reacting to violence, state violence."

I nodded, doing my best not to appear in awe of him. His understanding, however, was so clearly thought out and assured that I couldn't help but feel it.

"Half a million Irish people were trapped in Craig's *'Protestant State for a Protestant People.'* A state that blatantly declared itself sectarian and anti-Irish."

I nodded. "That's what the women were chanting. 'Don't abandon us again.'"

"Abandoned, aye." He took a deep breath, paused and pursed his lips. "I joined the Army because I couldn't accept the abandonment of Irish people. For thousands of years, we were all the same people. Then we weren't."

"Yes," I said enthusiastically. "How did Stormont think, after the civil rights marches, that it could continue oppressing half a million people simply because they wanted to remain Irish?"

"The oppressor must serve the function for which it was invented."

I huffed at the clarity of his thoughts. "It seems simple when you put it like that."

"Let me put it this way, in relation to how you see indiscriminate violence. If state violence does not yield to reason, does not listen to peaceful protest, then counter-violence is inevitable. That's a fact of life in any society." He looked at me questioningly. "Stormont ignored and quashed peaceful protest, the civil rights protests."

"Yes, I understand what you're saying..." I was going to add, "But that doesn't address the morality of indiscriminate counter-violence."

"So, you tell me?" he interrupted, his thoughts in free flow. "Who's responsible for the counter-violence, the oppressed or the oppressor? The abused or the abuser."

"The abuser, the oppressor."

"Aye. Now, I can't tell you that the bombing campaign is right. But I can tell you that indiscriminate counter-violence has a cause."

"I understand what you're saying. But cause and

justification aren't the same."

"I'm not trying to justify. I'm saying, if you aren't open to changing your thinking, you can't change anything." This was followed by an inclusive, knowing smile. "There's more than one way to skin a cat. It takes Republicans to change Republicans."

I was struck by the thought that he was trying to recruit me for the very reason I hadn't been able to join the IRA. *Maybe,* I wondered, *he's looking for fellow Republicans to persuade other Republicans away from the bombing campaign?*

He rubbed his face with both hands. "I didn't mean to lecture. I'm sure you've more than enough of that in university."

"No. Jesus, no. If only we had lecturers with your insight. My Granny used to say, you can't learn to swim from reading a book."

He laughed. "Your Granny was a wise woman." Then, looking at his watch, his eyes popped with animated surprise. "Shit, I'm late. Well, *Conchobhar Mac Cárthaigh,*" he said, tapping the side of the table with both hands. "I have to be somewhere. But here's one for you now, before I go. Did you know that, throughout the time of the British Empire, it took more British troops per capita and per square mile to hold Ireland than anywhere else in their Empire?

"That's a good one. I didn't know that." I made a clenched fist salute, half in jest. "Brits Out."

"That's the truth of it. The fuckers are slow

learners. You'll never beat the Irish, as the soccer lads might say. Thanks for telling me about your Granda, it's been great chatting with you.

"Eh. Yeah, me too," I said, disappointed our conversation had come to a close.

He stood, stretched his back and put a hand on my shoulder. "Take care, Conor. It's good to talk to one of my own."

"Yeah, you too. G'luck," I said, and wondered what he meant by *'one of my own'—was it solidarity or something more?*

My mind buzzed with questions and altered perspectives, but mostly, I was giddy with the idea of having had an in-depth conversation with a real, live IRA Volunteer—who maybe tried to recruit me. I couldn't wait to tell Finn about him.

I watched Red Hugh leave, navigating the closely seated area, side-stepping shopping bags, giving way to wayward children and pausing for overweight women carrying trays. He avoided all eye contact and moved through the restaurant like a ghost who was only visible to me. Nobody saw him, nobody knew he was there.

He crossed the street towards the corner of Grafton and Wicklow, where a young woman was looking in the window of Switzer's Department Store. She could have easily stepped from the cover of a fashion magazine with her Sergeant Pepper jacket and knee-high black boots over tight, faded blue jeans. I noticed she had the same self-contained aura as my erstwhile companion and the same pale complexion, although her hair was more auburn than rust, and she wore it in a soft mullet style. They shook hands and pulled each other close in a warm embrace. She then stepped back and listened intently to whatever he was saying. I could see he was asking her something serious, to which she gestured her approval before they both glanced about the street and moved off. He then said something else that made her pause, and smiling, she looked towards McDonald's, straight at me. My heart jolted, and I felt I'd been caught spying. He continued to walk, but she stopped, broadened her smile and waved. I assumed she had mistaken me for someone else, although I was happy to return her smile with a shy wave.

There was something in the recesses of my mind that told me I knew her, some vague notion of familiarity. Gradually, her face began to emerge from the depths of my memory; it was her smile and trendy aura that surfaced first, but I couldn't quite grasp it. The emerging face was a different age, a teenager, with a different fashion style and... different hair. There was something about her hair... then it came to me. It was cropped tight. She was the teenage skinhead from our school dance, the night of the Christmas fight. I was nearly sure of it.

I was sixteen years old, with a group of my classmates, all dressed to the nines at the end-of-term school disco. We attended a Christian Brothers' all-boys school so just being in the presence of teenage girls was exciting. Gordon's Mobile Disco pounded out Slade's *Cos I Luv You*. Psychedelic lights covered the walls, and above our heads, a large disco ball hung perilously from the ceiling, showering us with rotating streams of multicoloured light while the main illuminations flashed in sync with Slade's stomping sound. This was our time, our place; all was right with the world. The girls in their tight white jeans and flowery tops were already throwing us sideways glances.

"It's lookin' good, Con," Finn shouted in my ear. "If we don't score tonight, we must be fuckin' queer."

Suddenly, the music stopped, and the dancers scattered, running past us as a commotion erupted at the entrance. Brother Christopher, a horse of a man, well over six feet tall, was holding his hands out wide across the doorway, shouting, "Yer not comin' in! No way!" The next thing, he was lying face down on the floor, and a gang of about 20 skinhead teenagers trundled over his body, not unlike a scene from a *Charlie Chaplin* silent film. They paused for a moment, as if they hadn't expected to get that far. Then they spread out across the floor, rampaging forward, indiscriminately kicking and punching every male in their path. Those who weren't dropping like flies were running for cover: into the toilets, onto the stage, some even got out the windows. I didn't move quickly enough, and for a brief moment, it was just me standing before them, a lone gunslinger facing down a band of desperados.

Jamie Lynch, an effeminate boy from my class, was directly behind me, too terrified to move. "Run, Jamie!" I shouted, giving him time to dart from my cover. Unfortunately, this meant I didn't have enough time to get out of the gang's way. I held my breath, hoping they would move past me. Of course, they didn't, and I was unceremoniously punched in the face. Instinctively, I returned the punch, drawing the wrath of five or six gang members who unleashed an avalanche of kicks. Within seconds, I was on the ground, and a kick to my mouth and nose splattered blood across the floor. I managed to get up, wildly kicking and punching the air before I was dropped again. Another kick caught me smack on the side of the head.

"Stop! You're going to kill him," a girl shouted from somewhere in the melee.

A long swinging boot slammed into my forehead, and for a few seconds, everything went black. I was flat on my back, but I could see my father reading the morning newspaper about a tragedy at St. Anthony's school dance, slowly realising that the dead teenager was his son.

"Stop!" The girl's voice commanded.

She was now standing over me, one hand outstretched, flat-palmed like a Garda halting traffic. I surmised from her well-polished George Webb shoes, red socks, and above-the-ankle parallel denim jeans that she was a skinhead. Although I could see little else from the floor, I sensed the gang didn't know her. A standoff quickly ensued between her and my attackers as she took a kung fu pose astride my crumpled body, like a female Bruce Lee.

I tried to get up, to stand beside her, but my head was spinning, and I stumbled forward, face down.

"Fuckin lezzer," one of the attackers shouted, followed by some posturing from the others. None, however, stepped forward to take on my mysterious protector. They headed up the hall to join the rest of their gang, who were making an unruly exit through the emergency doors.

Finn immediately pulled me from the floor. "Jesus, man, I'm sorry. I thought you were behind me. Are you alright?"

My head was still swirling, and the next face I saw was Jamie Lynch; his eyes were full of tears. He held a cold, wet hanky to my nose. "Are you hurt?"

"I'm OK, Jamie, thanks."

A crowd quickly gathered with a plethora of questions: "Are you alright? What happened? Who were they? Did you see Brother O'Neill?"

The skinhead girl moved away without introduction or explanation. I ignored all the questions and looked around, trying to see where she had gone. Then, I caught a glimpse of her heading towards the emergency exit. She was tall and elegant with striking eyes, and she smiled at me over her shoulder before disappearing into the hustle and bustle.

The girl on Grafton Street was my teenage

protector; I was nearly certain of it, and I had to meet her. "Sorry. Sorry. Excuse me," I muttered, leaving the table in a hurry and rushing clumsily through the packed restaurant.

When I got to the corner of Switzer's, there was no sign of them on Grafton Street. I wondered if they had doubled back and headed down Wicklow Street. My reason urged caution, suggesting that it was foolhardy to follow two possible IRA operatives. Then I saw them turning into Clarendon Street at the far end of Switzer's. She slowed and looked back over her shoulder, creating a photo opportunity worthy of David Bailey. They were only seconds ahead of me, and I broke into a run, nearly upending a young female cyclist. When I got to Clarendon Street, they were gone. It didn't seem possible. There were only a handful of people on the street, so I looked into the few small shops that were open and walked as far as the grey, foreboding church of Saint Teresa, even though I knew they couldn't have covered that distance in a matter of seconds.

It was a puzzle, and as I stood looking back and forth, bewildered, my reason told me that if they were that determined not to be followed, it was best to leave them be. I zipped up my combat jacket and headed home.

CHAPTER 3

I was sitting side by side with Emily in the vaults of Trinity's Buttery, having an afternoon pint. It was a popular, dimly lit cellar that dated back to the 1740s, with low arched ceilings, timeless granite pillars and scarred wooden benches enclosing old wooden tables in discrete cubicles. It could have been a gothic Dungeon if it wasn't for the smell of sausage and beans coming from the fluorescently lit cafeteria area. There were a few other students dotted about, eating, drinking, smoking. All were nicely closeted in their own cubicles, with only the occasional snort of laughter drawing attention to their clique.

Sipping her pint, she looked as beautiful as ever. The dim lighting made her brown eyes bewitchingly black, jumping out from her pale skin and newly acquired short blonde hair. Her erstwhile long black tresses were the last vestige of the prissy middle-class girl who entered university the previous year with a hesitant air of privilege about her.

"What are you smirking at?" she asked.

"I'm still getting used to your hair."

"Oh, I forgot. Do you still like it?"

"Yeah. It's lovely." I couldn't say I preferred the old style. The deed was done.

"Truthfully?"

"Yes. It's lovely."

"Mummy nearly had a canary. You would think I had become a Catholic."

I started to laugh. "That's funny."

"Seriously." She was playing to the gallery now with acquired haughtiness. "She'd have you all neutered, culled."

My laughter became unrestrained. "Jesus, you're funny."

"I do my best," she said, pleased with my reaction. "On a more serious note, did you go to the Hunger Strike protest yesterday?"

"Yeah. It was huge. I met this IRA guy, full-on Che Guevara type, and he just blew my mind."

"Were you involved in the riots?"

"No. I only heard it on the news this morning. I think the Belfast crowd tried to march on the British Embassy, but the Guards had it cordoned off. Apparently, the Army Rangers had a security ring around the Embassy and were issued with live ammunition. So, I guess it's good they didn't get through."

"Yes. Gosh. I wouldn't want to lose you. What was the IRA man like?"

"One head, no horns."

"Funny." Her cheeks dimpled. "Did he have blood on his hands?"

"Yes. Covered in it."

"I thought so."

"I know it's not your thing," I said, "but he was such an intelligent guy, with a lived philosophical perspective."

"I wouldn't say, 'it's not my thing'. That sounds very detached given the current situation. People dying on hunger strike for their principles is shocking." She took my hand in hers. "I know you care, ergo I care."

"Ergo, I care. Really?" I said, playfully, avoiding a pseudo-intellectual conversation about the strikers. Her intentions were well-meaning but the subject was too raw, too visceral. "I know you're a cold-hearted West Brit Prod," I added with a grin.

She leaned away from me and assumed a faux aristocratic posture, cocking her head to one side. "Was I cold-hearted during our last little tryst?"

I grinned, coquettishly, and kissed her hand. "No, my lady, you were not."

"As for this Protestant fixation you have, Messrs. Tone, Emmet, and Parnell were Protestant. Even your illustrious literary idol, Yeats, was Protestant. Wherever would you people be without us?"

I laughed. "That's true, all Protestant."

"And, may I add? While Daddy is a Church of Ireland minister, I have long disavowed my allegiance to the Church of Ireland faith and Christianity in general. Have I not?"

"Yes, you have. Countless times. Usually under the influence of intoxicating substances."

She withdrew her hand and, with a flick of her wrist, shooed away my comment. "As for me being a West Brit, you think everyone beyond Sandymount is a West Brit, nay beyond the Liffey." She started to laugh. "Peering... at the gentry, from out of your little Northside hovel."

"That's a bit close to the bone. You know I come from a very proud line of peasants." I tipped my forelock, "Ma'am."

"How the mighty Trinity College has fallen, once the bastion of all things English in Ireland. Now overrun with Northside Papist peasants."

"Jesus, you're on a roll. The further up the tree the monkey climbs, the more you see its arse."

"What?" She shook her head. "You've lost me. Who's the monkey, you or me?"

"I'm not sure," I said, putting a finger to my lips with a gobdaw expression.

"Suits you. But," she said, wide-eyed, running her hand along the inside of my thigh, "I like the monkey business."

I let out a grunt of surprised pleasure. “Begob Ma’am, there’s nothin’ I’d like better than pullin’ the knickers off the Fine Lady. That’s now if it’s suitable to the Fine Lady?”

“It’s suitable.”

“Really?” I wasn’t sure if she was still joking.

“Yes,” she raised her eyebrows and moved her hand higher, gently squeezing and dispelling any doubt I might have. “Ingrid will be out until around 10 p.m.; she has choir practice.” Ingrid was her older sister by two years and they shared a flat while Emily was in college.

“Great! I have a lecture at 4 p.m., but I’m sure he won’t miss me.”

“I wouldn’t want you to miss your lecture on my account.” She had a salacious twinkle in her eye, but there was no indication that under the table her squeeze had become a fondle.

I puffed, a long puff, as my mind clouded and my loins quivered. “I think it’s OK, if I miss this one.”

“Sure?”

“Sure. But if you keep that up, it’ll be game over here and now.”

“Oh, bloody hell!”

“What?”

“I forgot. I have a meeting with my tutor at 3.30 p.m. It’s about the grading of my continuous assessment essay. I can't miss it."

"Eh, OK."

"The essay, it's about the influence of sport on culture. You said 'game over.' That's what Cassady said about Kerouac."

"OK?" I'd heard of Kerouac, but that was it.

"Kerouac was a big sports guy?"

"If he wasn't in the GPO, he's nobody."

Her face lit with amusement. "You're so cute. With your little disappointed republican head."

I loved her humour and the way her mind worked. She was studying Hiberno-American literature and was taken with obscure perspectives rather than the usual Yeats' "Innisfree" stuff. "It's grand," I said, trying not to look too disappointed. "I'll finish my pint and chill out for a bit." The clock through the doorway said 3.15 p.m. "Jesus, you better get your skates on; you don't have much time."

"Again, I'm really sorry." She stood and grabbed her bag and coat.

"It's grand." I pulled her forward and kissed her pretty bow lips. "See you at Jeremy's this evening."

"Apparently, Jer has acquired some amazing hash oil."

"Great," I said, half-heartedly. "Good luck with your tutor."

"Thanks. Gotta fly. Byeee."

She was gone, and I was left to consider my relationship with this wonderful woman. I'd never met anyone like her before. She was so carefree, everything was in the moment, and her mind could fly anywhere at any time. Yet, when she was serious, Jesus, could she pin you to the wall? I thought I was smart, but she was smarter, and she had this uncanny ability to transform simple moments into ones of profound intimacy.

We had been dating for months before we made love. Afterwards, we talked until the morning sun peeped through her bedroom window, and we joked about how sneaky it was. I told her all about Granda, my Irish spirit, my dreams, and my ethereal experience in Poulnabrone. I even told her about Jonesy thinking he had been possessed by a demon. Other than Finn, she was the only person I ever told about my experience in the tomb. She was fascinated with the possibilities of what it might have been.

"Gosh," she said, leaning on her elbow and running her finger from my chest to my belly button. "You were touched by an otherworldly entity when you were only ten. You need to open up your mind again to harness that spiritual energy. Perhaps your bright light overpowered the dark demon. That's so exciting. Do you think it was your ancient spirit?"

"I don't know. It probably sounds strange, but I never really thought about it afterwards, in any meaningful way. It was just, sort of, part of my childhood. In a way, it became how I think about my self-identity as being Irish."

"Your ancient Irish spirit is the essence of who you are?"

"Yes. I guess, that's what I'm trying to say."

"You people are so inarticulate," she said, in her best Anglo-Irish accent.

Her jibes about my "peasant origins" always made me laugh because I knew her politics were anti-imperialist, anti-monarchy, and pro-proletariat. "Begob now, Ma'am," I said, "aren't ye wonderful entirely for makin sense of me gibberish."

She climbed on top and straddled my stomach, her long black hair falling discreetly over her slender figure as she pulled the quilt snug around her shoulders. "Never mind your gibberish. What about your dreams?"

"Hmm... my dreams? Ah, that's a horse of a different colour."

"I'm serious." Her voice was soft yet insistent, as her face beamed with wonderment. "Is there no end to you—ancient spirits and Celtic kings? Jung would be orgasmic if he got you on his couch."

"I never dreamt about my mother—before you start spouting Freud."

"Seriously, Jung would have a field day with your dreams. He said dreams are a way into the unconscious mind. They convey messages from the collective unconscious and offer the potential for true personal growth. Pay no attention to Freud, everything was sex, sex, sex, with him." There was a salacious twinkle in her eyes.

"Is there no end to *you*?" I mimicked. "Rock chick, literary aficionado, sexy bum, and now psychology buff. Did you study psychology?"

"Not exactly. I... I dabbled in my early teens. So, you think I have a sexy bum?"

"Maybe."

"Maybe?" She gripped the hair on my chest. "Think again?"

"Ouch! Definitely. Sexiest ever."

"Oh, you charmer you." She kissed my lips soft and sweet. "What's a girl to do?"

We made love again.

Later, we chatted about her family—the confinement of being a Minister's daughter in a small town and the difficult conformity of her teenage years.

"Mummy was more austere than Daddy. She was always guilting me about disappointing him, about him wanting me to be a young lady, to set an example as the Minister's daughter. I tried. I tried constantly, but I invariably failed. She often introduced me as an anxious child. Sometimes, she called me highly strung. Often, wilful. And when I just couldn't get it right, downright bold."

My mind slipped back to the Buttery, where I sat

staring vacantly at the two half-full pint glasses. I was struck by the thought that what I remembered most about us making love for the first time was lying in each other's arms, chatting and laughing. It was the intimacy of our embrace that felt magical, and the feeling that I'd known this wonderful woman for a hundred years.

Someone laughed loudly, my focus changed, and the glasses begged me to put them out of their misery. I knew I had to make a decision. If I drank both of them, there would be little point in going to my 4 p.m. lecture. On the other hand, it would be a terrible waste of money if I didn't. With that thought, I looked up, and there was Finn walking towards me.

"I met Emily leggin' it across Front Square. She said I'd find you here. She got her hair cut?"

"Yeah."

"Looks great. Soft, sexy feminist look. Very alternative Trinners."

"Is that what you came in from Maynooth to tell me? That you fancy my girlfriend?"

He sniggered. "Touchy, touchy. I was lookin' for you in the library."

"I'm on an extended lunch break. How did you get into the library?"

"I bumped into Dave. He lent me his card." Finn sat on a stool at the opposite side of the table and looked at the glasses. "Is one of them for me?"

"Yeah, she'll hardly be back. She's meeting her tutor."

"Fair enough." He lifted her glass. "Slainte. I hope I don't catch posh off it."

"Very funny. You don't have to drink it."

"I'll take me chances."

"I didn't see you at the march on Saturday," I said, ignoring his teasing. "I was lookin' out for you."

"I was with the *Ógra Shinners* from Maynooth. Were you part of the riots?"

"No. I had no idea until I saw it on the news. It was a huge crowd. Were you part of it?"

"No. I think the Belfast crowd was heading back to the buses and only then decided to head for the embassy."

"Yeah. That's what the *Times* said. I saw the Maynooth banner alright, but it was too far away. Where did you go after?"

"A few of us went to O'Neill's. Where were you?"

"I met this fella at the end of the march. An IRA Volunteer. Coolest fella I've ever met. He blew my mind.

"Sounds interesting." He spoke the words but didn't actually sound that interested, and I was surprised.

"We ended up going to McDonald's," I said, finishing my pint. "We had this amazing conversation." I decided to order two more pints before telling him how Red Hugh might have been trying to recruit me into an internal anti-bombing wing. "Will you have another one?" I asked, as I shifted along the seat to stand up.

"Eh, no. I have a meeting in an hour."

"A meeting? With who?"

"That's why I was looking for you. I'm going to America."

"What!"

"I'm going to America. I've got a job."

"Wait a minute. You're going to America? What about uni?"

"I'm packing it in. I'm struggling anyway."

"Just back up a minute and tell me from the start. When did you decide you were going?"

"Saturday, after the march. There was a fella there from Noraid—he owns a chain of pubs in Boston and New York—and we got talkin'. I told him about working part-time in Madigan's, and he offered me a job, there and then. He'll pay my fare over and set me up in an apartment."

"Will you be working for Noraid as well?"

"Yeah, I guess so."

"Are you sure about this? It's a big move."

"If I stay here, I'm joining up. It's gone too far. I

can't sit on my hands any longer." His eyes filled with tears. "They're fuckin' starving themselves to death. That's the only weapon they have left. All they want is political status."

"I know." I put my hand on his forearm. "It's fuckin' awful."

"I can't watch Irish Republicans killing themselves. Ordinary people who'd be bus drivers, plumbers, and nurses. Just ordinary married people with kids, if it wasn't for the British occupation of our country. Now, they have to starve themselves to death. I didn't think Thatcher would let Sands die. I really didn't. May she rot in hell for all eternity and all belonging to her."

I decided there was no point in trying to dissuade him. "When are you headin'?"

"He says he can sort a visa for me in about a week, so fairly soon. I think he's well connected in the Embassy."

"We'll have to organise a few pints before you go."

"Yeah, definitely. But no going-away do. I want to keep it low-key. If anyone asks why I dropped out, Emily included, just say college wasn't for me."

"Grand. No problem," I said, knowing it was only between us. "What are you doing later this evening?"

"Nothing much. Are you not working in the restaurant this evening?"

"No, tomorrow afternoon. They shifted my hours. There's a bit of a party in Jeremy's flat—if you want to drop in."

He huffed. "I'd prefer to stab myself in the eyeball with a sharp pencil."

I started to laugh. "That's a no, so?"

"What are you doing with those pricks? Jeremy, 'Jer Jer,' is an arsehole."

"I thought you liked him," I said, teasing. "I know. He's a complete cretin. But he's Emily's cousin."

"A complete dope head and soon-to-be junkie." He shifted on the stool, looking concerned. "Emily and you smokin' your brains out is one thing. But she's on a slippery slope, droppin' acid. That goes for you, too."

"I know. For the record, I only did it the once."

"I am not my brother's keeper," he said, shrugging his shoulders.

"I'd prefer Bob; He ain't heavy, he's my brother."

"You've been warned. You heard it here first, folks. Drugs will kill you."

"Says the man going to buy guns for the IRA."

"I don't think Noraid buys guns."

"OK. Raise money to buy guns for the IRA."

"No. Raise money for the strikers' families, the prisoners' families, for food parcels."

"I know. I'm joking."

"I blame you, with all your Granda stuff about us

not losing our ancient spirit. And all your guff about Tone and Pearse and Yeats. You really did a number on me. *'This is not your country. We are not your people.'* I would have been quite happy being a busman or a carpenter, like me auld fella, until you opened the door in my head."

"That sounds very accusatory. As Buddha might say, 'the finger pointing at the moon, is not the moon.' Or, in your Jesus parlance, I was merely the messenger of the Lord. Or..."

"You're shitein' again," he smiled tenderly, swilling the remains of Emily's pint.

We shared a knowing smile that covered a lot of unspoken territory between us. This was, without doubt, a significant milestone in our friendship.

"It's probably good that you're getting out of here. You'll be safer over there. Out of harm's way."

He managed a chuckle. "If my Ma and Da knew, I think they'd have me locked up." Mr and Mrs Mulcahy were staunch *Fine Gaelers.*

"Do you remember us going to Prendergast's door? He must have had a good laugh."

"I remember," Finn said, highly amused, "the look he gave me: '*Who are you? I'm his blood brother*!'"

"I can still see you standing to attention. You were so funny."

We started to laugh at our innocence and naivety.

"What am I going to do without you?" I said. "There'll be no *craic*."

"You'll probably become a West Brit and be best buggers with Jer Jer."

"Ha fuckin' ha. Very funny."

"I have to be off. I'll catch up with you during the week. Give my best to Jer Jer!"

"I will, yeah."

"I hope Emily is great in the sack. Because you're paying a heavy price having to suffer that arsehole."

"Fuck off!"

"Right. See you later."

"Yeah, see you."

Now, I was looking at two empty glasses, and no longer in form for more pints or for a tedious history lecture that would be irrelevant to the making of new Irish martyrs only a hundred miles up the road. I checked to see how much money I had in my pocket and decided to go to the early showing of *The Blues Brothers*, in the Savoy. This would give me enough time to get something to eat after the film, have a pint, and arrive at Jeremy's around 9 p.m.

It was probably closer to 10 p.m. when I arrived, having had a couple of pints in the Palace Bar with a nice auld fella hellbent on reminiscing about Dublin, "*back in the day*."

Jeremy opened the hall door to the Georgian

house. "Hi, man." He giggled. "I'm high man."

"Good to see you, old boy," I said, walking past him. "Ra ra and all that."

His giggles were interspersed with snorts. "Balls to you, Bertie."

I had no idea what he meant. He was the real rugby boy, about 6' 2" tall, broad shoulders, blonde hair, beady eyes, and a chin as big as his chest. I'd been to his flat once before—it was on the first floor of a three-story house and was more of an apartment than a flat: two ensuite bedrooms, living room, kitchen and dining area. He lived there with another guy, both worked as advertising executives, and both had a few bob. Emily said Uncle Reggie, Jeremy's father, was loaded.

When I entered the living room, there were six or seven people, including Emily, sitting on the floor around a lava lamp that was throwing fluid paisley patterns onto the ceiling. A couple were sprawled intertwined on the cream leather couch and there was a guy standing in the corner, staring at the wallpaper. Everyone was obviously out of it. Bob Dylan was on the record player singing about the hard rain that's gonna fall.

Emily waved. "Hey, handsome." Then patted the floor beside her.

I sat, and we gave each other a little peck. "Sorry, I'm late."

"Are you?" She sounded irked, and I guessed from

her intensely dilated pupils she had taken acid.

Roger, Jeremy's flatmate, reached over, holding a very large joint.

"Keep it, man. You gotta catch up."

I was certainly way behind, and, taking his advice, I inhaled deeply, only to cough and splutter, which was followed by everyone's giggles and laughs. "It's... eh... laced," Roger said, slowly. "Sorry, eh, I should have..."

There was silence.

"What, Rog?" the girl beside him said.

Roger looked at her very precisely. "What?"

"What?" she said, looking bewildered.

"Eh." He narrowed his eyes as if to help him think. "What do you mean, 'What Rog?'"

She started to giggle. "You said... what did he say?"

Everyone laughed, including me.

The guy at the wall turned and said, "He said, '*Sorry, eh, I should have...*' That's what he said." He then turned back to the wall, and everyone went into stitches of laughter.

Emily linked my arm. "It's laced, baby, so you gotta take it easy."

"Yep, got it." I inhaled deeply and cautiously. She took my face in her hands, and I exhaled slowly into her mouth. The rest of the room was oblivious to us, taken by whatever slow-motion minutia that was going on in their heads.

After a prolonged moment, she said, into my ear, "Thanks for coming."

"Wouldn't have missed it for the world."

We both started to laugh. "You're the best," she said, in fits and starts. "I know, these are not your people. Love you, though."

We hadn't said the love word before, and I wasn't sure if she knew she had said it. "Love you too," I whispered, not wanting to leave her hanging.

She opened her eyes wide in recognition of the love word and kissed my lips tenderly. Then, there was empty space that needed to be filled, but it wasn't the right time or place to elaborate on my love for her.

"I think,' she said, "Jer Jer thought he was in with a chance if you didn't show."

"Was he?"

She slapped my shoulder, playfully. "Uuhhhh!"

I offered Roger the joint, and he stared at me from a faraway place before slowly opening a wooden pencil case, similar to one I had in primary school, revealing three or four more fat joints. "It's cool, man."

"Cool," I heard myself say before continuing to smoke deeply and cautiously.

By the time I finished the joint, Emily and I were lying side by side on the floor, holding hands. I was mesmerised by the lava lamp patterns on the ceiling. "Jesus," I said, slowly. "That's some heavy-duty hash. The shapes… shifting and turning are amazing."

There was a long pause. "I dropped some acid before you came."

"I thought you did."

"I don't like the…" She pointed her finger upwards. "The monster things… eating the little ducks. Stop! Leave them alone."

I put my arm around her, and she snuggled into my chest. "It's OK, Em. They'll be gone in a minute."

"Shoo them away, Con," she mumbled.

"Shoo, shoo, go away.

Without any warning, she jumped to her hunkers. "Oh, my God, you're bleeding!" She was waving her arms over me. "Leave him alone! Get away! Get away! You can have the ducks. Get away."

"Shhh… Em, I'm OK. Look, I'm fine."

"You're bleeding, Con, you're bleeding. Jesus Christ! We need something to stop the bleeding." She sprinted to the kitchen, and I ran after her, whereupon she pressed a dirty t-towel to my neck. "I'm sorry, Con. I'm so sorry."

"It's OK, Em. Look, you stopped the bleeding. I'll be fine. Thanks."

"They're in the room. I can smell them." She turned full circle with a pointed finger and rigid outstretched arm. “They’re hiding. But I can smell them.”

The others were gawking at her, perplexed and amused in equal amounts. Jeremy had a strange, complicit look about him as if wondering how this scene might play out. Roger stood. “Conor is all better, Emily. You saved him.” He looked at me. “Best if you take her out of the room. You can crash in my room for the night.”

“No,” Emily whispered in my ear, “they’re in there too.”

“Alright,” I said, “let’s get out of here. We’ll be safe outside.”

“Yes, all right. If you think that’s best?”

“I do.”

We walked for about an hour, ever watchful for monsters, until we reached Sandymount, where she was living with Ingrid. Ingrid was very much the Minister’s daughter and, of course, disapproved of me. I knew she’d have a fit if she saw the state of Emily, so we walked and sat along the strand for another couple of hours, waiting on Ingrid to leave for work.

Huddled on a bench, the sea breeze chilled me to the bone as Em slept, curled into herself, her head on my lap. My mind was shaken by her hallucinations, and other than gently stroking her hair, I didn't know how to comfort her—how to protect her from the monsters. She hadn’t spoken in more than an hour, but I knew she wasn’t at ease—her eyes darting, her body twitching, the occasional whimper.

It was another hour or more before she spoke. “How long are we here?”

I held her closer. “A couple of hours.”

“I’m freezing.”

“I was waiting for the Christian Soldier to go to work.”

“What time is it?”

“Eight.”

“She’ll be gone in half an hour.”

“Are you back?”

“Yes, I think so. Oh, my God, I’m so cold and thirsty.”

“You were really gonzo last night.”

“Was I?”

“I wouldn’t take anything from Jeremy again.”

“Why?”

“I don’t trust him.”

“Was everyone else—OK?

“Yeah, that’s what I mean.”

“All right. You know this is the exact spot where Bloom was ogling Gerty MacDowell?”

I started to laugh. “Jesus, Em, you’re something else. After all that, you’re thinking about *Ulysses*.”

“It’s better than monsters.”

I kissed her hand. "It certainly is." Unlike her, I wasn't a Joycean scholar, but a particular line came to mind: *"Are we walking into eternity along Sandymount strand?"*

"I hope so. For ever and always."

"Forever and always." It felt as though we had passed through a liminal challenge: the die was cast.

She gathered herself and looked directly into my eyes. Her eyes were tired and bloodshot but mostly questioning. "*I asked you with my eyes to ask again yes and then you asked me would I yes to say yes my mountain flower and first I put my arms around you yes and drew you down to me so you could feel my breasts all perfume yes and your heart was going like mad and yes I said yes I will Yes.*" She sighed and hugged my arm. "Yes, I said to you, yes, a thousand times yes to you, but I am not Molly."

I knew it was a famous Molly Bloom quote but I didn't know its context and could only guess the depth of its meaning for her. My eyes filled with tears. "I love you, Em."

"I'm sorry about last night. Please, don't ever leave me. You are the only light in my darkness."

"Never. For ever and always."

After tucking her up in bed, I sat by her side until she was sound asleep. She looked so beautifully innocent, a sleeping angel, that it was difficult to comprehend she was fleeing monsters only hours before. I lightly stroked her hair and recited Yeats because she deserved the most beautiful words I could think of:

"Had I the heavens' embroidered cloths,

Enwrought with golden and silver light,

The blue and the dim and the dark cloths

Of night and light and the half-light,

I would spread the cloths under your feet:

But I, being poor, have only my dreams;

I have spread my dreams under your feet;

Tread softly because you tread on my dreams."

There were books strewn across her room, and, other than the incongruous Cat Stevens poster, the space was dominated by a bulging bookcase. I pulled out a well-thumbed copy of *Ulysses*. It had sections underlined, with dated notes in the margins. One underlined piece, dated from before we met, had my name written beside it.

Yes, it was her he was looking at, and there was meaning in his look. His eyes burned into her as though they would search her through and through, read her very soul.

Before leaving, I wrote a note and, placing it in the book, left it beside her pillow. "Yes, a thousand times yes. Yes, I watched you, yes—to your very soul! Hope you are feeling better. I had to go to work. Love forever and always, Con."

CHAPTER 4

I was in the middle of summer exams; my social life was on the back burner, and I hadn't been on a night out since Emily lost the plot in Jeremy's a few weeks earlier. Her courses were mostly based on continuous assessment, with some set exams around Easter time, which meant she was still fitting in the odd party without me. We were meeting three or four times a week for coffee, a quiet pint, or a trip to the cinema, but we hadn't discussed her bad trip in any great detail. I didn't want her to feel that I expected her to conform – she had enough of that from Mummy. Nevertheless, I was concerned about her, particularly her continued use of acid and her altered moods even when she wasn't taking it.

I'd spent the morning in the Berkeley library studying, and I was now sitting on a bench in College Park with a pint of milk and a dodgy egg sandwich, debating whether I'd soak up the sun, which was doing the proverbial rock-splitting, or watch the cricket between Trinity and Queens. Apparently, it was a friendly match—or game, I didn't know which term was correct—and with that conclusion, I decided to soak up the sun.

Pulling off my Rory Gallagher T-shirt, I stretched out on the park bench, feeling reasonably confident about revealing my physique after months of training with the Trinity hurlers. Unfortunately, our training regime didn't match our skills, and the inter-college Fitzgibbon Cup remained a pipe dream. We were slaughtered by Carlow Regional, who lined out with half the Kilkenny County Team. We then suffered ignominious defeat against UCG and were even beaten by Letterkenny Regional, where one of their lads caustically suggested, "Ye should stick to cricket boys or a spot of tennis." He seemed affronted by the very notion of a Trinity team daring to play hurling.

"Where do you think you are, St. Tropez?" Emily said from behind the bench.

My heart gladdened, and as I sat up, I quipped, 'St. Tropez? Hah, more like Dollymount. Brittas Bay, at a stretch.'"

She stayed behind me and kissed my ear. "Sorry, I forgot you were a peasant." Then she rubbed my chest and bit my ear with a faux sensuous growl. "Sexy body, though."

I held her hands on my chest, and she placed her chin on my head. "This is a nice surprise. I've been buried in the library with Wolfe Tone for the past four hours. I could do a *Mastermind* on him at this stage."

"Did you know he was a Protestant?"

"Very funny. What brings you in?"

"I scoured the library looking for you until I

realised it was lunchtime and you'd be slacking in the sun. Then I saw your jacket and bag. You're not in your usual seat?"

"No. It's quieter in the Law Section."

"The girl sitting opposite you is very pretty."

"Which girl?" I knew who she meant: a beautiful Spanish girl with sultry looks.

"Seriously! Are you going to tell me you didn't notice Miss Boobies?"

I couldn't help laughing, but I wasn't going to admit I noticed her because I'd grown wary of Emily going all paranoid over inconsequential things. "Is she the smelly one with the straw hair and buck teeth?"

"You're such a cad. '*But I like you.*' As that comedian guy says."

"Glad to hear it. You still haven't said why I have the pleasure of your company. If it's to steal me away for a coffee in Bewley's and a stroll around Stephens Green, you won't have to twist my arm."

"Unfortunately, not." She gave a big, heavy sigh. "I have to meet Mummy and Daddy for lunch."

"Really?" I led her around the bench without letting go of her hands, and she sat on my knee. "Wow, aren't we looking very pretty? I don't know if I ever saw you with makeup. And a dress! What have you done with my feminist?"

"It's serious," she said. "I want to make an

impression, or rather, dispel an impression."

"Sorry. You look gorgeous. What's wrong?"

"Apparently, Ingrid has snitched on me to Mummy." She held an invisible phone to her ear and affected an even posher accent. "Who is this boy I hear you are in love with?"

"Shit. It was bound to happen sooner or later."

"As far as I could gather from her hysterical state, she's been given a scurrilous report. Apparently, you are Catholic, poor, a reprobate, a drinker, a carouser, and overall bad influence."

"You left out sheep-shagger."

"It's serious, Con. You don't know what she's like."

"Sorry. I'm actually a bit surprised that Ingrid would hang me like that. I know I'm not her favourite, but she could have told Mummy about me months ago, and she didn't."

She scrunched her face with a guilty expression as if she was concealing a frightened emotion. "What?" I asked. "Is there something you're not telling me?"

"Last Tuesday... I had a flashback when I was with Ingrid."

"We met on Wednesday?"

"And you said I didn't seem myself."

"Em, you should have told me."

"I thought I got away with it." She had a peculiar,

forced, childlike smile. "I don't want you to think I'm nuts." Her face changed and big pearl tears rolled down her cheeks. "I don't want to lose you, Con."

"Oh, Em, you're not going to lose me. Forever and always. They're not just words to me. I mean them with all my heart."

"I know you do."

"That has to be the end of droppin' acid? Really, Em."

"Yes, I know."

"What happened? Where were you?"

"We were in the flat. A lot of it is a blank. I thought there was blood coming out of the shower, and I started to scream and took a fit on the floor. Ingrid didn't know what was happening to me. Then people started getting out of the TV. I don't remember much after that."

"What did she do?"

"She didn't know what to do, so she phoned Jeremy at work."

"Jeremy?"

"She knows him from childhood, they're the same age, and... I don't know why she called him. She just did."

"OK. And what happened then?"

"He gave me something to make me sleep, and I don't remember much until I woke up the next day."

"Did Ingrid stay with you?"

"No. Jer. I vaguely remember him..." She looked frightened, as though some memory was coming back to her.

"Vaguely remember what?"

"Nothing. I'd prefer not to remember anymore, and put that day behind me."

"Yeah, of course. I wish I could have been there for you."

"Me too."

"Do you want me to go with you, to show them I'm none of those things?"

She looked me up and down and laughed. "I don't think that's one of your better ideas."

"Yeah, maybe not. But we could arrange another day. I can lose the Che Guevara look, shave the beard, cut my hair and put on a suit. No problem. I polish up well."

She pinched my cheeks and kissed my lips. "No, baby. You look beautiful. More Cat Stevens than Guevara. But thanks for offering."

"Think about it, Em. It's only a look. I can grow my hair again and look equally scruffy again. I can impress them if you give me a chance. I'll tell them about my career prospects as a university lecturer. I'll show them I'm a highly intelligent, respectable peasant who's more than capable of taking care of their daughter."

"No, baby. Let me deal with them. They're my parents."

"I don't want you taking any shit from them over me. They're not even horse-protestants, just middle-class snobs."

She grabbed my beard in both hands and shook my head from side to side. "Not even horse-protestants! Gosh. Where in heavens did you pull that one from? So, we're not good enough for you now."

I laughed. "Well, if the cap fits. The McCarthys have a noble and royal heritage dating back over 600 years. We can spot a jumped-up protestant from a mile off, minister or not."

She pulled my head to her bosom, "I love you, Conor McCarthy."

"I love you too, Emily Williams, and I'll be damned if I let Daddy, Mummy, Ingrid or Jeremy come between us."

"That won't happen, baby. Don't worry." She looked at her watch. "I'm meeting them in the Shelbourne at half past. I'd better go."

"Remember plan B. I can look like Mr Corporate, no problem. I'll even let him convert me. That would get him brownie points upstairs."

"I suspect you'd self-combust and take Daddy with you. But don't worry, I'll remember, just in case. I'll meet you in the library after, not sure how long it will be."

"Grand. There's no rush, I'll hang on."

"Love you. Byeee."

"Love you too. Good luck."

"Thanks."

As I watched her walk away in her summer floral dress and respectably heeled sling-back shoes, my love for her was weighted with sadness. I could see her free spirit trying desperately to conform, trying to please Mummy. She looked beautiful, and a garbled line from Pearse entered my thoughts. *Her beauty in the world hath made me sad, this beauty that will pass.* I felt nervous, sensing that our bubble had been punctured and she might be passing from me.

Back in the library, I couldn't sit still. My mind was anxiously fixated on the lunch and on what Mummy might be saying to Emily. *If I was there,* I thought, *I'd tell her how much I loved her daughter and how I would always protect her. I'd speak properly, dressed in a suit and tie, and I'd hold my cup correctly if we were having tea, remembering to say yes, please, and thank you.*

No, I reasoned, *that all sounds way too grovelly. Maybe it would be better if I just let rip and told her a few home truths: how she didn't understand her own daughter, didn't recognise the beautifully unique person she is, and how she made Emily doubt herself and feel sad. I'd tell her, we're two grown adults, and if she couldn't accept us, she could fuck off and never get to see her grandchildren.*

Miss Boobies was obviously distracted and irked by my restlessness. She displayed her displeasure with heavy sighs interspersed with frustrated tapping of her pen on the desk. Feeling guilty, I took a book and sat by the General Reference shelves where I could keep an eye on the stairwell and wait for Emily's return. Her luncheon was taking longer than I expected. I thought she would have been back by mid-afternoon, but my watch was telling me 5.45 p.m. I went to check the clock at reception, and it also said 5.45 p.m. At 6.15 p.m., my sultry studier left, and I went back to my desk, more worried than ever.

It was about 7 p.m. when Emily appeared. She was crying, and my heart sank. Her mascara had stained her blotchy cheeks, her nose was red and runny, and my stomach churned with fear at what she might say. I met her halfway, and she fell into my arms, exhausted.

"Oh, Con," she said, gasping between sobs, "I thought I'd never get here. I thought you'd be gone."

"I'm here, Em. It's OK, I'm here."

Some students lifted their heads, annoyed at the interruption but curious about the commotion. One glanced at Em's feet, and I realised she wasn't wearing any shoes; her feet were filthy, and one of them was bleeding.

"Jesus, Em, what happened?"

My question didn't register. Her body trembled like a frightened bird, and she kept whispering, amid sniffles and quivering gasps. "I thought you'd be gone... I thought you'd be gone."

At this point, every head in the place had popped up like meerkats. "C'mon, Em, let's get out of here." I didn't want her to be a spectacle.

She clung to me as a drowning man might cling to a buoy, and as we moved towards the stairs, I noticed she was limping. Eager to get her away, I swept her up in my arms and left the prying eyes behind. "I'm here, Em, I'm here. Everything will be OK."

Outside, I stood on the library steps with her in my arms, at a loss as to what I was going to do. After racking my brain, all I could come up with was Dave. He wasn't a close friend, but he was a generally sound guy, and he had rooms on campus.

"Hey," I said, when he opened the door.

"Hey." He looked surprised and gave Emily the once-over. She was standing, but her body was limp, and she clung to me for support. "Is she OK?"

"Not really. Can we use your room?"

He took a deep breath, looked at Emily again, and exhaled with an extended puff. "Eh, sure. For how long?"

"I don't know. Eh, just until she gets her head together."

"Are you OK?" he asked Emily, but she didn't respond in any coherent way. I knew she didn't want to start explaining her situation. "Does she need a doctor?"

"No. Just some space."

Again, he took a deep breath and exhaled with a long puff. "Eh, well. I can crash with Paddy. But you owe me, man."

It was one of the tiny rooms, hardly changed since the 19th Century: single bed, table, two upright chairs, one armchair, wash hand basin, and a small closet. Emily sat on the edge of the bed. She had stopped crying but was still sniffling. There was a large poster of Black Sabbath on the wall behind her, together with a few magazine pullouts of Led Zeppelin and Deep Purple.

Dave pulled on a heavy jumper and took a denim jacket from the back of a chair. "There's a first aid kit over the sink. I don't know what's in it, it came with the room."

"Thanks, man."

He paused in the doorway. "I have an exam at the end of the week and I study in the room. You need to be out of here in the morning. Sorry."

"Yeah, definitely," I said, as he was closing the door behind him.

Emily still wasn't saying much, but she seemed to be gaining a greater awareness of where she was and what was going on. I wrapped her in the bed quilt and gave her a cup of hot coffee before washing and dressing her feet. The cut was minor, mostly scratches, although she had also grazed her knees.

"This might sting a bit," I said, dabbing her knee with soapy water.

She didn't flinch or react, other than a small embarrassed smile. 'I jumped out of the car.'

"How do you mean?" I asked, trying to sound very non-alarmist."

"They were taking me home." She started to sob, quietly, as though she was afraid the sound of her crying would betray some secret vulnerability. "I told them I wouldn't go anywhere without seeing you." The sentence proved too much, and she broke into uncontrollable sobbing, gasping and moaning between tortured words. "They said, I wasn't well, that I was, making myself sick again."

"Shhh. Calm down, Em. You're safe here. Nobody is taking you anywhere."

"I panicked and jumped out of the car." Her face was distorted with anguish and defiance. "Then I ran and ran. I had to see you before they took me away."

"I'm here, nobody is taking you away." With every passing moment, my heart sank further, and my anxiety grew faster, but I tried to keep a calm exterior. *They must be searching for her.* I thought. *Probably, terrified of what might have happened to her.*

"Then I got lost, and these little urchins chased me, but I was too fast for them. I ran and ran, and they threw bottles after me. I was afraid I'd never see you again. I was afraid of..."

I waited, hoping she was going to reveal whatever that secret vulnerability was, but she didn't finish her sentence. "You don't have to be afraid, Em. I'm here. I'll protect you." I kissed her forehead. "I just have to go to the bathroom. I'll be back in a minute; it's at the end of the hall. Two minutes, and I'll be back. Is that OK? Two minutes?"

She nodded.

I flew down the granite stairwell to the public phone in the hallway.

"Hello. Ingrid?"

"Yes?"

"It's Conor. I want to let you know Emily is with me, she's safe. I'll phone you again in the morning."

She started to cry. "Oh, thank you, Jesus. Thank you, Conor, thank you for phoning. Is she... is she well in herself?"

"She's upset, but she's... I just wanted to let you know that she's safe."

"Thank you. Thank you for all your kindness. I should tell you that Mummy has reported her missing and... unwell. She has given the police your address. It was in Emily's diary."

"Eh, OK. We're not there. I'll call you in the morning."

After hanging up, I phoned home. Dad answered,

"Hello."

"Dad, the Guards might call looking for Emily. Everything is fine, you don't have to worry."

"Are you alright, son?"

"Yes, I'm grand. Just a mix-up. Nothing to do with me."

"Emily is a lovely girl, son. But don't get on the wrong side of those people."

"I won't, Dad. I'll talk to you tomorrow."

On returning to the room, Em was sitting four square at the table. "I want you to know who I am." Her posture was terribly forced, and I could see she was summoning all of her strength.

"OK," I said, sitting opposite her.

"When I was fifteen, I fell in love with a boy. He was a little older, one of Jeremy's friends. He meant everything to me." She reached across the table and held my hand. "It was a huge teenage crush. But..."

She wiped her eyes. "I let him have sex with me. We were drunk. I was drunk. The following day, he sent me a note saying he was breaking up with me, but one of his friends wanted to go out with me. I was heartbroken, inconsolable, and when one of his friends offered to pay me "for a fuck" I lost my mind, literally. I wanted to die. I was only fifteen. I couldn't understand the betrayal, and I couldn't cope knowing everyone was talking behind my back, calling me a whore. I became very unwell and..."

She swallowed hard, and silent tears cascaded down her face, dropping onto the table. "They put me into a psychiatric hospital...Your girlfriend is mad."

I was crying, and took her in my arms. "No, Em. You're not mad. You were only a child. Oh, poor Em."

"I was afraid if you found out, you might leave me."

"Jesus. God, no, Em. Forever and always."

"I'm not a whore. He was the only other one."

"Oh, Em. You were only a child. You don't have to explain anything to me. I love you, Em, with all my heart and soul."

We talked and cried for a while longer until she fell asleep in my arms. The following morning, she looked wrecked. Her eyes were blinking rapidly and she had developed a disconcerting tick in her neck.

I have to go home," she said, with sad clarity. "I need to take my meds. I'm not well, Con. I forgot to tell you that your mad girlfriend takes prescribed medication every day."

"Don't say that, Em. You're not mad."

"You are a fabulous human being, and the past eight months have been the best of my life. But I'll only drag you down unless I go home and recuperate. I don't want you to see me helpless."

I was in floods of tears. "OK, Em. Whatever you want. I can come down and visit you. Mummy won't have to know."

"Yes. It's for the best." She gave me the bravest smile I'd ever seen. "And when I'm all better, we can get married, have babies and live happily ever after. That's if you still want me."

"Yes, Em. A thousand times, yes. I'd marry you tomorrow. Yes."

"Con, you're such a dote." She gave a loaded chuckle. "Don't rush me; you're getting a catch here."

"Don't I know." I tried to sound light-hearted.

"That's what I'll think about when I'm getting better, a little Conor running about."

"Our little Conor, or Emily."

"Yes, our little Conor, or Emily." She kissed the palm of my hand. "I love you, baby, more than life itself."

"I love you too."

CHAPTER 5

Two days passed, and I heard nothing from Emily, so I called out to Ingrid.

"She's being cared for," Ingrid said, standing in her chunky plaid dressing gown at the hall door, as an early morning breeze swished about us.

"Where? Can I see her?"

"The doctors say her episode was brought on by the use of illicit drugs, and provided she stops, she should make a full recovery. They want to observe her for a few days, reassess her medication. If all goes well, she'll be home by the end of the week."

It took me all my time to swallow the lump in my throat. *She's going to be OK.* "Can I visit her?"

"No. I'm afraid not. Not at the moment." She sounded less hostile than I expected.

"When?" I barked. "Sorry, when can I see her?"

"If you phone me on Thursday evening, I'll have a better idea."

"Thursday evening. Is 7 p.m. OK?"

"Yes."

"Thanks."

Just as she was about to close the door, she said, "I know you love her. It wasn't me who phoned Mummy."

I couldn't think of what to say. I nodded. The door closed.

On Thursday evening, she told me Emily was well. She was coming home on Saturday morning and would meet me on Sunday at 2 p.m. by the old round tower overlooking the river. "It's only five minutes from the train station."

The train arrived-in ten minutes late, and I hurried to the round tower, which was clearly visible from the platform. Emily sat on a green slatted park bench with her back to me, overlooking the river at the bottom of a grassy incline. The river's outwardly calm currents reflected a brooding sky, and my heart beat ever faster as I approached her along a narrow, tarmacked path. I was nearly upon her when she saw me and stood. Instantly, the seriousness of her face dominated what I had hoped would be a joyous scene, and my stomach churned with anxiety.

We hugged. "Em, Em. I'm so happy to see you. Oh, I was really scared. How are you feeling?" She didn't speak and clung to me so tight that I thought we might topple over. "Ingrid says you're doing great."

She sniffled and stepped away from me, one pace, and then a second. "I need to tell you something."

I didn't want to hear anything other than happy

resolutions, but the gravity of her tone and the distance she had created between us told me I wasn't going to get what I wanted. I moved closer. "OK. You can tell me anything. Do you want to sit down?"

We sat on the bench, with an unusual space between us, and she looked at the river for what seemed like a long time. I stayed silent, thinking she was trying to find the words to tell me whatever she needed to tell me. She took two quick breaths through her nose and turned to me. "I'm pregnant."

My jaw swung open, and my mind raced. *I'll have to drop out of college. Get a job. A proper job. We could go to America. Over to Finn. Better prospects in America. Say something. Quick.* "OK. A little Conor or Emily sooner..."

"Stop, Conor!" Her face inflamed with angry guilt. "It's not yours."

A searing spike shot from my anxiety and stabbed through my heart. I couldn't breathe. "I don't understand. How could... Are you sure?"

"Yes. I'm sorry, Con." Her face was solemn, deathly calm, but her bloodshot eyes were wrought with pain.

"Sometimes condoms don't work..."

"It's not yours," she snapped.

"I don't understand, Em... how? Who?"

She shook her head. Her eyes, now washed with shame, breached her unfamiliar exterior, and a huge tear rolled down her face, followed by another. She wiped them away.

"Who, Em? I deserve to know."

She hung her head. "Jeremy."

"Ah, Jesus. No. No, Em. I don't understand. Please... I don't understand."

"When he put me to bed, after Ingrid called him." She looked back to the river. "I don't really remember. I have a confused image of him on top of me, telling me to turn over. I wasn't wearing my pants when I woke up, and I was sore. Ingrid said he left during the night."

"He raped you. The fuckin' bastard raped you." I leaned towards her, and she pulled back. "Please, Em, let me hold you."

We held each other in silence, then walked along the riverbank, beyond the path and under the overhanging trees, until we came to a small clearing. "This is where I used to come when they were calling me a whore. And here I am again."

"No, Em. Here we are—together."

She smiled, a sad hollow smile, as if dismissing my naivety. "What am I going to do?" The despondency in her voice was crippling.

"Are you absolutely sure I'm not the father?"

She nodded, looking at the ground, struggling with the weight of something that was all too obvious to her. "I had my period."

She looked defeated, broken, and I felt compelled

to find a solution. "We can get through this. You can have the child adopted. Or you can have an abortion in England. I can get the money. We'll get through this together."

An ironic snigger curled her lips. "Money won't be a problem. As soon as Mummy knows, I'll be on the first plane to England, and she'll be vindicated. Emily, our highly strung whore child."

The following morning, I raged into Jeremy's office. It was an open plan with six desks beyond a reception area. I saw he was at the second desk and charged towards him, picking up a marble desk clock on the way before crashing it into his mouth, sending him tumbling from his seat with a look of shock still evident through the pouring blood. He steadied himself and lunged at me like a Leinster flanker, trapping my arms in a bear hug, lifting me off the ground. I slammed my head into his nose, once, twice. It cracked and gushed blood. On the third headbutt, he staggered and released his hold. I grabbed him by the hair and whacked his head against the wall repeatedly, until he was about to go down. I then pulled him forward and continued to smash his face against the desk. His dead weight was too much for my grip, and he slid onto the floor.

Everything in the office appeared small, as though I was towering over it all. He was now slumped between desks. I lifted a heavy typewriter and hurled it at his head, but he managed to raise an arm and block it. I then looked about for another weapon and saw two women screaming.

"He's a fucking rapist!" I shouted, feeling the need to tell them. "A fucking rapist! He raped his cousin. He raped her when she was unconscious."

"We've called the police," one of them whimpered.

"Call the fucking police. He's a fucking rapist." I was still shouting, but their terrified faces had confused and abated my rage. "A fucking scumbag." Things began to resume normal proportions. Jeremy was crumpled on the floor with terror in his eyes, and my mind blanked as to what to do next. I leaned over him. "You're a fucking rapist," I said, and spat in his face before walking out the door.

Outside, there were a number of rubbish bins for collection on the footpath, and sticking from one was a metal pipe, about two feet long. My mind flashed with an image of him on top of Em, turning her over, and a feeling of icy retribution ran through me. I took the pipe and went back inside the building, intent on taking his life. When he saw me, he hobbled into a side office and locked the door. I noticed, for the first time, that there were three women in the office and two men, one of whom was Roger. No one interfered with me. There was some crying and shouting, but I was oblivious to what they were saying. My heart was cold, unemotional, and I pounded the locked door with my shoulder.

"Alright now, calm down," a commanding voice said. "Nobody needs to get hurt." It was one of two

Gardai who appeared with their batons drawn.

I dropped the bar and walked towards them. "He raped my girlfriend, his cousin," I said, by way of explanation.

"That may well be," the older Garda said, calmly. "But we can't be takin' the law into our own hands, sure that wouldn't work at all. Hands behind your back now, like a good man."

* * *

After being processed and remanded on bail, I was sitting at home, staring mindlessly at the telly. Mam and Dad were tiptoeing around me, worried sick. They knew I'd been arrested for beating the shit out of some fella but little else. I didn't feel like talking.

The phone rang in the hall. "Con," Mam shouted, "it's for you. Finn."

I sat on the stairs and picked up the phone. "Hey."

"Hey. Your Dad called, and said you might need to talk."

"So, you know the story?"

"No. Other than you beat the shit out of some fella."

I told him all that happened, and he was horrified. "I'm really sorry, Con. Poor Emily. I told you he was a fuckin' prick."

"My solicitor says I'm most likely facing a custodial sentence given the level of violence, and the victim's unblemished record."

"So, you really gave it to him?"

"I went animal on him."

He nearly laughed, but knew he shouldn't. "Good."

"But it's not good. I'll be in Mountjoy when Em needs me. She's being very calm and collected about everything. But that's on the outside. On the inside, I know she's in bits. She's really hurting. I'm such a fucking idiot. I could have done him in the dark somewhere."

"Maybe you won't have to do time. What did Granny Bubbles used to say? 'God is good, but the Devil is earning.'"

"I thought I'd be visiting you in Sing Sing, for gun running. Now, here's me heading to Mountjoy."

Two days later, my solicitor phoned. "Good news, counsel for the other side was in touch. They want to drop the case in its entirety. Apparently, a Mr. Prendergast had a meeting with the victim's father, Mr. Reginald Hutton, and matters were brought to a satisfactory conclusion."

I phoned Em immediately, on the off chance that she might pick up, but there was no answer. I tried a number of times until I kept getting the engaged tone and guessed Mummy had taken the phone off its hook.

Before Ingrid answered the hall door of her flat, I was buoyed by relief at my narrow escape from prison and felt that my love could overcome whatever the future might hold. I couldn't wait to tell Em I wasn't going to be incarcerated. I also knew Ingrid understood how I felt about Em and guessed she would be open to organising another meeting—without Mummy knowing.

The door opened. She was crying and looked puzzled to see me. "How did you know?"

"Know what?"

"I've only put the phone down." There was a dazed, puzzled look in her eyes.

"Know what?"

"Emily is dead." She spoke the words with numbed disbelief.

"What!?" My knees buckled and I had to hold onto the wall.

"Emily is dead," she repeated, disbelieving her own words. "They found her down by the river."

I don't remember much after that; my mind collapsed, and all that is life became a tormented haze.

* * *

On the day of her funeral, I stood discreetly inside the gates of the small churchyard, my heart broken, and watched as they carried Em's coffin from the hearse into the church. A big white Mercedes pulled in by the gate, with Jeremy in the passenger seat, about to alight. Reason drained from me, and I instinctively hurried to open the car door. His arm was in plaster, and his face looked as though it had been trampled by horses.

"You're not going to desecrate Emily's funeral," I said, incensed. "You fucking abomination. If you step foot out of this car, I'll take your fucking life."

Neither of them looked at me, and my blood boiled with barely repressed rage. I looked at Uncle Reginald. "If you get out of this car, I'll fucking burn everything you own to the ground. Shame on you for letting this piece of shit get away with raping your niece. You're fucking despicable."

"Drive, for Christ's sake," Jeremy implored, and the car sped away.

I kept my distance from the graveside, not that anyone would have recognised me; clean shaven, short hair, suit and tie.

At the end of the burial, Ingrid came over and hugged me. "I'm sorry for your loss, Conor." Her voice was raw, her eyes sunken and bloodshot.

"Thank you. It's so awful. I'm sorry for your loss too. I don't know what... is there anything that... did she leave a note or something?" My lip began to quiver, and I had to steady myself.

"She had a note from you in her pocket. I'd like to think she was reading it before she... It said, 'Yes, a thousand times yes. Yes, I watched...' I can't. I'm sure you remember it."

I nodded.

"I didn't know if you would want it back. I thought you would probably like it if she were buried with your love, so I placed it inside her shirt, over her heart."

I bit my hand and blurted through snot and tears. "Yes. Thank you."

"I was talking to her the night before, she knew you had been calling out to me, and she asked me to tell you that she loved you"—her words broke down between desolate cries—"forever and always." Shaking her head, she groaned. "I should have known. Her voice was different. I should have heard it."

We hugged. "It wasn't your fault," I said, cursing God for not letting her hear it.

"I know, but... if I hadn't called that bastard. I'm surprised he didn't come to show he had nothing to hide."

"Did she talk to anyone else?"

"Mummy."

"She phoned me about Em having an abortion."

"Mummy phoned you?"

"Yes. She didn't want me to stand in the way."

"I didn't know."

"I told her I wasn't the father. Does she know that Jeremy raped her?"

"Emily told Mummy. But she didn't believe her."

"Ahh, no." I broke down into uncontrollable weeping, choking on my words. "Oh, Em... Em. We could have got through it. We could have, Em—together."

CHAPTER 6

It had always been my room, the room where Yeats found me after Granda died.

Come away, Oh human child! To the waters and the wild. With a faery, hand in hand. For the world's more full of weeping than you can understand.

Only ten, and I was captivated. The same room where I made love to Em, and we laughed like giddy children because she was so nervous Mam and Dad would arrive home early.

Now, curled in my bed, I wasn't feeling giddy or captivated. Her death had crushed my heart and all I wanted to do was burrow and hide, to be solitarily numb. Yet the more I burrowed, the more she was there, inside my brain, inside my soul.

The door knocked. "Are you getting up today?" It was Mam.

"Maybe later." I hadn't been out of the room in days. It was a small box room with a single bed tucked behind the door, a free-standing clothes rail, a disproportionately sized chest of drawers, and a couple of precariously held DIY shelves stacked with books. The back of the door was loaded with coats and jackets, and when it opened, they overhung my pillow.

"Will you come down for some breakfast?"

"No thanks." *Go away, Mam, please.*

The door opened, but I couldn't see her behind the coats. "Will I bring you up a cup of tea?"

"No thanks."

The door closed. I turned onto my back and stared into the abyss.

Nietzsche came to mind. *If you stare too long into the abyss, the abyss will stare back into you.*

I didn't care.

Sometime later, hours, I guess, the door knocked again and Mam came into the room. "There's a letter for you. From America. It says, Finn Mulcahy on the back."

He apologised for not being able to make the funeral, explaining he hadn't yet got his visa, and if caught re-entering the States, he would be deported. The envelope also contained a bank draft for $2,000 "in case you need to find headspace on the Burren—recharge your spirit."

We had hiked around County Clare when we were teenagers and had found a deep connection with the Burren's karst landscape. Finn was never a man for poetry—James Connolly and Fintan Lawlor were his strength—so his concern for my spiritual wellbeing was all the more touching when he quoted Yeats at the end of the letter.

Whether man dies in his bed or the rifle knocks him dead, a brief parting from those dear is the worst man has to fear.

It was a line from *Under Ben Bulben*, but he couldn't have known that it was the poem I had discussed with Emily only days before she went to lunch with Mummy and Daddy, only days before our world imploded.

"There is life in death," she said. "If we can resist the fear of temporary loss, love can be eternal."

Never in my wildest dreams could I have imagined that her interpretation would soon have such personal meaning.

The Ennis bus wasn't due to leave for an hour, so I crossed the road from the station to Molloy's pub for a coffee and to idle away the time. The bar had two intermingling layers of cigarette smoke; a stale, dull grey and an undercurrent of expectant blue-grey drifting in and out of a slanted sunbeam.

My watch said 11:45 a.m., yet all the stools along the old wooden counter were taken by a row of hunched male backs, save for one empty stool at the far end. There were also a few people sitting at tables, male and female, all seemed to be smoking. An unstated atmosphere of fellowship prevailed, where morning alcohol was the common denominator. One woman, about the same age as Mam, lifted her glass gingerly, and I saw the tremor in her hand steady as she sipped her first sip. A fragile mask of ease came over her addiction, but her weary eyes betrayed the hollow comfort.

I moved across the bare floorboards without making eye contact with anyone and sidled my way to the empty stool. The barman lifted his eyebrows in recognition of my presence. “Pint of Guinness,” I responded, without sitting on the stool, because I told myself, *I’m only passing through.*

A vacant minute or two passed, and the barman placed a creamy pint in front of me. I remembered the last pint I had with Em in the Buttery, and wanting to hold onto the thought, I eased myself onto the stool.

There’ll be other buses, the voice in my head said.

“Do you have nothing smaller?” the barman said, as I handed him IR£20. “I’m a bit short on change.”

“No. Sorry.”

I drank the pint, quickly. As one might if they were going to catch a bus.

“Same again?” the barman asked, clearing the empty glass.

I nodded.

He placed another pint in front of me and counted out 85p from the change and notes that were on the counter from the first pint. He then tidied the notes together and stacked the coins on top. I observed his endeavour, but didn’t lift my head.

“That must be a fierce thirst ya have,” the man

sitting to my right said.

I half turned my head, without lifting my eyes. “Yeah.”

He shifted on his stool and repositioned his feet on the footrest. “Sorry. I didn’t mean to intrude.”

“OK. I’d prefer not to chat.”

“No problem. I’m often like that meself.”

“How’s Desie?” a man passing behind us said and patted my chatty neighbour on the back.

“Good man yourself,” he replied. “I see you’re still with the quare wan.”

“Ya know yerself,” he didn’t stop, yet continued talking, raising his voice as he went. “A glutton for punishment.”

There was other intermittent banter going on in the background, but I ignored it.

On my third pint, I needed to use the toilet. “Where’s the jacks?” I asked Desie, who was now facing away from me, giving heed to my preferred solitary drinking.

“Just there,” he pointed, “on your right.” There was no umbrage in his voice.

“Thanks.” I looked at the money on the counter and wondered should I take the notes.

“Safe as a house,” he said. “It’ll be here when you get back.”

When I returned, he winked, transferring the safekeeping of my money back to me. "Thanks."

"Not a problem. It'll be better before you're twice married."

I looked questioningly at him. *What will be better?*

He was fifty-ish, with a donkey jacket over a denim shirt that was struggling to contain a porter belly beneath a pockmarked face and boozy nose. "Whatever's troublin' ya," he said. "You're too young to be carrying the weight of the world."

"It's none of your business." My words were quiet, nonconfrontational.

"You're right. I'm sorry." He turned his back to me.

"My girlfriend is dead," I barely whispered to myself, staring absently at the counter. *Em is dead. Em is dead,* I repeated over and over in my mind, but it still didn't make sense. *Em. Em. What am I going to do?*

"Are you alright there?" the barman asked.

I wondered why he was asking me, then realised I was crying. I sniffled and wiped my face. "Yes."

Desie must have overheard or was watching in the mirror behind the bar. "My own son would have been about your age. I have two daughters and they're..."

"My girlfriend is dead." *Leave me alone.*

"Oh, Lord save us," he blessed himself. "May she rest in peace."

I nodded, tight-lipped. “Thanks.”

“I’m very sorry for your troubles. I’m Desie, by the way.” He offered his hand.

“Conor.” We shook hands.

“Can I buy you a drink?”

I looked back at the counter. “No. Thanks.”

“Maybe you’ll have a small one? A Jemmie?”

I didn’t respond quick enough, wondering how best to deal with his well-meaning intrusion.

“Pat,” he called to the barman, “two Jemmies.”

The drinks were put before us, and I downed mine in one swallow. “Thanks.” Then returned to the counter, hoping my minimalist interaction would result in him leaving me alone.

“That’ll do ya good,” he said and, hesitating, as you might before jumping into a cold sea, drank his Jemmie all at once, followed by a pleasurably anguished gasp. “Jaysus, it’s too early in the day for that.” He put his broad, flat palm on my back. “My advice, Conor. Pace yourself. Or you’ll be too drunk too quick. There’s no one here will bother you. I’ll make sure of that.”

I heard him, but I wasn’t listening, and I spoke softly to Emily, “And still I dream you tread the lawn, walking ghostly in the dew.”

Desie slid his hand to the nape of my neck. “Did you write that?”

"Yeats." I knew he meant well, but I wished he would go away.

"Bewdaful. Bewdaful. I'll leave you be."

He left me be. And my mind raced towards alcohol-induced oblivion.

Time drifted, and someone leaned into Desie. "Me auld flower. I thought you were unloadin' the French boat."

"Easy," Desie said, half hushed. "Our friend here is grievin'. Come round the other side of me."

"Oh, sorry." He patted my back. "Sorry for your troubles."

I nodded, without looking.

"I thought you'd be unloadin' the French boat," he repeated, from the other side of Desie.

"I am," Desie said. "Bilocation."

"Very nice. Ya can get tablets for that now. Will ya be out with it long?"

"Ya know yerself. Terrible hard on the auld back, so it is."

"I could write a book on it, so I could."

"Whacker is lookin' after my end."

"Whacker? Tiddle-the-ropes?"

"Yeah."

"No better man. There's some nice clobber on it.

Top end."

"Don't I know. Give us a shout on Saturday, and we'll get somethin' sorted."

Over the next few hours, under Desie's wing, I was absorbed into the fellowship of North Inner City morning drinkers. Various people, on route to the toilets or stopping to chat with Desie, patted me on the back and expressed their condolences. But other than these brief expressions of clannish compassion, I wasn't bothered; for the most part, everything beyond my thoughts remained distant—exterior.

Several drinks later, I went to stand and stumbled backwards, bumping awkwardly into two men passing behind me.

"Jaysus! C'mon, pal." He steadied me. "Steady on. It's too fuckin' early for that messin'."

"Sorry."

"Yeah?"

"Yeah, sorry," I said, looking him in the eye, then taking in his friend. Both were in their early twenties and had an edgy aspect to them, with long, greasy hair, narrow faces, and pointy noses.

"He's with me, Tony," Desie said.

"No probs, Desie, no probs," the edgy man said, adopting a suddenly jocular tone and holding my shoulders. "You OK, pal? Here, sit back down there."

Standing straight, I raised my open hands to chest

level, and he released my shoulders. "I'm grand."

"Fair enough, pal. No probs. Listen, Desie, you're the very man I came in to see. I hear on the bush telegraph there might be a bit of nice gear floatin' about."

"Haven't heard," Desie said without looking at him.

"No? Some French ship, full of Gucci and Armani?"

"No. I've been out sick."

There was a long pause, during which I plonked myself on the stool and reengaged with the counter.

"Right, so," Tony said, sounding sceptical. "Well, if ya hear antin', ya let me know, yeah?"

"I can't tell ya what I don't know."

"Fair enough, Desie." There was pronounced irritation in his tone. "Fair enough."

Tony moved up the bar, and Desie spoke under his breath. "Fuckin' toerag."

I gave no indication that I heard him and slipped back into my thoughts. To the same old paths where love had walked with hope, and memory fed the soul of love with tears.

Several whiskies later, I heard the barman say, "He'll be scuttered in no time."

"How we doin', Conor?"

I looked at Desie through bleary eyes. "Grand."

"Maybe you should have a little kip." His voice

rose. "Can he have a kip in the snug?"

"Fire away," the barman said. "Old Peter and Sally are in there."

"Stick that money in your pocket, and we'll get you sorted in the snug."

He took me by the elbow, but I removed my arm from his hand. "After you," I slurred, not wanting to be manhandled, yet ready to follow his lead.

"How's Old Peter? Sally?" he said. "I'm goin' ta leave this fella here – he needs to rest his head for a bit. Will ya keep an eye on him?"

I was standing in a small room with ornate wooden panels and frosted glass in a wooden swing door. There were two round tables, no chairs, and a wooden bench skirting the walls. Old Peter and Sally were sitting beside an end-of-counter hatch, through which I could see the full length behind the bar.

"I will," Old Peter said. "Will ya be comin' back for him?"

"No. I have to see a man about a dog."

"Off ya go. I'll keep an eye on him."

"Lie down on the seat," Desie said, to me. "Have a bit of a kip. You'll feel the better of it later. Take off your jacket, and put it under your head."

I did as was suggested, not because I was stupid drunk, but because I didn't care. I was tired and detached, and I was indifferent to being awake-drunk or asleep-drunk. As long as I didn't have to talk to anyone.

"What's that you're drinkin'?" Desie said, to Old Peter.

"No need, Desie."

"Now, you were never one to look a gift horse in the mouth."

"You're a terrible man," Old Peter quipped. "A ball of malt so, and a Sandyman's for herself."

"I'll sort that," Desie said. "Keep an eye, and don't let anyone interfere with him. There's a few toerags in the bar."

"Rosie Brennan's son," Sally said. "God rest her. A toerag is right. How's herself?"

"She's doin' good. Thanks for askin'."

* * *

When I woke, Tony was standing over me, holding my jacket and looking surprised. "Ah, yer awake." He turned to his companion, who was sitting where Old Peter and Sally had been.

"Here, Snotzer," he said, hastily placing my jacket over me, "he's awake."

"He thought ya might be getting cold," Snotzer said.

"Yeah. Ya were out for the count," Tony said, and sat beside Snotzer.

I put my feet on the floor and my face in my hands, remembering how I came to be asleep on the seat.

"We're friends of Desie's," Tony said, "we were chattin' earlier."

I nodded and moved to the end-of-bar hatch.

"Any chance of a pint?" Tony said, with clumsy guile. "I'm a bit short; I don't get me Labour till Thursda'."

A new barman came to the hatch.

"Two pints," I said, and looked at Snotzer.

"I'll, eh, have a brandy?"

"Ya will in yer hole," Tony scoffed. "Are ya tryin' to fuckin' fleece the man? He'll have a pint."

The evening continued in the same vein. I bought the drink, and they kept to themselves, careful not to disturb their golden goose.

"Time," the barman called, from beyond the snug. "Time now, Ladies and Gents."

"Do ya fancy goin' on somewhere?" Tony said, to me.

"Yeah, where?"

"Eh, a friend of ours has a free house."

"Yeah," Snotzer chimed in, "a free gaff."

"Where?"

"Eh, Mary's Mansions," Tony said. "But eh, ya

know, we couldn't go empty-handed. We'd have to bring a bottle."

On route to the free gaff, they lost me somewhere around Foley Street, absconding with a bottle of Smirnoff and leaving me with a bottle of Jameson. I wasn't familiar with the location, so I headed to the Five Lamps landmark and then turned up the North Circular Road in the direction of home. By the time I passed O'Connell's School, a place where Finn and me had attended numerous school dances, I knew I didn't want to go home.

A few more strides, and I stopped at the top of the steps onto Mountjoy Parade—three flights of deep, broad concrete steps. It seemed like a fitting place to sit and gather myself. But there was nothing to gather on the cold concrete. Emptiness swirled about. I opened the bottle of whiskey, put it to my mouth, and guzzled it like it was a bottle of lemonade. I slurped and gurgled between breaths until the bottle was half empty. A cold sweat broke on my brow, and I waited for the alcohol to wallop me senseless.

The next thing I knew, my bulging eyes opened, and I struggled to my feet, disoriented. I had been asleep on an old discarded mattress, beside a builder's skip, in a vaguely familiar laneway. Morning had broken, and all was quietly still. I barely remembered navigating the steep steps in search of a place to relieve myself.

Swaying slightly, I left the lane.

After climbing to the top of the steps, I leaned heavily on my thighs for fear of passing out from exhaustion. Sporadic people were already moving with a steady purpose along the North Circular Road. The city was waking, and I was unable to decide on where to go, what to do. To the right was home, a shower, a soft bed, and a caring family. To the left was an early pub, more alcohol, and drunken numbness.

I turned left.

* * *

The summer of 1981 was a drunken blur interspersed with snippets of clarity. Another hunger striker died, and another, and another, and the world continued.

Finn told me he had joined the IRA, and I envied his self-assured purpose. An Indian doctor in the Mater Emergency Department realigned my broken nose and was aghast I had no recollection of how it happened. A baby-faced Garda arrested me for urinating in a shop doorway and kept me overnight in a dank cell beneath Fitzgibbon Street Garda Station. I wet my trousers while I slept in an abandoned car. I roared Emily's name and cursed Christ outside St. Patrick's Cathedral. I bragged about my blood brother in a republican bar in Dundalk. I woke in a doorway in Thomas Street with three teenagers urinating on me. Mam cleaned vomit from my bedroom floor. Dad sat on the side of my bed to make sure I didn't vomit and choke during the night.

"You can't continue like this," Dad said. "Emily wouldn't want you to destroy your life. You said she told you that you were the only worthwhile thing in her life – don't make her responsible for you destroying yours."

He was right.

"But I miss her so much, Dad."

"I know, son, I know." He took my hand, and I felt like a little boy again.

Sniffles quickly turned to sobs. "I'm sorry," I said, wiping my tears, becoming uncomfortable with the tender moment.

"Big boys cry too." We both smiled at the memory, and he released my hand.

"I don't want her to be responsible for me turning into a drunken shit."

"No. She deserves more. Talk to Finn, he's been ringing, looking for you. He's worried about you."

"I will." I hadn't spoken to him in weeks, months, because I didn't want to hear what he had to say. I guess I wanted to wallow in my sadness.

Finn suggested I talk to Professor Ryan, my tutor, about sitting the repeat exams in September. "Just sit them, Con. You don't have to study; you only need a pass. It's what Emily would want you to do."

My first repeat exam wasn't difficult. There were two separate questions on the 1798 Rebellion, including one on Wolfe Tone, and I finished the paper with a couple of minutes to spare.

Outside Trinity's Front Gate, the newsstand's headline screamed: 'Hunger Strike Broken – Devlin Taken Off. I immediately felt terribly sad for the men, coupled with deep-rooted anger towards the British Government. Thatcher hadn't budged an inch on their demand for political status, and after ten excruciating deaths, the strikers' families began taking them off their strike. Devlin was the third to be taken off and effectively ended the strike. A song that Granda used to sing about 1916 whispered in my thoughts.

The world did gaze, in deep amaze, at those fearless men, but few, who bore the fight that freedom's light might shine through the foggy dew.

Two days later, I was lying on my bed trying to study when the doorbell rang.

"Con," Mam shouted up the stairs, "it's Mr Mulcahy for you."

Finn's father stood wan and ghostly at the front door. "Will you come in?" I said, surprised that Mam hadn't already brought him into the sitting room.

"I won't. I have to get back. I didn't want to tell you on the phone. Finbar was killed last night." His delivery was steady and unbroken—these were words he needed to get out. We looked at each other, speechless, as silence stretched between us. I put out my hand and he gripped it like a lifeline from a nightmare. "I wanted to tell you meself."

"Yes. Thank you," I said, barely recognising my voice. I was having an out-of-body experience, but I knew I had to come back because he was drowning in sorrow. "Eh...? Will you not come in?"

"I won't. I have to get back. She's not..."

"OK. Eh. How did...?" Straight away, I was sorry I asked the question and, trying to ignore it, I pulled him into a hug, with our hands still tightly gripped.

"He was shot."

The incomprehension in his voice slithered into my ear like a snake. I released the embrace, but he didn't let go of my hand.

"Shot?" I said, sounding more surprised at the manner of his death than his actual death. My heart, already full with the sorrow of Emily, felt encased in a protective film, unable to bear more pain.

"That's what the police said. An Irish cop from Boston's Homicide Unit phoned me. He said he knew Finbar. 'A mugging that went wrong,' that's what he said. I rang the Embassy and they checked—he was killed in South Boston."

"I don't... eh. It's terrible news." I began to shake his hand, my emotions still encased. "I'm so sorry."

A couple of nights before, I had a Jonesy dream where he was leering from the far side of an open coffin, but this time I could see the corpse—it was Finn. I didn't recognise the dream as portentous and thought no more of it until I wondered if this ominous prelude had somehow smothered the shock of his death. "I wanted to tell you meself," Mr Mulcahy repeated. "Finbar would want me to."

We let go of each other's hand, and my world was instantly emptier.

"If there is anything I can do? Eh, I'll call around this evening. Or whenever you want me."

"This evening. You might ring the Embassy and stuff. To get him home."

"Yes, of course. Don't worry, I'll do all that."

"Margaret is beside herself," he said quietly to someone who wasn't there.

"You look after Mrs Mulcahy. And I'll get him home, don't worry."

* * *

Finn's funeral took place in our local church about two weeks after his death. The repatriation of his remains went smoothly, and I was involved in all the funeral arrangements until just a few days before his burial. Apparently, Mrs Mulcahy began to consider me partly responsible for Finn's death. She felt that I had encouraged him to go to university, and when he couldn't get into Trinity, I left him alone to struggle at Maynooth.

"He wasn't cut out for university," she told Mam. "He would have been happier as a carpenter, like his father. And whatever possessed him to go to that Godforsaken country I'll never know."

I knew she was in shock and needed someone to blame for his death, so I accepted her misplaced reproach without protest. However, it hurt when she asked her brother to deliver the eulogy and I was left to read one of the short prayers.

The church was nearly full with family, neighbours, and friends, including those from Maynooth University, *Ógra Shinn Féin*, Trinity, the local GAA club, old school friends, and a number of people I didn't recognise. As I stood on the altar reading my prayer, I noticed Mr Prendergast and Malachy McGinley, a suspected former member of the IRA's Army Council, standing at the back of the church. Their presence surprised me, but I also felt a sense of honour on Finn's behalf to see Malachy McGinley marking his passing.

Outside the church, as the coffin was placed in the hearse, I stood to the left of the door with Mam, Dad, and a few other mourners. The family stood to the right with Mrs Mulcahy, who was surrounded by a sea of sympathisers. An elderly neighbour grabbed my hand and said, "All done now, bar the shoutin'. You'll miss him." I responded with a frozen half-smile, knowing he was right. The ceremony was over, and all that awaited my blood brother, my best friend, was a cold, dark hole in the ground. Ghosts wandering here and there had already gone to their wormy graves.

I didn't want to think about these words, so I conjured the memory of Mr Flynn playacting as he recited the same line when we were children. I remembered Sherlock spilling the lemonade on the bus, the look Finn and I shared, and how we laughed when he said, "I'll give you a kick in the mickey."

Mr Prendergast approached me with McGinley, and the three of us instinctively moved to the side of the crowd. All eyes were on McGinley. Prendergast shook my hand. *"Ar dheis Dé go raibh a anam dílis."*

I nodded. "Thank you. Thanks for coming."

"I'm sorry for your loss," McGinley said, taking my hand and drawing me into his presence. He had a naturally pleasant and disarming face with an incongruous twinkle in sharp, unyielding eyes. His Derry lilt was soft and a little nasal, anchored in an unmistakable aura of authority. "I never met him," he said, "but his comrades in America, who couldn't be here today, asked me to represent them. They thought very highly of Finbar."

"Thank you. He'd be very honoured that you are here."

He shook his head. "It's me who's honoured to be here. Our loss is Ireland's loss."

"It's probably best if you don't go to the graveside," Prendergast said to McGinley with a knowing look.

"I have time. I'd like to be there."

"Ceart go leor," Prendergast replied.

"He's like a cluckin' hen," McGinley said with a warm, familiar smile. We shook hands again. "I'm happy to have met you, Conor, and to let you know that Finbar is a big loss to the Army." He turned back to Prendergast. "I'll let Tom know I'm staying," then he headed to the church gate where a man in a black leather jacket was standing.

The absence of McGinley's presence allowed Prendergast and myself to stand down… at least, that's how it felt to me. "I never got to say thanks," I said to him.

He looked questioningly.

"For having a word with Hutton."

"Oh, yes. Finn asked me. Ye must have been good friends. He thought the world of you."

"Blood brothers!" I smiled at the memory of the two of us at his door.

"Yes." He chuckled. "I remember the pair of you well."

"Do you know what happened? Was it a mugging?"

He ignored my question. "Did he say what he was doing in America?"

"No."

"No? But ye were so close? He once said he would trust you with his life."

His tenor had changed ever so slightly, as though he might be considering the possibility that I had leaked information on what Finn was doing. "I knew he worked in the bars and was doing some work with Noraid. He didn't tell me anything else. I didn't even know for sure that he had joined the IRA. When he didn't tell me what he was doing, I knew not to ask."

"I'm only curious, Conor. There's no need to be agitated."

"I'm not agitated." The hair was actually standing on the back of my neck, and I had repositioned myself directly in front of him—ready to defend my blood loyalty. "The reason he didn't tell me wasn't because he didn't trust me. We knew everything about each other. He didn't tell me to protect me."

"You're not in the frame, Conor," he said, with a calm demeanour that was disconcerting. "But we have to be curious about everyone."

Thou art a traitor—false to thy gods, thy brother, and thy father. It was a quote from King Lear, our school play for the Leaving Cert. and it echoed incongruously in my head.

I wanted to tell Prendergast to fuck off. I wanted to say, *How dare you even consider me having anything to do with Finn's death?* I wanted to say, *I'm not a traitor. I'm a republican, the same as Finn.* But I knew I wasn't the same as Finn, and I knew he knew I wasn't.

"Can you tell me how he died?" I asked bluntly. "Or would that put me in the frame?"

"I'm sorry if I've caused offence. I have a habit of asking questions. It comes with the territory."

"You didn't. I understand."

"Finn was assassinated by MI6."

My mind exploded, unable to process what he had just said. Finn, my childhood friend—the one I had played Cowboys and Indians with, made my Communion and Confirmation with, laughed uncontrollably with while watching *Laurel and Hardy,* spooned in a ditch with when we got lost on the Burren, the one I had done a million idiotic things with—had been assassinated by some James Bond-type character. "MI6?" I said, flabbergasted.

"MI6 turned a member of an Irish American gang, and he assassinated Finn."

"Why?" I asked, my head still spinning.

"I can't say."

I nodded. "OK." Immediately accepting he couldn't say.

"If it's any consolation, the shooter was found yesterday, with a bullet in the back of his head."

"Who…? Sorry, I know. You can't say."

"I spoke with Mr Mulcahy last night, and he agreed that the IRA would take charge of the funeral once it entered the cemetery. I explained to him that Finn was a Volunteer of *Óglaigh na hÉireann*, and it's what he would have wanted."

"Does Mrs Mulcahy know?"

"I don't think so. He agreed on the condition that you and him would be lead pallbearers. He said it's what Finbar would have wanted. Is that alright with you?"

"Yes, of course."

"Special Branch don't know Finn," he said, nearly gleefully. "We've caught them on the hop."

When the hearse reached the gate of Balgriffin Cemetery, four men in paramilitary uniform, with black berets over black balaclavas, appeared from nowhere. They removed the coffin and placed it on a bier, whereupon a woman dressed in black, with a beret and sunglasses, unfolded the Irish Tricolour over the coffin, carefully positioning a black beret and a pair of black leather gloves at its centre.

Mr Mulcahy got out of the first mourner's car, and I quickly joined him. "Were you talking to the Prendergast man?" he asked.

"Yes. He said you were OK with it."

"What could I do? If he was in the IRA, this is what he would have wanted. Isn't it?"

"Yes, I think so. Yes, it's what he would have wanted."

"Are you in the IRA too?"

"No."

"I said we should carry the coffin, as well as them. I know for certain he would have wanted that."

"What about Mrs Mulcahy?"

"I'm sorry about the church, Conor. She's not herself. I had no say with the eulogy."

"There's no need to be sorry. Really. I understand.

But what will she say about this? Does she know?"

"Jesus, no. We'll deal with that later." There was an unfamiliar steadfastness about him. "He's my only son. You're his best pal. If he was foolish enough to join the IRA, then this is what he wanted. I'd have no truck with them meself, but I'm not going to go against his wishes." His bottom lip quivered, and he put a shaky hand to his mouth. "Not in death."

One of the IRA men gestured for us to come forward. After a bit of manoeuvring, we carried Finn, shoulder-high, to his final resting place, slow-marching behind a single piper playing a haunting lament. Each note floated on the air like the echo of an ancient Irish spirit, carrying an unyielding belief in the sanctity of Irish unity. The mourners were spellbound by the paramilitary display, especially since no one knew Finn was in the IRA.

Father Talbot said the prayers, apparently unfazed, as six IRA men stood to attention a few feet behind him, one holding a flagpole with an unfurled Tricolour. The scene was starkly beautiful, backlit by the brittle morning sun—a detail not lost on the photographers vying for the best-angle shot, likely for the US media.

"Now," Father Talbot said, as though conducting any ordinary funeral, "the Rite of Committal. We commit the body of our brother Finbar Terence Mulcahy to the earth, for we are dust, and to dust we shall return. But the Lord Jesus Christ will change our mortal bodies to be like his in glory."

One of the six IRA men moved to the head of the coffin. "*Réidh*!" he ordered. Two men and a woman in paramilitary uniforms stepped forward from the mourners, handguns at their sides. "*Eirígí!*" he commanded. They raised their weapons. "*Seasaigí*!" They held their positions. "*Cuir!*" The crack of gunfire shattered the stillness, reverberating among the headstones. "*Seasaigí!*" They kept their weapons raised. "*Cuir!*" The second shot rang out louder, reaching high into the clear sky. "*Seasaigí!*" They held their positions. "*Cuir!*" The final volley, as if bearing the weight of Finn's last farewell, splintered my encased emotions. A cold loneliness crept like ice through my heart. I began to weep.

PART TWO

CHAPTER 7

It was 1999, the year following the Good Friday Agreement and five months before the new millennium. I was sitting in our back garden having a beer, reading a newspaper article about the 1913 Lockout. Granda had joined the Volunteers in 1913, and I felt obliged to read it. But I struggled to concentrate—my heart wasn't in it.

Bees buzzed among the flowers, hovering as they moved from the geraniums to the lavender, to the roses, and back again. The geraniums were new, while the roses were ones I had planted last year. Two butterflies fluttered back and forth over the boundary wall, undecided about whose property to land on.

"Dad!" Helen shouted from the swing at the far end of the garden, "Kate won't push me."

"Don't be a baby," Kate responded, putting down her book and splashing her feet playfully in the paddle pool. "You're nearly 12."

"Dad. What age is Kate?"

"Nearly 15," I said.

"Going on 25," Mary, my wife, chimed in without moving her head. She was sunbathing on a recliner, enjoying the start of her vacation from nursing.

"You're nearly 25!" Helen teased Kate. "That means you have to push your little sister."

"OK. Three pushes. But only if you go up to my room and get my Nokia."

"Six pushes, and it's a deal."

"OK. Deal."

On the surface, it was a picture of suburban bliss. But life and happiness are seldom surface dwellers, and I was anything but happy. The previous week, I had a chance encounter with Mrs Mulcahy on a busy Grafton Street. I was about to say hello when she shouted, "Don't you come near me. You and your IRA murdered my son."

"It's me, Mrs Mulcahy," I said, shocked and disbelieving her outburst. "Conor McCarthy."

"I know well who you are," she spat her words with contempt.

I hadn't seen her or anyone from the old neighbourhood in years and I had no idea she harboured such thoughts. This was the woman who made popcorn for Finn and me, who tended my grazed knees, who consoled me when Granda died. She was the mother of my second childhood home.

My first instinct was to comfort her, to calm the situation. But as I moved closer, she began to scream, "Murderer! Murderer!"

Panicked, I fled the scene, shaken to my core. I couldn't get her accusations out of my head, and as the butterflies disappeared over the wall, I considered if she had lost her mind or if there was some truth in what she was saying.

If it wasn't for me, I thought, *he would never have joined the IRA.*

My thoughts of Finn were soon followed by memories of Emily—the ghosts of times past had only been sleeping. For eighteen years, I had managed to keep them at bay, but since Mrs Mulcahy's onslaught, Em and Finn had flooded my mind with both the happiest and the saddest emotions. My life was grey, unbelievably grey. Yet when I thought of Em and Finn, I saw them in colour. Not only that, I saw the unquenched embers of my long-lost ancient spirit, and I longed for my old self.

As if all this wasn't enough to fuel my discontent, I hated my job as an inconsequential middle manager, stuck and sinking in the bureaucratic swamp of the Department of Agriculture and the Marine. The last straw, however, was Mary's suggestion that we divorce when Kate finished her Junior Cert., and I couldn't find any good reason why we shouldn't. Our marriage had come to its natural end, with its energy behind us.

I first met Mary in the emergency department of the Mater Hospital when she attended to my sprained and swollen ankle, after I'd twisted it hiking in the Wicklow mountains. We got chatting and it turned out we had a mutual acquaintance who was having a birthday party that we were both invited to. After a night of drinking, we woke up the next morning, naked, in the same bed. It wasn't a big deal for either of us, but arranging to meet the following week seemed like the civilised thing to do.

Eventually, we settled into a regular dating pattern, which led to pregnancy, which led to matrimony. Unfortunately, our marriage never really found a natural rhythm. I think it was our different ideas of happiness that stopped us from being happy. Divorce seemed the next logical step.

"This isn't working," she said, the week before my encounter with Mrs Mulcahy, her sing-song Cork lilt cutting through the quiet of our usually silent breakfast.

"What isn't working?" My mind was trying to think of some faulty household appliance.

"Us."

"Oh. How do you mean?"

She sighed. "We don't gel together anymore. I don't think we ever did. Not only are we living together separately. We diminish each other."

"We diminish each other?" I hadn't heard that expression before.

"Yes. We're meant to be stronger together, to be more than our separate selves. But we're not. We diminish each other."

"OK?" It seemed the inevitable conversation had finally landed, although I hadn't been expecting it there and then.

"Can you tell me that you are happy. With me? With your life?"

I thought for a moment, just in case I was being blindsided. "No. I can't."

"Neither can I." She looked validated and relieved.

"So, what do we do?" I asked, disinclined to be the problem solver.

"I think we should get a divorce."

"A divorce? What about the girls?"

"We could wait until Kate finishes her Junior Cert. and Helen starts First Year."

"So, you're thinking next August-September?" I can't say that my head was spinning, it wasn't. But I was somewhat taken aback by her certainty.

"Yes. We can work everything out. It doesn't have to be a big trauma."

"Eh. If, you're sure?"

"I'm sure. It will be better for all of us."

"OK. Once we have equal access and parenting of the girls."

"You're their dad. You'll always be their dad. Equal everything."

"Is there someone else?" I thought it unlikely, but I

was curious given her certainty.

"No. You?"

"No."

There was no animosity, no recriminations. In fact, we still liked each other, we still cared for each other. We had simply run out of road. Nevertheless, I knew she'd be keeping the house, at least until the girls turned eighteen, and I was facing the reality of a tiny grey apartment or bedsit.

* * *

Beside the newspaper article, was an old grainy black and white photograph showing a large crowd being baton-charged by the police. I wondered if Granda was in the photo. There was also a reference to Yeats' poem, *September 1913*, and I automatically whispered the lines:

"Yet they were of a different kind,

The names that stilled your childish play.

They weighed so lightly what they gave.

But let them be, they're dead and gone,

They're with O'Leary in the grave."

The words seemed pertinent to my memory of Granda and I could see him, plain as day, with his hand on my head, saying, "Never lose your ancient spirit."

Mary looked up. "What did you say?"

"Nothing, just reading something to myself." I

glanced at the photograph again, and thought about how much the country had changed. *"All changed,"* I quietly recited, *"changed utterly, a terrible beauty is born"*.

What would Granda have thought of the Good Friday Agreement? I wondered. The Free State Government, officially recognising Ireland as two separate countries—how would that have sat with him? My thoughts turned to Red Hugh and his role in the negotiations. There had been photos and clips of him entering and leaving Downing Street and St. Andrews with the Republican delegations. But he had always kept a low profile—a mysterious figure, always in the background. I wondered if it was his inner circle of Republicans who had led the shift from bombs to a negotiated peace. On the rare occasions that I saw him on the telly, I invariably regretted not following up on our McDonald's conversation—but my head was a mess back then, with Emily and Finn.

The sun was distractingly warm, and as I closed my eyes to enjoy its penetrating heat, my thoughts grew distant. I began to doze, floating peacefully away from my surroundings, away from Red Hugh, away from my mundane, grey life. A burst of giddy laughter from the girls bolted me to the present, and their exuberance made me smile despite myself. They're the future, I thought, untainted by bombs and bullets. Economically, politically, or socially, Granda could never have envisaged this new independent 26 County Ireland, standing proud, educated, and wealthy, among the nations of the world.

A line from the 1916 Proclamation interrupted my thoughts.

We declare the right of the people of Ireland to the ownership of Ireland and to the unfettered control of Irish destinies, to be sovereign and indefeasible. Cherishing all the children of the nation equally.

It sounded like something Finn might say, he was always quick to balance my romanticism with pragmatism, always quick to claim unfettered ownership of all Ireland.

OK, I said, silently. *I know what you're saying. Where are the ideals of 1916 in this new truncated Ireland? Where is our ancient spirit?*

The words *ancient spirit* registered deep in my soul, like a huge crashing wave excavating buried emotions, and I had a queasy sense that my Irish genie was awake after years of sleep in a greasy till.

Before I could consider the feeling, I mouthed the line: *The Irish genie is but a burning fire, shut up in your bones, a pain, a protest against shame and defeat, a morbid condition which a healthy man must shake off if he is to keep sane.*

It was a quote from Shaw that I read in the newspaper article, and I was surprised I knew it. There seemed to be an internal voice telling me to rekindle the dying embers of my long-lost ancient spirit, to unshackle myself from my morbid grey life before it was too late.

I wondered if, after nearly twenty years without Em and Finn, I was metaphorically dying between my two eternities. The thought stemmed from one of my favourite Yeats' quotes.

Many times we live and die between our two eternities. That of race and that of soul. And Ancient Ireland knew it all.

As with most things Yeatsian, there were numerous literary interpretations, such as, death is an illusion, spiritual immortality is the only reality, and ancient Ireland knows the truth between life and death.

If spiritual immortality is a reality, are Finn and Em still with me? I asked myself. *Is that what the internal voice was telling me—that Finn and Em are still with me? That my ancient spirit is still alive—guiding me towards my old self?*

These were strange thoughts, even for me—who loved to indulge the esoteric. I re-read the Shaw and Yeats quotes and pondered the idea of a burning fire, a protest against shame—where I might live and die between my two eternities. I didn't understand it, but it felt profound.

That night, I watched a broken string of cumulus clouds outside my bedroom window. They slipped across a perfect half-moon, playing peep. Now you see me, now you don't. Otherwise, it was a black sky dotted with twinkling stars.

"Can you not sleep?" Mary muttered, turning on

her back, still mostly asleep.

"No."

"Is everything OK?"

The question was rhetorical and, judging by the soundness of her sleep up until that point, my predicament would need to be fairly serious to warrant a detailed response. Anything less than a mild stroke would have been derisory. "Yes, everything is fine, go back to sleep."

My mind was in that place where I thought I was more awake than I was, edging towards sleep with eyes wide open. I wondered about the quotes in the garden, about Mrs Mulcahy's accusations, about my marriage ending, about my promise to Granda not to lose my ancient spirit. I wondered what Ireland would be like if 1916 had never happened?

Was it for this, I silently recited, *the wild geese spread the grey wing upon every tide. For this that all that blood was shed?*

The words seemed external to my thoughts and I pondered the quote. *Was it for this, was it for this that all that blood was shed?* My musings began to dissolve, floating majestically towards sleep. *For this divided country... for these scattered people... for the poor uncherished children?*

I saw wild geese drifting on a calm tide under the glow of a silver moon as gentle waves lapped a sandy beach on a ravaged island. When the geese turned to look at the shore, they transformed into a fleet of sailing ships, thronged with downcast soldiers. They longed to fight on but knew their time was past. Their hearts still dreamed of battle and love, and the cry of the hounds on the hills of old.

I was among them—yet also watching them from a high cliff. A woman in military uniform, with greater presence than the rest, beckoned me to leave the ship, and I was no longer among them. I was standing on the cliff's edge watching the dejected fleet sail away.

All at once, I galloped off on a raven black horse of flowing mane. A pearly white deer passed me by, chased by a hound and a beautiful woman who rode like the wind, holding a golden apple in an elegant hand. She was followed by a handsome man with a quenchless gaze and fluttering hair. They looked at me as they passed, their eyes asking, *are you of this place?* I stopped my horse and watched them until they faded into the moonlight, and I wondered, were they people of Dannan, and had they ever breathed mortal air?

The next morning, dawn peeped in the window over a fading mist, its rays bidding farewell to the last remnants of darkness in the creeping corners of an illuminating sky. I mused over the beauty of the scene while pulling my awakening thoughts back to my earthly body.

Still half asleep, I couldn't help but search my mind for the geese, the ships, the galloping horses, only to find they were gone and I was left to consider their passing. I assumed the soldiers in the boats were Sarsfield's defeated Irish army, the Wild Geese of

1691. The rest of the dream was straight from Yeats' *Song of the Happy Shepherd.*

I hadn't dreamt like this in years. Not since I lost Finn and Em. Certainly not about Ireland. However, there was something more noteworthy about this dream. I had a sense that it wasn't me who dreamt it. It felt as though, somehow, it was dreamed by someone else in my head, a separate internal voice.

I had always given my thoughts free rein and allowed any number of counter-thoughts and internal arguments to swish about in my mind. The contrasting opinions usually came from two perspectives, my heart and my head. Will and reason. However, with the advent of my garden quotations and my recent dream, it now seemed I had a third source, as though from the perspective of Finn, or Granda, or Emily. I didn't know which, if any. Nor was I concerned; it was just another string to my cognitive bow.

Standing in my boxers, looking out at the back garden, I wondered what Finn and Em would think of my humdrum domesticity.

Not much, I thought.

They'd like that you're dreaming again, the other voice said.

I remembered when we were kids—I'd regale Finn with my nighttime adventures: riding with Celtic warriors, running with the Fianna, or hurling with the magical Tuatha Dé Danann.

I smiled at the memory of us riding around the neighbourhood on our imaginary horses, slaying the foreign foe at *Cath Fionntrá* and racing the best of the *Tuatha Dé Dannan* at *Emain Macha*.

Jesus, he loved the Celtic mythology—before he found Connolly, Fintan Lalor, and Marx.

"Will you put the kettle on?" Mary asked from beneath the duvet.

"Before or after I have a shower?"

"After will do. Will you call me in half an hour?"

"Yeah. I'm finished work early today, so do you want me to pick up anything in town? Sun cream? Insect bite stuff?"

"No. I have all that stuff," she mumbled, still with the duvet pulled over her head. "The cases are packed."

"Great," I said, surprised at my enthusiasm. "Are the girls looking forward to it?"

Her head emerged, as if to check I was me. "Yes."

"I'll give you a shout in half an hour."

Looking at myself in the bathroom mirror, I wondered, *at what point do different perspectives in my head become psychotic voices in my head?*

I don't care, I told myself. *I'm tired of my grey life, sick and tired of it.*

Mrs Mulcahy's outburst had jolted my thoughts back to a time when I was at one with my ancient spirit, at one with Ireland, at one with the hopeful rhythm of life. She had sparked a new voice in my head. I didn't know if it was Finn, or Em, or Granda and it didn't really matter. I longed for my old spirit.

CHAPTER 8

Over the years, the Algarve's golden coast had become one of my favourite holiday destinations, with its scattered coves and inlets concealed between promontories and cliffs, chopped and crafted by millennia of Atlantic waves.

As I strolled along the untrampled sand by the water's edge, a gentle breeze merged seamlessly with the hues of the morning sun. Each step brought a wave of harmony, fusing my thoughts with the tranquil surroundings. Overhead, two seagulls appeared, their wings slicing through the air as they swooped and dived. Playful squawks echoed like laughter, and I found myself entranced by their aerial ballet until they vanished into the horizon. My eyeline dropped to the winding trail of footprints I'd left on Mother Earth's pristine canvas, stirring a fleeting memory of an old *Robinson Crusoe* film I'd watched in Finn's house. I remembered how we ate fresh popcorn with TK lemonade and speculated about what we would do if we were stranded on a desert island.

It wasn't long before the incoming tide swallowed the dry sand. My planned route soon became blocked by small headlands jutting into the sea. But I didn't mind and happily settled into a secluded tidal cove, my own idyllic castaway refuge. I watched as deceptively calm barrel waves rolled covertly towards the shore, then crashed enthusiastically at my feet. I imagined they called out, "Look at me," as they crashed before being pulled back into the anonymity of the ocean. Another, "Look at me," and another, and another. Swell and crash, swell and crash, swell and crash.

Spellbinding serenity filled the isolated cove, and I sat on the warm sand with my legs stretched in front of me, hidden from the disappointments of a grey world beyond my *Robinson Crusoe* refuge. My feet were about a meter from the edge of the swash, and I idly observed the outer rim of water advancing on every second or third wave. Lost in the moment, I lay back and basked in nature's warm caress, half-hoping a sly wave might catch me unawares and wash over my hot, sandy toes. The sun's rays tingled through my body, radiating through every muscle and bone, while my thoughts wafted back to sunny childhood memories on Dublin's Dollymount Strand—swimming, catching pinkeens, digging sandcastles, jumping waves, throwing seaweed. The rhythm of the waves echoed with a poem I couldn't quite remember, one from Granda's library...

When I was a child of ten, my internal voice recited. *I went down on my bare knees and promised God that I would devote my life to an effort to free my country.*

Eh, Pearse? I queried.

Yes, Padraig Pearse. Ten years old, he promised. The same age as you promising Granda that you would never lose your Irish spirit.

I wasn't in form for this internal conversation. The voice was interesting, but I felt the less recognition it got the less I would have to rationalise having another voice in my head. Anyway, I wanted to absorb the intoxicating sun as it flowed through every neural path in my body and surged throughout my physical and ethereal being.

I have kept that promise, the voice persisted, continuing the quote. *I have kept faith with the past and handed on a tradition to the future.*

The Provos, I thought, sceptically, irritated by the voice's persistence. *They certainly took what he handed on, minus the self-sacrifice.*

It was a snide remark, and I knew it wasn't true. Finn gave his life. The hunger strikers had suffered agonizing self-sacrifice. Prisoners had spent unrepentant lifetimes in English gaols. Ordinary men and women did and endured unspeakable things.

But how many could name them—the strikers who died? I asked myself and felt honour bound to name them.

Bobby Sands, Patsy O'Hara, Francis Hughes. Eh. Kieran Doherty, eh... There were ten; Sands, O'Hara, Hughes, Doherty, McCreesh, Lynch, McDonnell... McDonnell...

The focus of my thoughts drifted into the intoxicating sunshine, half here, half there. Swell and crash went the waves, swell and crash. Their constant rhythm lulled my mind's internal chatter. As the swash inched closer, it gently lifted and floated my legs until the water was sucked back to its vastness, and my legs resettled on the wet sand. Again, the wave spilled up the beach, this time reaching my waist and swaying my hips before the undertow pulled it back to the ocean. It was an enjoyable sensation, and I relaxed my body in preparation for the next gentle swash.

Whoosh! went the wave, rushing forward and lifting me effortlessly. I was floating.

"Maith an fear," cried the seagull from the clifftop beside the tattered green and gold *Éirinn go Brách* flag.

That's very strange, I thought.

Without warning, a huge wave crashed over me, pounding the air from my lungs. I was turned head over heels, gulping and spewing water as it sucked and pulled with all its might. My belly and face scraped along the sandy bottom of sharpened pebbles and shells. I tried to dig my fingers into the sand, but a powerful undertow had me, determined to pull me into its vastness. Another huge wave crashed, turning me every which way. Legs and arms flailing until I was bent and twisted like a rag doll.

The seagull swooped down—screeching, *"Éirinn*

go Brách! Éirinn go Brách!"

But how can I hear the seagull if I'm drowning?

I opened my eyes to find I was lying on the beach with my hands behind my head, still above the swash of the waves and not even my toes wet. An empty smirk of bravado crossed my cheeks, pretending I hadn't been frightened when in fact, as the wave tossed me about, I thought that was the end of me.

The sun was high in the sky, and the heat of the morning was building, so I moved into the cliff's shade at the back of the cove, far above the reach of the water. Again, my mind started to drift, its sleepy recesses unsatisfied by my abruptly ended snooze. I welcomed the approaching doze, closing my eyes, and settling my back against a smooth, comfortable rock. It wasn't long before wafting dreams snatched my thoughts.

* * *

A woman of slender build in an oversized beach dress with long, straight, silky black hair, like Emily's, stood by the water's edge. My sleeping heart jumped at the prospect of it being Em, but on seeing her dark skin, I quickly realised it wasn't her. She seemed captivated by the sky and her gaze travelled past me to high above the cliff. I followed her line of sight but I couldn't figure out what she was looking at. When my eyeline returned to where she was standing, there were two young children running towards her, a boy and a girl, one no more than a toddler.

She bent and embraced them without taking her gaze from the sky behind the cliff. Then, she looked out to sea and pointed, directing their view beyond the undulating waves—maybe further, to beyond the horizon. The dream began to fade as I followed their eyes, and I sensed she was also quietly directing me, aware that I was concealed in the shadows.

* * *

After I woke, the image of the woman and children remained in my head, and I wished I could have stayed a while longer in the dream—to explore her resemblance to Em and my feelings of connection to her.

I headed back to the apartment and my family, at least until after the Junior Cert. It turned out to be a great day, including a couple of swims and a lovely long walk with Kate and Helen.

Later, there were a few beers, nice food, and even a bit of dancing. As the evening closed, the four of us strolled along the coast road, overlooking shimmering moonlight on a glass ocean. Alcohol had loosened my tongue, and I unintentionally told Mary about my dreams and the voice in my head.

"I wouldn't go around telling people you're hearing voices."

"Well, I'm sorry I told you," I said. "Jesus, you're always worrying about what people might think."

She smirked at my defensiveness and shook her head. "You're drunk."

"Aren't *we* very observant tonight?"

"Your obsession with this silly promise to your grandfather is bad enough, but now you have a voice in your head."

"I didn't even mention my Granda. Anyway, it's not an obsession, it's..."

"Are you guys fighting?" The girls had been a couple of meters in front, but Helen dropped back.

"No, Hun," I said. "Your mother is just langers drunk."

Mary started to laugh and slapped my shoulder. "Don't mind him. I am not. Your father is talking through his bum again."

For the next week, things remained uneventful. No dreams or voices. Midway through the last week, we were at dinner in our favourite restaurant. To finish, I consumed a very generous cheese board.

"A bucket of wine and a pound of cheese," Mary said pointedly. "That's a good recipe for dreams."

She was right.

* * *

Stars flickered in a cloudless sky. The woman and children were standing by the water's edge, on a beach I didn't recognise. I watched them from an oval-shaped, primitive boat and simultaneously from rocky cliffs that enclosed a horseshoe beach. The boat was made with leather-stitched animal skins stretched over a main structure of interwoven tree branches.

A gust of salty sea spray hit my face, and I was alarmed, realising we were heading to the open, innocent, murderous sea.

Before I could consider the situation, an old man, crooked and haggard by life, stood beside me on the clifftop. For a moment, he looked like Granda, and my pulse quickened. Then he didn't. Around his waist was a skirt of long, colourful feathers, and his otherwise naked torso was splashed with brilliant yellow and blue paint.

"Who are you?" I asked him.

He ignored me, mildly irritated.

The boat was occupied by three women and four men, each with dark skin and clear blue-green eyes. I was among them but not of them. I didn't have a physical presence. Two men sat on each side, paddling with ornate wooden oars, while a woman stood in the centre, mastering the sail. Like the woman earlier, I was struck by her profound similarity to Emily, despite her skin colour."

"Hello," I called. "Is that you, Em?" My heart beat excitedly in the hope of talking to her. But she was busy at her tasks, whatever they were, and didn't appear to hear me.

"Standing like drops of frozen rainbow light," the old man said to me, "they will ponder upon their shadows in the tide. For their journey is the feathered eye, guiding their vessel to the land where the great spirit dwells."

His eloquence took me by surprise. I think he was quoting Yeats.

"Eh, do you mean the ancient Irish spirit?" I asked, confused. "I don't understand. What is the feathered eye?"

He looked equally perplexed. "The feathered eye guided us—to the land where the great spirit dwells."

"I don't understand."

"Twice in the long cycle of the sun, the skies turn dark with feathered travellers," he said. "From land they come, to sea they go. From sea they come, to land they go. They guided us on our journey to the land of the great spirit."

"Do you mean migratory birds?" I asked, reaching for some kind of explanation. "Do you mean you follow the path of migratory birds? How do you know they, eh...?"

He nodded slightly. "Your woman of the sail was a See-er, a knower of the feathered travellers. She marked their beaks and saw that those who left for the sea were the same feathered travellers who returned to the land. She knew they had to feed on land. She visioned a land beyond the vast ocean—the land of the great spirit."

"Did she survive the journey?" Strangely, I felt protective of this woman, concerned for her well-being.

He didn't answer. Silence settled between us, and we walked together from the cliff edge until he stopped by a white boulder with a painted black arrow pointing me back to the cliff face. I returned to the very edge of the cliff and, looking down at the sea below, goaded the wind to displace me. It was a moment that echoed with a premonition of deep anxiety and destiny. The boat, the woman, and her children were gone—departed to another shore, a better place—and I deeply regretted not being with them.

"Goodbye," I said, waving to the now empty spaces they had filled.

The dream ended, and my thoughts went elsewhere to dreamless sleep.

* * *

The next morning, I felt muzzy-headed from the previous night's wine, and I was keen to take an early morning swim. The pool area was still partially shaded and empty of sun worshipers, save for a smattering of blonde, pale-skinned continentals who were staking claim to their sites of homage, covering sunbeds with multi-coloured towels and various inflated floating devices.

Lebensraum was my first thought, but no—they were Dutch and Scandinavians, as far as I could tell.

Without hesitation or pause of stride, I dived straight into the cool, clear water, and my entire nervous system tingled with a sensation that invigorated my body and soul as I glided beneath the captive sea. On the second lap, I paused in the middle of the pool and floated on my back, my ears bobbing in and out of silence.

I remembered the woman at the sail, slight and straight-backed, her face and raven-black hair wet with spray. Her upper body was statuesque as she studied markings on the sail, and her bare feet rode the undulating twists and turns of the primitive boat. It was a Stone Age craft, which meant she was a prehistoric female mariner—a rose among the stones. The thought of her filled me with a sense of awe and a longing for Emily. I remembered Emily sitting astride my nakedness *"dreams are a way into the unconscious mind,"* she had said. *"They convey messages from the collective unconscious."*

Collective unconscious? I mused.

The cool, clear water wasn't conducive to floating— it was chilly, and I got out of the pool to dry in the warming sun.

Wrapped in a soft beach towel, my goosebumps retreated from the advancing solar warmth, but my thoughts were elsewhere. I regretted leaving the dream and not talking further with the old man, not getting closer to the woman.

On the flight home, most of the passengers were asleep, including Mary and the girls. All was quiet, and I flicked through the in-flight magazine for the want of something better to do. One page showed the Aer

Lingus flight paths between Ireland and Europe. Many of the routes went: Spain, the Basque Region, Brittany, Cornwall, Ireland, and back again. It was strikingly similar to the path I had imagined my dream migratory birds took, and it made me think about an *RTE* program that showed the flight paths of birds who flew north from Iberia to spend their summer in Ireland. A lightbulb went on in my head, connecting the birds and my dream voyagers with Ireland's original settlers.

Mr Flynn used to say that ancient Irish mythology told us the first settlers came from Iberia. *"Milesians* in wellies," he called them.

Was the primitive boat going to Ireland? I asked myself. *Were they the first Irish? Were the Great Spirit and the Ancient Irish Spirit the same? Was Em trying to show me a direction, a way back? Did Stone Age people have boats? Could they navigate the open sea? Did the first Irish come from Iberia? Is there historical evidence, archaeological facts?*

There must be.

I sat back, excited at the prospect of researching the tangible links to my dream world—and perhaps rediscovering Emily, Finn, and my old self.

CHAPTER 9

A few weeks after my in-flight epiphany, I was sitting at a microfiche monitor on the ground floor of Trinity's Lecky Library, opposite the lending counter. The reference numbers of the old manuscripts were still in the process of being transferred to digital files and it was taking me forever to find what I wanted. Tired, I stretched my arms in the air and stared at the darkening sky through the slanted glass roof wondering if I should call it a day. The clock on the bare concrete wall told me I was already five hours in the library and it was time to go home.

I tidied my reference slips and made my way to Geraldine at the lending desk. In her early thirties, she reminded me of a rosebud yet to bloom. Over the past week, we had developed a warm rapport, and she smiled as I approached the counter.

"Hi," I said, with a reciprocal pleased-to-see-you smile. "Another long day?"

"Opus fac et veniet."

"What?" I said, with affected surprise.

"Do the work and it will come. It's something our Latin teacher used to say."

"Latin! OK." I laughed. "I haven't quite mastered English yet."

"The wonders of a classical education."

"Ah. But can you say it in Greek?"

"Poiei ergon kai hēxei," she said with a playful, self-satisfied grin.

"Now, I'm impressed and humbled in equal measure."

"Classics. It's my secret weapon."

Her marble-grey eyes flickered with uncharacteristic mischief and I felt a flutter of curious anticipation in my stomach.

"Well, it works," I said. "I'm feeling quite uneducated."

"Gosh, no." She gave an understated coquettish smirk.

My stomach sank. That was Emily's word. I hadn't heard anyone say 'Gosh' since she died. My chattiness crashed, and we looked at each other, disappointed. Her eyes dimming and gradually mirroring my own.

"Eh, any chance of getting these for the morning?" I asked, handing her my reference slips.

She separated the slips with her usual efficiency, and God himself wouldn't have known we'd just had a flirtatious moment. "These two, yes." Her demeanour remained pleasant. "But these two are in the Old Library stacks. They're not on general access."

"OK. That's grand." They were old Celtic manuscripts written in Latin or Old Gaelic, neither of which I could read. I only wanted to touch them, to feel them, like touching a spiritual bridge to my ancient past.

"Sorry." Her eyes were gentle, kindly. "The early manuscripts are restricted to scholars and staff."

"Ah, I see."

"I'll put the other two on the top of the call list and they'll be here for you first thing in the morning."

"Thanks", I said, with a half-smile and turned to walk away.

"You're welcome. Sorry again."

I paused. "That's OK. They're not central to my research."

"If you don't mind my asking," she said, deliberately halting my retreat, "What are you researching? You've had a few long days yourself?"

"I suppose I have. It's a long story."

"Sorry. I didn't mean to pry. Curiosity got the better of me. You're not the typical research student."

"I guess not. Eh, you're not prying, not at all." She was looking directly into my eyes, waiting for my reply, and I didn't know what to say. "I'm working on, eh, it's... let me see. The origin of the Irish, I guess, and the Irish spirit."

"That is a long story."

We laughed, like friends might, and I was delighted she hadn't allowed my unhealed loss of Emily to darken a rare moment of light.

"Opus fact eh..." I tried to recite her Latin. "Nope. It's gone."

"Opus fac et veniet."

"That's it. Do the work and eh... you will succeed?"

"Close enough. Are you studying full-time?"

"No. I'm a civil servant. Took a bit of sick leave."

"You don't look very sick."

"Eh, well..." I did a short comic limp. "A bit of shrapnel in the leg: acts up every now and then."

She laughed. "I understand. You're one of the un-sackable mandarins."

"Hmm... I wouldn't say un-sackable."

"Securely employed... on the backs of the taxpayers?"

"You're making me feel very guilty," I said, feigning remorse and liking her repartee.

Offer to buy her a coffee, I thought. "I'd be happy to buy you a coffee, in recompense."

She glanced at the clock on the wall, apparently considering my offer.

While the offer wasn't in jest, it wasn't wholly serious. Nevertheless, I automatically took the ball on the hop. "What time do you finish your long day as a downtrodden taxpayer?"

"Twenty minutes," she said.

"Would you like to grab a coffee?" I was all in now.

She seemed undecided.

"If you have time," I added, giving her an escape route.

Whatever her doubts were, she overcame them with a slight smile "My bus isn't for an hour. I could do with a coffee. Yes. Why not. If you're prepared to wait twenty minutes?"

* * *

A deepening twilight darkened the rich colours of Bewley's stained-glass windows, casting a hush over the clinking crockery and murmured words. We chatted effortlessly, like old friends reacquainting, and sipped milky coffee. I explained my impromptu research, and she was intrigued by my "Portugal dreams."

"They are all about direction," she said. "About new beginnings. The woman pointing. The boats leaving. The idea of them travelling back to your past, in ancient Ireland, to find new hope, new beginnings. To find your ancient Irish spirit."

"Yes," I said, "I think so too. But I'm not sure what to do."

"*Somnia vestra sequimini.* Follow your dreams."

"You're showing off now."

She seemed slightly embarrassed by my comment. "Before I say any more, let me preface my remarks with some context. The only reason I'm a librarian is because I love books. Hodges Figgis is my second home."

"OK. Not a crime, as far as I know."

"I just finished one last week about Carl Jung and dreams."

"Really? That's very interesting. The famous psychologist?" I smiled inwardly at my childish urge to show I knew who she was talking about—and at the memory of Emily, sitting astride my body, telling me about Jung.

"He was actually a trained psychiatrist and a Professor of Psychotherapy at the University of Zurich. Sorry, I'm being academically pedantic now. Yes, the famous psychologist."

"That's all right. If Trinity's Keeper of Knowledge can't be academically pedantic, who can?"

"You're right. Thank you. Back to your dreams, the Jungian school believes that dreams are a way for the unconscious mind to communicate with the conscious mind, often through symbolic imagery. Guiding the dreamer through a process of individuation—an ongoing journey of becoming one's true, whole self."

"Talk about hitting the nail on the head," I said with raised eyebrows. "That's it. I want to find my old Irish spirit—the old me, the whole me."

"Well. You should really try to interpret those dreams. There's a lot of stuff in there."

"I'm trying. That's why I'm back in Trinity after nearly 20 years. I think if I follow the practical stuff in the dreams, the ethereal might become more apparent."

"Good luck with finding your ancient Irish spirit in Trinity."

I laughed heartily, caught unawares by her dry humour. "Not the most likely place, I'll grant you."

"The College," she said copper-fastening her quip, "was actually founded by Queen Elizabeth I, to forever propagate Englishness among the Irish."

"I know. My friend Finn was always poking me with that. But the one he really liked was Cromwell's intelligence officer, Henry Jones, plundering the Book of Kells and giving it to Trinity to forever prostitute its Gaelic soul."

"It's true. The College makes a fortune off it."

"Surely Trinity can't be all bad. It did give us Tone and Emmett."

"But did they have the spirit of Irish individuation or the spirit of French enlightenment? Were they Republicans by reason or Irish Republicans by spirit?"

"That's a very valid point. I never thought of that. You've obviously read more than the Classics and Jung."

"My Masters was in Roman History. Nearly as useless as Greek and Latin."

"OK. Now I'm humbled and intimidated."

"What was your degree? Let me take a wild guess. History?"

"I did History, back in the 80s. But I never finished. My life took a turn and I dropped out."

"I knew we had a common thread. We've both had useless Trinity educations."

I sighed, unsure if I should tell her what happened. "In 1981, my girlfriend, who is maybe the woman in the dream, committed suicide. And a couple of months later, my best friend was murdered."

"Gosh! I'm very sorry. I didn't mean to be frivolous. That must have been awful for you."

"It was. My light went out. Sorry, that's all a bit glum."

"Don't be sorry." A faint smile crossed her full cheeks. *"Upon the wharves of sorrow, you heard ring. The bell that calls you on; the sweet far thing."*

I continued the quote, it was Yeats. *"Beauty grown sad with its eternity, made you of us, and of the dim grey sea."* We smiled knowingly, sadly, as fellow admirers of the great poet.

"I can't believe I told you about Emily and Finn. I never really talk about them."

"Talking can be cathartic," she said with gentle

encouragement. "I'm a good listener."

"Oh, what can I say? They were my heart and soul. My light. Then my life turned upside down and I dropped into this dull grey world. I've been in it ever since."

"The woman in your dream, the one pointing you in a new direction and taking you on a Voyage—you saw her as your girlfriend. Right?"

"Yes. I think so."

"Oh. Gosh. I've got goosebumps. It sounds like she's telling you to seek the new. To find a new direction. A way out of your grey world. It's so romantic." Her eyes were intensely curious. "I wonder why she waited eighteen years. It could have to do with the new millennium. The realigning of cosmic energies." She winced theatrically. "We're down the rabbit hole now."

I smiled politely at her humour. "A few weeks ago, I had an encounter with an old woman from my past, and it seems to have jolted my thoughts back to when Emily and Finn were alive."

"That could be it. I'm not a psychic or an augur, but I definitely think you need to work on interpreting everything in those dreams."

"What's an augur?"

"Oh. That's my Classical education again. In ancient Rome, it was someone who interpreted the will of the Gods by studying the flight patterns of birds."

"No!? The woman in my dream read the flight patterns of birds. That's how they knew where the new land was, where their Great Spirit was."

"Look." She pulled up her sleeve. "I've got goosebumps again." Her watch was now plain to see and she glanced at its face. "Whoops. If I don't get the next bus, I'll be sleeping in College Park."

"Are you in work tomorrow?" I asked, wanting to continue our conversation.

"No. I'm going home. I have some annual leave I need to take. This millennium."

I smiled. "Where's home?"

"Achill."

"I wouldn't have thought that. I saw you more inside the Pale. More Ascendency."

"I'm afraid not. Small sheep farmers. Mountainy people."

"Where does the Classical education come in?"

"Wasted scholarships. My poor parents thought I was destined for dizzy heights."

"I'd say they're happy enough with you. *Is fearr cairde ná ór.* It's not Latin. One of my Granny's."

"Friends are better than gold. That's lovely."

"I thought I might catch you out with our native tongue."

"I'm afraid not. Honours Leaving Cert. Sister Aloysius. I'm also afraid I have to go. I'll be back in work Monday week. If you're around, we could get another coffee. My treat. Sometime during the week?"

"I'd love that," I said.

"Wonderful. I'll see you then. You can tell me all about your research and augury interpretations."

"Looking forward to it."

CHAPTER 10

My research told me that by 8,000 BC, the first Irish had already settled on the island. They were Stone Age hunter-gatherers and small numbers of them had crossed the open seas in animal skin boats, having travelled along the Atlantic coastline from as far as Iberia. The historical accuracy was so precise, it felt as though my Algarve dream was unfolding before my eyes—these pilgrim voyagers might have been the first Irish. They might have been the first people to find, create, or imagine the ancient Irish spirit.

The historical evidence was encouraging, but I hadn't even begun to scratch the surface of the spiritual, the mythological. I felt I needed to delve deep into the essence of the ancient Irish spirit before I could begin to interpret my "Portugal dreams." I needed to understand the meaning of the spirit that Granda saw in me—the spirit he said had cracked an empire, the spirit he made me promise never to lose.

Not surprisingly, this path of research dragged me away from factual archaeological and genetic evidence and into the realm of mythology and legend. Especially into the ancient Gaelic annals of *Leabhar Gabhála,* the Book of Invasions—a collection of early

Gaelic manuscripts that explain the origin of the Irish. They weave a complex tale of mythology, legend, supernatural beings, great battles, and broken treaties—stories of good and evil, loyalty and betrayal, sickness and death, and much more. Central to this history of origin is a series of invasions and the struggles between five seminal tribes: the *Fomorians, Nemedians, Fir Bolg, Tuatha Dé,* and *Milesians*.

The *Milesians* from Iberia were the last to arrive, and many believe they are the ancestors of the modern Irish. Their legacy is deeply ingrained in Irish culture and identity, symbolizing the final chapter in the mythological history of Ireland's early settlers. The tale of their journey highlights themes of perseverance, conquest, and the fulfilment of destiny, marking the transition from mythical beings to the lineage of humans who would go on to shape Ireland's history.

Researching this area was heavy going, and after a week of full-on study, I found myself bogged down in a mire of myth, legend, and superstition. It was strangely unsettling and my mood became agitated. The more I tried to go beyond reason, the more I was pulled into the mystical depths of the dim-dark Celtic twilight, deep into the pulse of an ancient island people. Nothing was clear. My emotions and reason clashed, and it seemed I was trying to shoehorn my mind into a place it didn't want to go. At the same time, I had a nagging thought that I wasn't even on the right track, that this wasn't what my inner voice wanted from me. I sensed it wanted me to touch and feel the essence of the Irish, to experience the ancient Irish spirit, not just research it.

To give life to a dream, the voice explained. *That was dreamed in the heart, and that only the heart can hold.*

However, I didn't know how to hold it in my heart—to give life to a dream, to open my mind, to go beyond reason—without losing my grip on reality.

* * *

That night in bed I wondered if it was a trade-off between finding my ancient spirit and losing my mind. It was probably the last waking thought I had before I sleepwalked into the black limitless space.

"Con," a familiar voice said.

I turned, excited, realising who it was. "Finn!" He looked gaunt, a spectral figure, and I was overcome with a desire to embrace him.

He halted my approach with an open hand. "It's good to see you."

"Jesus, I've missed you. I'm sorry, Finn. I'm sorry I led you into joining the IRA. I'm sorry you were murdered. Your mother blames me."

"Listen to me, Con," he commanded, his voice severe. "We don't have time for sorry. There are dark forces after you."

A chill ran down my spine. "What? What dark

forces?"

"Listen!"

"OK. Sorry."

"Jonesy brought a malign energy into Poulnabrone, and it conjured a dark spirit that possessed him. It's a very powerful spirit that draws on the evil of his ancestors, Henry Jones and Cromwell. You saw it the same day in the Dolmen, but it wasn't able to possess you. For thirty years, it has yearned for your soul. Con, it ate Jonesy's soul."

My blood ran cold. "What about Mulligan?" I asked, in an attempt to bring reason to a nightmare.

"Mulligan didn't see the dark shadow. He went in before Jonesy. Con, it means to harm you. But there is something protecting you."

"Protecting me? What?"

"I don't know. The evil couldn't possess you, so it took the lives of the two people you told about its existence. The two people who were entwined with your soul."

"You and Em? Are you telling me it killed you and Em?"

"It has taken my life, but it hasn't eaten my soul yet." The fear in his voice carried the weight of inevitability.

Terrified, I managed to ask, "What about Em?"

"I don't know. Your Granda has been hiding me."

"Wake up! Wake up!" a female voice shouted.

"No!" I screamed. "I can't leave. I have to..."

Mary was shaking me. "Wake up!"

"OK. OK. I'm awake." My heart was thumping at a phenomenal rate, and my trembling body was drenched in sweat.

"Holy Christ! You were groaning and twisting. I couldn't wake you."

"I had this insane dream about Finn and Granda and... crazy stuff. It was so real."

"Crazy!? It was a bit more than crazy. You sat bolt upright, like something from *The Exorcist*. You frightened the life out of me."

"Sorry... eh..." I was sitting cross-legged on the bed. My pillows were on the floor. Morning light filled the room. "What time is it?"

"6 a.m.," she grumbled.

"OK."

She gave a long, disgruntled puff. "I'm awake now."

"Sorry about that," I said, reorienting myself to the bedroom.

"Gerry from the Department phoned yesterday looking for you. He said you haven't been in all week."

"I took some time off."

"Yeah?" She was tetchy. "For what?"

I flopped back onto the bed and sighed. "Here we go."

"It's a simple question."

"I'm doing some research on Celtic and pre-Celtic history."

"I see. You know you're waving goodbye to any promotion prospects. They don't promote people who are lame in the head. I told Gerry you had the flu. You could have at least phoned in sick."

"It's not a problem. I'll get a Cert... for being lame in the head."

She smirked. "Lame and thick."

"OK." I put my hand on her back. "Sorry, again. I'll pass on your medical diagnosis to the doctor."

"Do. And you might add annoying."

"Got it. Lame in the head, thick, and annoying."

When I came home that evening after a long day in the Berkeley Library, the house was empty. I put the kettle on, stuck a tuna and cheese toasty under the grill, then sat in semi-darkness. The vacuous silence of the tiled kitchen made me think of my Finn nightmare, and I wondered if Mary was right—was it all getting a bit too crazy, too real?

The door flew open. "Dad," Helen said excitedly, "I did six lengths."

"Swimming night," Mary explained, turning on the light.

"Widths," Kate corrected Helen.

"Widths," Helen echoed, rolling her eyes to heaven. She plopped onto my knee, took a bite of my toasty, and mumbled, "Silly me," licking relish from her upper lip.

We all laughed.

"That's brilliant," I said, giving her a squeeze. "You'll be like a fish next year in Portugal." Then it dawned on me—we might never be in Portugal again as a family. I looked at Mary, and I could see she was thinking the same thing.

"Time for bed, ladies," Mary said. "It's late. Night to Dad. Brush your teeth. In to bed. And I'll be up in a minute. First in bed gets a story."

Helen gave me a quick kiss and was gone like a bullet. "Night Dad."

"I did two lengths, back crawl," Kate said, before kissing me.

"That's great, Hun. The back crawl! Two lengths! That's not easy. I couldn't do that."

"Could you not?" She was delighted.

"No way." We hugged. "Night Hun."

"Night Dad." She was about to move away.

"Are you OK?"

"Yeah. All good."

"Why were you sitting in the dark?"

"No reason. Saving electricity. Off to bed, see you in the morning. Love ya."

"Love you too."

When Mary came back downstairs, she joined me at the table. Her face was drawn and not much darker than her white cotton top.

"Kate is worried about you," she said. "I'm worried about you. It's time to let go of whatever you're researching. Time to let go of your childhood promise to your Granda."

Usually, I didn't like being told what to do, but I was pleased with her intervention because I knew my research was sucking me ever deeper into a mental swamp. I reached across the table and put my hand on hers. "I know what you're saying, and I can't disagree with you. You're right."

She exhaled heavily through her nose. "Good."

I think she expected me to put up an argument. "Listen," I said, "I'm grand, you don't have to worry. I let my mind run wild, and all the stuff got muddled. My dreams, my ancient spirit, Granda, the poetry, the history, everything." I tapped my forehead. "It was a flight of fancy. Looking for a bit of colour in a grey world. I suppose I didn't want to go back to work after the holidays."

"I'm really glad. Is it to do with the divorce—the grey?" There was relief and sadness in her eyes, maybe even a hint of pity.

I definitely didn't want her pity, so I gave a brave smile of acquiescence, hoping to conceal my sense of disappointment—maybe even failure. "No, I'm OK on the divorce."

"Good. I think it's for the best."

"I'd prefer not getting into it right now. I know I've been a bit preoccupied, but it's nothing to do with the divorce. Emily and Finn have been on my mind."

"I didn't mean for us to get into it now. We have plenty of time to figure everything out... about the house and maintenance and the nitty gritty things.

"Yeah. OK," I said, realising she had her side well figured out. "No more research. Back to work on Monday."

"It'll be good to get back into the swim of things." She wanted to move the conversation on quickly in case I changed my mind. Ever forward, that was her style.

Is that it, I thought? *Back to work. Back to the grey. My dreams, my promise, Finn, Em, Granda, all gone?*

This must not be done with haste, the voice interjected. *For night's swift dragons cut the clouds full fast, and yonder shines the Fomorian harbinger.*

Fomorian harbinger? I scoffed. *This—this is the dark force Finn warned me about? The Fomorians, for God's sake.*

"Hello," Mary said.

"Sorry. I was thinking of something else. Yes, it will be great to get back to work!" I made a wide-eyed startled look.

She laughed. "Well, Gerry is dying to get you back."

"To tell you the truth I'll be happy to forget about the dreams and to get the quotes out of my head. Mr Flynn, my old teacher, would be proud of me, with all the quotes. He used to say, 'McCarthy, you've buckets of ability, but you're dog lazy.'"

"Ah, now," she said, "fair is fair. I wouldn't agree with the lazy." Her smile was large and warm, and for the briefest moment, it felt like she loved me.

I grinned with feigned modesty. "Buckets of ability though?"

"How about large cups? No. Mugs?"

"OK, mugs of ability." The brief moment had passed and we laughed, like actors. "I'll be happy to get my mind clear again. But it felt like I was so close to discovering something. Would you believe, on the bus this morning, Yeats was telling me; *When a man is fighting mad, something drops from his long blind eyes to complete his partial mind.* It felt as if he was urging me to complete my partial mind—to see the truth of my dreams, the truth of my ancient spirit."

"It's only a poem," she said, crestfallen. "He wasn't telling you anything."

"I know," I said, regretting my words. "I didn't mean he was actually telling me. It was just an example, you know—like..."

"You have to stop the nonsense. Kate is worried you're losing your mind." Her words were shrill, sharpened by my irritability and neglect over the past few weeks. "Poems are just words in a book, and dreams are for when you're asleep. Your promise to your Granda has no meaning in reality. It's a childish memory that you need to leave in your childhood."

I wanted to kick myself. "Listen, it doesn't matter. I know what you're saying and I agree with you. But why is Kate worried about me? I hope you're not manoeuvring the girls on the divorce. If that starts, you can forget about it being easy."

"God, no. I was worried about you not going to work and not telling me. I asked Kate what she thought. I know, it was a stupid thing to do. I'm sorry. She said she was worried because you didn't seem happy."

"She didn't say she thought I was losing my mind?"

"No. I'm sorry. She didn't say that. But you have been in very strange form since you met the old woman, Mrs Mulcahy."

"I don't want you talking to the girls about me like that. The divorce is going to be hard on them, and they have to see us in agreement, not divided. There's no need to undermine each other."

"I didn't mean to. I was worried about you, that's all."

"OK. You don't have to be. I'll go into work on Monday—no more dreams, no more poems, no more ancient spirit."

"Promise? You'll let go of your dreams and your research?

"Yes," I said. "I'm not losing my mind and I'm sorry that I let it go this far. I'm sorry I worried you and Kate. It's just... it was a bit of an escape. A flight of fancy that went too far."

"You'll stop the nonsense, the flight of fancy, and live in the real world?"

"Yes... Do you want me to write it in blood? No more nonsense. My head is out of my dream world."

She smiled. "No blood required. I'm glad we had a talk." Her face was relieved and a bit sad, as though she saw what might have been. "I'm off to bed. I have an early start tomorrow. Don't stay up too late."

The following morning, I dropped the girls off at summer camp, and headed to Dollymount for a walk along its white sandy beach. My intention was to clear my mind and return to being a responsible adult with a family and job to look after. Dollymount was my go-to refuge, woven into every stage of my life, through every joy and sorrow. It was a place where I could be just me, talk to those who had passed, and ask the universe questions I couldn't answer.

The beach was nearly empty, a few scattered people lost in its wide expanse. The tide was retreating, with scraggy waves breaking reluctantly along once-conquered sands, their tips sprayed by a fresh, erratic breeze. I stood motionless, looking out across the cold grey sea from my resurgent grey world. Wispy white clouds drifted across a blue-grey sky that sloped and bent over the horizon, until the sea and sky met, just before Wales. It seemed like a good day to clear my head of random quotes and fantastical dreams. But as the tide retreated, I wondered if my ancient spirit, my old self, was slipping away with it."

I took a deep breath and released it slowly, listening to the exhale as it left my body—it reminded me of when I turned to Buddhism the year after Em and Finn died. I continued, breathing in and out, slowly and deeply, listening to the rhythm of my breath. After ten breaths, a sense of calm began to loosen the tightness in my mind, and I started to walk, synchronizing my steps with my breathing. A natural rhythm soon took over, and my thoughts gave way to the present moment of sand, sea, and sky.

By the time I reached the end of the beach, I was acutely aware that the channels of my mind were clearing of unintelligible promises, confusing mythology, fantastical dreams, and disjointed quotes from dead poets. The inexplicable, the irreconcilable, the unfathomable all dissolved into irrelevance. I stopped, perfectly still, as a moment of meditative clarity came over me, clearing my mind of all obstructions, residues, obligations, and confusions. The unimportance of the things I once thought important became blatantly obvious, including my talk with Mary.

To achieve pure understanding, the voice said, *you must be free of all knowledge, concepts, ideas, and views. Only then do you have the power to enter the other shore of freedom, emancipation, and eternal peace.*

I'd read these Buddhist words many times before, but this was the first time I'd truly heard them. "OK," I said, aloud. *To achieve understanding I need to be free of knowledge, free of ideas. My ancient spirit isn't unique to me, it emanates from a communal Irish spirit, a collective consciousness that exists on the other shore of freedom, emancipation, and peace.* I stopped my musings and gathered my thoughts. *The ancient spirit isn't words on a page. It isn't a reasoned concept. It isn't knowledge. I can't reason myself into it.*

Suddenly, I realised that to understand my ancient Irish spirit, I needed to be in its presence, and with this realization came a vision. I imagined a vast space bounded by a towering black wall. In the centre of the wall, a bright yellow light squeezed through a rectangular crack, tiny amounts of light at first, but enough to widen the crack and steadily push open a door—a gateway to the other shore. Beyond this gateway, I envisioned an ancient twilight over a vast tranquil dark-blue lake, surrounded by shores awash with merriment and magic, mythology and lore, knowledge and truth, emancipation and peace. It was a place full of magical things, patiently waiting for my senses to grow sharper, waiting for me to taste, feel, and see the truth, because I couldn't reason myself into it. Intuitively, I knew the gateway should not be open. The crack pulled back against the brightness and closed seamlessly.

The space disappeared from my mind and I stood in the present moment, on Dollymount strand. I felt I had glimpsed the place where my ancient spirit dwells, a place of eternal peace. I sensed Em, or her spirit, was there. I reasoned, this was where the boats were heading, where she was pointing. All the mythology, frightening dreams, and dark spirits were leading me the wrong way. I needed to touch and feel the essence of the Irish, to experience the ancient Irish spirit, not just research it.

My thoughts instantly turned to how I might find a tangible gateway to an ethereal world, and all roads in my mind led to Poulnabrone.

Driving home, I devised a plan to avoid any accusations of backsliding. I'd go back to work, and be on my best behaviour for a week, without any mention of my dreams, ancient spirit, or Granda. I'd pretend I received a phone call from Donal, my cousin in Kerry, saying he had broken his leg and needed my help for a few days while he organised someone to manage his farm. Mary and Donal didn't get along. They didn't talk, so I thought there was little chance of my deception being discovered. Anyway, I didn't really care. I was entitled to a couple of days to reconnect with the spirit of my old self. To try and shake the ubiquitous grey from my world.

CHAPTER 11

The Department buzzed with anticipation of the disastrous mad-cow export ban being lifted, but my mind was elsewhere. According to the guidebook, *Poulnabrone is a portal tomb, a stunning piece of Irish heritage that rises from the karst landscape of the Burren. Culturally aloof, it reigns spiritually from a bleak outcrop, drenched in mystical time and mysterious history. This mass burial site has sheltered the remains of our Irish ancestors for six thousand years, encompassing two hundred and forty generations of Irish souls.*

I told Mary about Donal's needy predicament and, to avoid any interrogation, I got out of the house as quickly as I could. Outside, it was a damp, grey Saturday morning. The front garden had a bedraggled look about it, yet amid the unruly evergreens and thriving shrubs, there were vibrant blooms of colour. Bright yellow daisies swayed in the gentle breeze, and clusters of budding white roses stood in a stoic show of rebirth. I wondered if this indomitable display of nature had anything to do with my ancient Irish spirit. The vibrant buds seemed to be an affirmation of ongoing life, of regeneration, and they gave me an extra spring in my step.

Nevertheless, I was aware my excitement was as much to do with escaping my marital and work situation as it was to do with finding an ethereal gateway—or recovering my former self. I knew I was indulging my desire to feel young, free and hopeful again, if only for a few days.

Your soul can recover radical innocence, the voice said, *and learn at last that it is self-delighting, self-appeasing, self-affrighting, and that its own sweet will is heaven's will.*

I didn't know the quote, but it didn't matter; I didn't need anyone to advocate for the recovery of my will— or my spirit. I was more than happy heading west along the N4, self-affirming my own sweet will and excited at the prospects. I settled back, listening to a compilation of rock and blues tracks from my college days—Rory Gallagher, Jimi Hendrix, Peter Green, Gary Moore.

I first saw Em at a Rory concert in the National Stadium. Her long, silky black hair swung from her bowed head as she played air guitar with frenzied rhythmic motion, rocking and bopping to *"Cruise on Out."* Her slender body moved as if possessed by the electrifying riffs and raw pulse of Rory's guitar. I think that was the moment she stole my heart. The next day, while waiting for Finn at the Campanile in Trinity, I was floored to see the daytime version of this free spirit walk across Front Square.

"Do you know who just walked past?" I said when Finn arrived.

"Who?"

"The little one, with the long hair, at Rory."

"The one you had the hots for?"

"Yeah. It looks like she's in Trinity. She went into the 1937 Room."

"Did you say anything to her?"

"No. I didn't get a chance. She was too far away."

I saw her a few times after that, but it was nearly a month before we spoke. She was standing in front of me in the Buttery's lunch queue. "Not listening to Rory today," I said, inanely.

"Excuse me?" She replied with affected confusion and knowing eyes.

"You're a Rory Gallagher fan. Right?"

"Yes." Her face was now exaggeratedly quizzical and her eyes unashamedly flirtatious. "But how do you know that?"

"I can tell by the way you stand."

"Seriously?" She smirked, and tilting her head looked directly into my eyes.

"I don't know where I'm going with this," I admitted, thinking I had headed into a conversational cul-de-sac.

She laughed, sweeping back her raven hair. "Are

you into Rory?"

"Yeah. I saw you at the concert last month. You were really letting go."

"Gosh." She feigned embarrassment. "I was out of it. I must have looked nuts."

"No, you looked great. Still do." We both blushed and my heart melted.

So long ago, I thought, *and I still miss you so much.* A sudden gust from a passing truck jolted me back to the road, my hands tightening on the wheel.

Overall, it was a pleasant drive, my thoughts meandering down memory lane—until I passed a sign for Athlone, marking the halfway point. Anxious thoughts surfaced through the poignant lyrics of Gary Moore's *Parisian Walkways* and the practicalities of uncovering an ethereal gateway began to dawn on me.

Will I just stand in the tomb, I wondered, *like I did when I was a child, and hope for something to happen? What if there are other people there? Tourists? Poulnabrone is a major visitor attraction now, and tourists are a strong possibility. What if Jonesy's demon is there, waiting to suck me down to hell and eat my soul?*

I shook my head. *Jesus Christ!—it was just a dream.* Nevertheless, the thought put the wind up me. It wasn't long before the exit for Ballyvaughan appeared—just a few kilometres from Poulnabrone. I wasn't ready, however, to head straight to the site and decided to collect the keys to my accommodation first.

The woman on the phone had said I could pick them up in Ballyvaughan. "At the grocery shop, beyond the Post Office, left on Main Street."

The directions had sounded uncomplicated on the phone but somehow finding the shop was no straightforward task. After driving up and down the main street twice, I sought assistance from a woman carrying a telltale grocery bag. Ironically, she was a tourist but was able to direct me to the hide-away shop where I duly collected the keys, along with a few provisions and further directions to my accommodation.

"Ya go st'raigh out da Lisdoonvara road," the elderly shopkeeper said, handing me the keys. He had a cloth cap pushed back on his freckled bald head and the thickest, quickest, most unintelligible accent ever.

"Above-bee-yond-da-churrch. Kape-st'raigh-till-ya see-th'sine-far-dacalfs. Go-updalaft-n-kape-st'raigh. Kapegoin-n-ye'll-see-da-allway-sine. Bu-don-mind it, kape-st'raight. Da-dalmin-karpark-ill-be-n-yerlaft. Don-mind it, kape-st'raigh. St'raigh-thru-cahirconnal-to-ballydaarracross. St'raigh-on-don-mind it. Kape-goin-tillye-get-ta-da-T-a-leemmneh. Dan-laft-n-righ-n-laft-n-st'raigh. Dan-righ-at-daauld-cramry. Kapegoin-till-da-auld-yalla-sine. Ya-kant-miss-it."

I stood looking at him, my mouth open, wondering if I should ask him to repeat what he said, laugh, or just thank him and leave. There was a lone shopper watching us, a pleasant, middle-aged, roundy woman in wellington boots. She smiled, slowly shaking her head. "Holy God, Tom, sure he'll never find that. I couldn't follow that meself and I know where he's goin'." With a dismissive wave she turned to me, "Don't worry, it's not too far at all. A grand spot." Turning to Tom, she continued without drawing breath, "She keeps it lovely, Nora."

"She do-righly," Tom said, before looking at me, "She-was-n-hersalf-ta-da. Get-hin-da-plas-raddy-fir-ya."

Biting my cheek, I managed to stop my smile spilling into a laugh.

"Do ya not have one of them little tourist maps?" the woman asked Tom.

"Aye do."

"Show me one so. And give me that pencil from behind yer ear." She put the A4 photocopy map on the counter and beckoned me to stand beside her as she marked out the route. "Now! You can't miss it," she said, mocking Tom, who looked a tiny bit irked under his jovial exterior.

"Whar would we be witout da women?" he managed to say, semi-coherently. "I'm only givin' darections ta-da-cottege for turty years."

"Don't I know it," she fired back, "with half the country knockin on me door, and them lost."

He looked at me and cast his eyes upwards.

"Thanks," I said, laughing, and took the map from

the wellied woman. "Hopefully, I won't be knocking on your door."

"Well, if ye-arr," he said, "you'd want to bring yer own spuds. Because she's here half da day talkin', middlin', and hasn't bought a thing yet. Be God, pur-Paudy-has-ta-folly-da-crow-fur-abita-dinner."

"Aren't you the one too busy to serve me, with all the directions you're givin' to anyone that darkens your door?"

"Thanks," I said again, and left them to their banter.

Before the door closed behind me, I heard him say, "Be-gob-dayaknow-tabesur-hillbe-bakyet." And they both laughed heartily.

The map took me along a narrow, undulating road bounded by rough grass verges beneath old stone walls. Beyond the walls were small rocky fields with more stone walls and a few cows scattered here and there.

This is proper rural, I thought. It felt like I was entering an ancient heartland, an indigenous locality steeped in its own sense of place with an ambience and prehistoric essence befitting an ancient Irish spirit. After about ten minutes, a small sign for Poulnabrone loomed large, and it wasn't in me to drive past. I turned into the carpark, nearly colliding with a plethora of exuberant Americans spilling from a large tour bus, their cameras ready to capture some shadowy attenuation of their forebears. God knows

Irish America kept Ireland alive through some lean and difficult years, but my *Céad Míle Fáilte* was at a low ebb, and I backed away, retreating to O'Loclainn's bar in Ballyvaughan.

It was a pub I had frequented before with Finn when we hiked along the west coast — a perfect haven, out of step with the hustle and bustle of the wider world and oozing sleepy afternoon charm. The sort of place you could settle into on a drizzly afternoon, get chatting with the locals, and before you know it the barman is calling, "Time now folks. Have ya no homes to go to?"

I stood at the end of the counter and took in my surroundings. There was a man on his knees stacking bottles behind the bar. Two heavy-set men were sitting further along the counter, chatting and waiting for their pints to settle. A third man, slight of frame, with a sunken chest and gaunt face, was sitting closer to me, nursing the dregs of a pint beside an empty chaser glass. There were a few other people dotted about at tables, but I didn't have time for them because a fair-haired, broad-faced woman with a warm and welcoming smile came from the other end of the bar and tracked straight towards me.

"What can I get you?"

"Eh." I hadn't decided if I wanted a drink or a coffee.

"You have the look of a man that needs a drink," she said, with enticing familiarity.

"You're right. But I can't decide between a pint and a whiskey." I smiled. "It's a big decision." My indecision stemmed partly from the fact that I rarely drank anymore, except for the occasional social drink after work, and partly because I wasn't with Finn. The place held great memories of him.

"Or maybe a lemonade. I don't want to lead you astray."

"You've twisted me arm. I'll have both, a Jameson with a drop of red."

"Comin' up."

"Beware of the high stool," the man with the empty chaser glass said as he shared a half wink between me and the barwoman.

She looked at me with a jaunty eye, as if to say, *are you going to take the bait?*

"Ah sure," I said to the man, "I won't be here long enough."

He leaned closer, weighing me up. "Did you know, *the downward slope from the high stool is longer and steeper than from the top of Everest?"* His eyes blinked rapidly, and he scrunched his face to refocus. "According to John McGahern."

"That's a good quote," I said, surprised by the literary barfly. "*The Barracks* was a great book."

He was delighted with my response and, I guessed, the probability of landing me quickly.

"It wasn't *The Barracks*," he said, now with the authority of a learned scholar. "But God between us, I couldn't tell you what it's from. There was a time I could, but sure, the things of time are well hidden from me now. I'd say, a short story."

I could see his mind rummaging through alcohol-dimmed references.

"I have it," he said, slapping both hands on his thin shiny trousered legs. "The teacher, in *High Ground*."

The barwoman put the whiskey and red in front of me, and the man's eyes drooled at the sight. "Will you have a drink?" I asked, happy to give him the pleasure of landing me.

"I'll have a small one," he said understatedly but without hesitation. I gestured to the barwoman to give him the same again.

The first drop of fiery nectar had barely hit the back of my throat when a female voice with an English accent came from behind.

"Hello, we meet again." I turned to discover the woman who had given me directions to the shop earlier. "Did you find it?"

"I did, thanks. I would have been lost without you." She had vivacious hazel eyes, mid-thirties, shaggy blonde hair, and a radiant smile. Earlier, she was no more than a telltale grocery bag being carried by a hooded raincoat, with a woman inside.

"You're not from here?" She laughed at herself for

stating the obvious.

"How did you guess?" I countered, light-heartedly. "It would be a difficult place to get lost if I was a local."

"Unless you had one too many." Her banter was quick.

"Well, there is always that. Many a good man has been lost that way."

"And woman."

"Indeed. I didn't like to say. In case you might be lost."

"No. It's too early in the day." Her eyes sparkled.

"I suppose it is." There was a brief pause as we both tried to assess the interaction. "Are you on holiday?" I asked.

"We came over for a friend's wedding."

"Oh. Very good."

"Are you in Ballyvaughan for work?"

"Not really. On a little break. Recharging the batteries."

The barman placed a pint and a short on the counter and addressed the woman. "There you go. That's IRL£4.50, when you're ready."

"Oh, these funny Irish pounds," she said to herself, counting coins on the palm of her hand before giving him the exact amount. Then she turned to me with a brief side glance at the barfly. "I'm sorry, I hope I didn't interrupt."

"No. Not at all. A bit of small talk."

"Oh, good." She leaned in towards the bar to get her drinks, and I could smell her perfume as her hair brushed my shoulder. "Are you waiting for someone?" she said, righting her body and, somehow, standing closer than before.

"No. It's just me."

"You're very welcome to join us." She gestured toward a nondescript man sitting at a table. "George, my brother, is having a hair of the dog. One too many last night." She gave a girly laugh, which she was still able to get away with, but time was catching up on her. "Would you like to join us?"

"Yes, thanks," I said, lying. The prospect of a three-way hungover conversation had diminished her allure, but I couldn't think of an excuse quick enough. The barfly's face registered his disappointment, and we shared a knowing look of no hard feelings – it was a given that an attractive woman trumped public-house-talk.

"I'm Liz, by the way."

We shook hands.

"I'm Conor."

On reaching the table, she said, "Conor, this is George, my brother. George, this is Conor." He leaned forward and as we shook hands; I wondered if the second mention of "my brother" meant she was actually on the pull.

Hardly, I thought.

We took our seats, and she directed her conversation towards me, excluding hungover George. "We flew into Shannon yesterday morning. This is my first time in Ireland, and I'm hoping to see some of the sights."

"Very nice. Welcome." A flirty smile crossed my face, reminiscent of times past when me and Finn were having the *craic,* chatting up a couple of American tourists at the bar.

"Thank you. Everybody is so friendly." Her tone was playful.

"I hope you get a bit of sunshine, between the clouds. How long have you got?"

She squinched her nose. "We're flying back tomorrow, late."

"You'll see a lot so," I said, tongue in cheek.

Her head dipped and she looked coquettishly from under her eyebrows, Princess Diana style. "We went to see Poola-brown this morning."

"Great," I said, proudly. "What did you think?"

"It was nice. It reminded me of a little Stonehenge. Like one part of it."

After picking my jaw up off the floor, I enlightened her about the ancient heritage of the Poulnabrone Dolmen, including that it was built more than a thousand years before Stonehenge. She listened intently, apparently enthralled with my history lesson. George, on the other hand, was only half pretending to listen. I could tell this wasn't his first time being a spare wheel in his sister's company.

"You would be a great tour guide," she said. "We went to see it because the woman on reception at our hotel said some people believe it's where leprechauns live."

I raised my eyebrows and smiled, dubiously.

She buried her face in her hands, covering faux embarrassment, and chuckled. "That sounds silly, especially after listening to all your wonderful knowledge."

Her eye contact was magnetic, and I was enjoying her coquettishness.

"Sure, maybe they do," I said with my best Leprechaun accent. "Who knows now? Wisha, if you caught one of them little lads, you'd be going back to England with a pot of gold. Begorrah and Bejasus!"

"Stop!" She laughed. "You're mocking me. I never knew you had so much history in Ireland. The only Irish thing we learned in school was your tattie famine."

"Tattie famine?" The word tattie grated on my ears and dampened my joviality; it sounded so incongruous.

She looked at me questioningly, as if maybe I didn't

know about the Famine. "When the tatties stopped growing and the farmers didn't know how to grow other crops, a lot of poor people died because they only ate potatoes. It was very sad."

"Yes, indeed it was." I was flabbergasted and, surprisingly, offended.

"Is that wrong? You're looking at me as if I said something stupid." There was an edge to her voice, but she was still smiling.

Without warning, my mood changed. I was uncomfortable talking light-heartedly with English people about the famine. It somehow felt disloyal to the Irish in the North who were still under English rule, and to the MI6 murder of Finn.

He wouldn't tolerate 'tatties,' the voice said. *Stand up for the un-coffined masses.*

"Let's say, it's not quite accurate," I answered, not arsed to elaborate because any desire I had for flirtatious banter was gone. "Leprechauns and Guinness," I said, "that's an easier Irish topic."

Liz looked slighted. She didn't like my change f mood. "That's quite condescending." Her upper lip had stiffened, and her eyes flashed with a mix of anger and hurt. "I'm a marketing manager for a multinational brand. I have a degree from Oxford. I don't need to talk about Leprechauns. I simply asked, "Am I wrong about the tattie famine?"

"I'm sorry, I didn't mean to sound condescending."

All I wanted was a way out. I certainly didn't want argy-bargy about the Famine with a disgruntled, ill-informed, English woman.

She watched me apologise, and I think I saw her gloat at the humbling of a kiss-arse native. "Don't worry about it," she said, with gracious haughtiness, though her eyes betrayed a flicker of uncertainty. "The tattie famine was..."

"Please, stop calling it the 'tattie' famine. It's inappropriate."

"That's what our teacher called it," she said, without giving ground. "She was Scottish. Tatties is what they call potatoes."

Just give her both barrels, the voice said *That's what Finn would do.*

"Everybody in Ireland," I said, "knows about the Great Famine, which is sometimes erroneously referred to as the Potato Famine. We know about it because it is the lowest point, the deepest sadness, in our 10,000-year history. And, yes, I have to say, your view of it is inaccurate.

Rule Britannia! Finn sang, in my head. *Britannia rules her slaves.* It was a memory of the two of us sitting by a feeble campfire, sharing a flagon of cider, the glow of the flames barely keeping the night at bay.

"I'm only telling you," she responded indignantly, "what I learned from a highly qualified teacher."

I nodded to show acceptance of her defence but

continued to unload both barrels. "It was more a famine of convenience. I mean, convenient for the British Government. Ireland, without the Irish, would be easier for the British to govern and, of course, more profitable."

Tell them about the wilful neglect, the genocide, the voice urged.

"At best," I said, "the Famine was wilful neglect by the British Government. At worst, it was genocide. Ireland, by the way, wasn't allowed have its own government."

She was taken aback by my thinly veiled hostility and, to tell the truth, so was I.

"Genocide?" Her tone was incredulous.

"I said, at worst. But just to give you a flavour of English sentiment towards the starving Irish, the *Times* wrote, during the Famine: *'We look forward to the day when an Irishman in Ireland will be as rare as a Red Indian in Manhattan.'*"

George had the look of a man who was wondering if he had sleepwalked into an IRA pub. "I'm sure Liz didn't mean anything inappropriate," he said. "Tattie is a colloquial term."

Colloquial or colonial? I thought, as I sipped my drink, taking a pause to let my emotions cool.

His demeanour was middle management, with eyebrows furrowed just the right amount to feign compassion. "Unfortunately," he continued, "I don't know anything about your famine, but I can see how it must have been a very sad time for you, the Irish. Famine is always difficult."

Despite his obvious unease with the conversation, I felt he was patronising me, and I wanted to slap him—verbally. "In fact," I said, "it wasn't a famine, in the true meaning of the word. Famine is defined as an extreme scarcity of food. But thousands of tons of food were being exported from Ireland to England at the very same time that the Irish were dying of hunger."

I could see Liz was about to say something, but I ignored her, and she sighed heavily. "The government in London wouldn't allow the food to be diverted to the hungry poor, and over a million people died of starvation. A million people. With over a million more forced out of their country, my country, forever."

George's eyes were fully dilated, and he pulled himself upright in the seat. "As I've said, it's very sad. The poor always suffer the most. That's the way of the world, even today. I can't comment specifically on your famine because I don't know anything about it. Undoubtedly, it must have been a difficult time."

"Have you heard of Oscar Wilde?" I asked. They both indicated they had, and Liz seemed annoyed that I felt the need to ask. "This is from a poem by his mother, Lady Jane Wilde, *Speranza*. She wrote it during the Famine, and I learned it as a child."

I cleared my throat, settled myself, and delivered the lines slowly.

"Accursed are we in our own land, and toil we must still toil;

For the stranger reaps our harvest, the foreigner owns our soil.

Oh, Christ! How have we sinned that, on our native plains,

We perish houseless, naked, starved, with branded brow, like Cain's?

Dying, dying wearily, with a torture sure and slow

Dying, as a dog would die, by the wayside as we go."

There was stony silence when I finished and we each shifted uncomfortably in our seats. They avoided eye contact with me and, ill at ease, looked blankly at the table. George gathered himself, swallowing before speaking through a frozen smile. "Well recited, thank you."

Liz said nothing, her eyes seething from behind an impassive countenance.

I intended the poem to be an empathetic slap in the mouth before bringing our conversation to an end. But it touched my soul with indignation, and defiance surged within me. I needed to let loose a final round, for Finn. "Just to add one last thing," I said, steadying my aim, "you said the Irish farmers didn't know how to grow other crops. Well, that doesn't really describe the situation. The Irish were forced by the English to live on tiny plots of land, often smaller than a quarter of an acre, and the potato was the only crop with enough protein to sustain a family on such small plots."

I paused, letting my words sink in before continuing. "The English, of course, lived in grandeur. Huge mansions and vast estates, on land they had stolen from the Irish with brutal military force."

The atmosphere had gone from decidedly uncomfortable to tense. I could see they were personally offended, and George was considering a spirited response. I was ready. My blood was up. Ready to lay waste the English foe.

Stop, my reason cautioned. *Stop. You've gone too far.*

"But we're hungry," the poem continued in my head, *"very hungry, and we cannot stop our crying.*

And some of us grow cold and white, we know not what it means.

But as they lie beside us, we tremble in our dreams."

I took a deep breath, and reason prevailed. *Say something soothing,* it told me. *Say, That's all in the past now.*

But I couldn't. My heart was burning with a heightened awareness that the English were still occupying part of my country, and any soothing words would have been traitorous to my sense of Irishness – an affront to Finn's martyrdom.

Liz rose to her feet. "We have a long day, George." She looked at me, expressionless. "It's been...

interesting meeting you, Conor."

He stood and nodded in agreement. "A long day." We didn't shake hands, and they left without further ado.

I remained seated, waiting for my mind to take stock of what had happened. Everything in the bar looked the same, but something had changed in me – as though a switch had been flipped. I felt more defiantly Irish than I had in years.

The barman cleared the table. "Will you have another one?"

"Yes, thanks," I said, without thinking.

The hum of conversations and clinking glasses around the bar was distant, like a backdrop to my thoughts. I was sorry I had met them. I knew they weren't to blame for their ignorance. They were, I suspected, hapless by-products of an antiquated education system still producing middle managers for a long-lost empire. I felt no animosity towards them as individuals, but the wanton injustice of the Famine was an exceptionally raw nerve for me and Finn, and a fire had reignited in my brain – a righteous fire.

"They rose in dark and evil days," the voice quoted, *"to right their native land and kindled here a living blaze that nothing shall withstand."* It was from a plaque that had been presented to my Granda, on his retirement, by the men of his Battalion.

I saw the sitting room of my family home, as a ten-year-old child, the plaque taking pride of place on the mantel piece above the fireplace. I remembered myself crying in Mr Flynn's class when I learned the Jane Wilde poem, and I couldn't help but whisper the lines.

"Their whitening bones against ye will rise as witness, from the cabins and the ditches, in their charred, un-coffined masses. A ghastly, spectral army before the great God we'll stand, and arraign ye as their murderers, the spoilers of our land."

I remembered Jonesy mocked me for being a cry-baby, and I punched him in the face – not because he mocked me, but because he mocked *the charred, un-coffined masses.* It was the first time I had punched someone in the face. His nose bled, trickling onto his pale upper lip like a ritualistic loss of innocence. The raw, unfiltered reality of the moment was etched into my memory, and in retrospect forever altered the simple purity of my childhood.

The barman put my drink on the table. "There you go. That's two twenty, when you're ready."

"Thanks." I gave him a fiver. "You can take for a small one as well, for the scholar at the counter." I gestured towards the barfly. "Keep the change."

"A scholar, to be sure." He stalled, scratched his chin, and giving a kindly glance towards the barfly, lowered his voice to a secret. "A former principal. Brains to burn. Sure, that's the way of it. I'll do that for ya. Thanks."

I downed my drink in one go and headed for the door.

CHAPTER 12

A small thatched cottage with whitewashed walls and a yellow door stood at the end of a short driveway. Two yellow sash windows flanked the door, with flower beds under each, filled with vibrant asters and chrysanthemums flaunting shades of purple, red, and gold. It appeared to be an isolated dwelling, but I wasn't sure because low clouds had descended on the surrounding hills creating a misty twilight. The cottage was nestled among irregularly shaped fields of poor grass and thistle, separated by weathered stone walls and interspersed with dishevelled hawthorn bushes. It was probably built in the nineteenth century, post-famine, a tenant's dwelling.

I stepped out of the car and immediately felt welcomed, as though embraced by a tribal belonging.

You know the walls, the voice recited, *the flowers, and the birds, the green and rugged sides of many glens, and do but half remember words, in converse with the mountains, bogs, and fens.*

"Exactly," I said aloud.

But it was more than a feeling of belonging, of knowing. My senses were also enveloped in a lonely hankering for something that was past, something heroic, something Gaelic. I looked beyond the hawthorn bushes and imagined a band of battle-worn Gaelic warriors emerging from the misty twilight, en route to right a grievous wrong that had been done to my people.

A band of warriors, the voice said, sounding quietly theatrical, *loud with hope and windswept, spray-dabbled hair, had gathered at hand. 'Turn if you may from battles never done,' you called, as they marched by one by one.*

The imagery stirred my heart. I felt at home, alive, and destined to find the ethereal gateway. Destined to find Em and Finn. To find my lost spirit.

You know, reason said, *this flight to the country is no more than a homage to a past life that can't be relived.*

I know, I just want to feel their emotion again. If only for a minute. To feel my Irishness again.

Maybe pull back a little on the Irishness! Reason jibed. *You're a bit too old to go all Braveheart.*

Inside the cottage I was greeted by a small, tidy room with a glass-fronted stove that was already lit, casting flickering shadows across a flagstone floor. The shadows danced under an old oak kitchen table and chairs, behind a tweedy sofa, and over a green-cushioned rocking chair. A charming oak dresser, stacked with blue and white willow-patterned delph, swayed and postured playfully in the shadows. There were two stoop-your-head doors, one leading to a compact scullery and the other to the bedroom. Everything was clean, fresh, and welcoming. The wellied woman was right, Nora kept it lovely.

On the window ledge, a large water jug displayed a bunch of freshly cut flowers. In the centre of the table, a little note read: "Welcome. Homemade scones, butter, and milk in the fridge."

I made a cup of tea and enjoyed my scones while sitting by the fire. Geraldine came to mind and I wondered how she was doing on Achill: was she herding sheep, had she thought about me? I hoped I'd have something good to tell her when we met for coffee, other than my unintelligible shopkeeper. *I won't tell her about Liz and George, not both barrels anyway.*

Oh, to have a little house, the voice interrupted my thoughts, *to own the hearth and stool and all. The heaped-up sods upon the fire, the pile of turf against the wall. To have a clock with weights and chains, and pendulum swinging up and down. A dresser filled with shining delph, speckled and white and blue and brown.*

The scones were delicious—fluffy and buttery with a crunchy top. I wondered if Nora had baked them herself. Was this her homeplace before she married Tom? Or perhaps it was Tom's place before he married Nora. I flipped my shoes off, put my feet up, and relaxed watching the fire. The flames were mesmerising, swaying and bowing, jumping and swirling like ethereal dancers.

I could be quiet here at night, my mind whispered, *beside the fire and by myself, sure of a bed and loath to leave, the ticking clock and the shining delph.*

I thought about my encounter with Liz and George and decided I was too hard on them. Granted, they should have known better, but there was no need for both barrels. A slight twist of fate and she could have been on the couch beside me, sharing my scones.

No. I was content there, alone, searching the enchanted flames for the spirit of my Gaelic past.

Every passionate man, the voice said, *is linked with another age, historical or imaginary, where alone he finds images that rouse his energy.*

I liked the quote, but I didn't tell the voice that. *Every passionate man,* my thoughts echoed, *is linked with another age. Between two eternities. That of race and that of soul... A burning fire... A protest against shame.*

A double bed, dressed in starchy white and yellow linen that matched the curtains, dominated the bedroom. Nora had an eye for home décor, that's for sure, but it was a bit too dolly for me. A bit too incongruent with the essence of the cottage, and I felt compelled to spare a thought for the people who lived here down through the years. It was a lovely house, no doubt about it, for one or two people on vacation, but how on earth did a family of eight, ten, twelve, or more live here? They could never have imagined that their impoverished tiny home would become a tarted-up tourist rental.

If these walls could talk, I thought, *what dark tales their words would tell.*

The bed looked inviting, and I decided on an early night—hoping to get a head start in the morning and beat the tourists to Poulnabrone. The duvet and pillows were full and soft, so it didn't take long for sleep to come over me.

It was 10:45 a.m. by the time I woke. Feeling well-rested and in fine fettle, I brought my tea and toast outside to take in the surrounding countryside. Unfortunately, the view was impeded by a morning mist, but the freshness of the cool morning air streaming into my lungs was invigorating. I strolled through a couple of adjoining fields, inhaling deeply, trying to soak in every drop of Ireland's rural essence: every scrawny and lush blade of grass, every sweet, wet leaf on every windswept bush, every moss-drenched rock in every dilapidated wall, every bird song on every moist waft of air—everything big and small, tangible and ethereal—until I was drunk on it.

I was at one with my surroundings and felt twenty years younger. The stone walls and scraggy fields were perfect. The cottage was perfect. The flowers were perfect. The yellow door and windows were perfect. It was all perfect. I couldn't have been happier, and I was on the point of enlightening the hawthorn bushes about my feelings for them when a sharp breeze rustled the flowers.

You must be gone, the voice said, *there is a grave where daffodils and lilies wave. And you must seek the ancient crown, buried under the sleepy ground*

I took it as an otherworldly message, guiding me back to Poulnabrone, and I gathered my bits and pieces. The idea that maybe Em, Finn or Granda was spurring me onward to my destination gave me an adrenaline rush, and I eagerly hurried to bring the soul of a man to an ethereal world.

The road was narrow with sneaky turns, and I drove faster than I should have through a hazy drizzle that covered the land and sky in a uniform mild greyness. Colloquially, it was a soft day, and I hoped a discouraging one for sightseers. There wasn't a car or bus to be seen, and I wondered if it might be possible that I'd have the place to myself. Unfortunately, while it might have been possible, it certainly wasn't probable, and when I turned into the car park, I had to pass at least ten cars and three tour buses before I found a vacant space.

Undeterred, I parked the car and continued on foot. It was a short walk to the site, and while the path wasn't festooned with tourists, there were enough to cool my ardour. Ignorant people, I suspected, who might just as easily have been visiting Guinness or chasing leprechauns.

I ignored them. However, when the Dolmen came into view, my heart sank. It was much smaller, less awesome, and less mystical than I had imagined. The closer I got, the more my enshrined image of this most ancient, iconic site was assaulted by the truth. Bord Fáilte had forced it to feed the inane masses with the marrow of its spiritual bones. Prostitute itself day in, day out. Constantly photographed and tongue-lashed by the endless mindless hordes: *"Stand closer." "Make a funny face." "Do the rabbit ears." "Where to next?"*

These people are of a different kind, the voice lamented, *gone about the world like wind, with no time to pray.*

When I reached the site, one wobbly mountain of a man, wet with drizzle or sweat—it could have been either—was posing in front of the Dolmen. "Make sure you get the T-shirt, honey," he said. His T-shirt read: 'Been there. Done that. Worn the T-shirt.'

Christ! I thought.

My eyes searched the place for any semblance of spirituality. I could only see the formerly idolised Dolmen standing dejected inside a circle of tatty, faded rope, like a once majestic animal humiliated in a two-bit circus ring. Despondent, I walked around its circumference and gazed incredulously at its humiliation, doubting if this could be home to an ethereal gateway.

And each one said, the voice recited, *with a long, long sigh, O saddest pilgrim in all the world, sleep here till the moon and the stars die.*

The relevance of the line to my feelings of sadness surprised me, and the words lingered in my thoughts.

What are you saying? I snapped. You want me to

sleep here? Spend the night in the tomb until the moon and stars fade, until the sun rises? Are you serious!?

Yes, it replied emphatically, *for this was ancient Oisin's fate. Loosed long ago from Heaven's gate. For his last days to lie in wait.*

"OK," I said aloud, feigning boldness. "I'll sleep here."

All at once, I was nervous and excited at the prospect of spending the night in the tomb, in the black of night, and maybe, just maybe, finding an ethereal gateway. Interpreting my "Portugal dream" was turning out to be a wild journey, and I looked forward to telling Geraldine all about my antics—which surprised me. It had been a long time since I'd considered sharing my inner world with a woman. Then, Mary came to mind, and I chuckled. If she knew I was going to spend the night in an ancient tomb, she'd definitely have me committed.

My mind shifted to the practicalities of nighttime access. I looked around the site for security cameras or personnel. There were none, other than an elderly man in a high-viz yellow jacket with the word 'staff' stamped on the back. I decided it would be best to investigate further because I didn't fancy being savaged by a pack of guard dogs while snooping around in the dark. The high-viz jacket man seemed to be the only source of the required information. I meandered towards him, stopping every now and then, pretending to take in a particular view. I didn't want to make my approach too obvious.

He was in his early sixties, about six feet tall with broad shoulders and, as I got closer, an unexpectedly formidable presence.

"That's a damp one," I said, following his line of sight across the grey karst countryside.

"Liquid sunshine," he replied, without looking at me. "That's what a Kerry man would tell ya. But," he gave me an inclusive side glance, "they'd tell ya anything down there for the tourist dollar." He sniffed and pulled up his collar against the damp air. "They wiped West Cork's eye on that one, the tourist dollar."

"You'd want to get up early to wipe a Cork man's eye."

"But twice as early for a Cavan man," he said, appreciating his own wit, and repositioning his body so that we were facing each other. "Where do ya hail from yourself, before I put me two feet in it?"

"Dublin," I said, mildly apologetic, conscious that those from the big smoke were often viewed suspiciously in rural Ireland.

"There's nothing wrong with the Dublin man," he said, in my defence. "The real Dublin man, if you get me."

"I do. I know what you're saying."

"But the drug fellas and the robbers and the gangs runnin' wild above on the streets, the whole shower of them should be rounded up and put on the Curragh or Spike Island. Then leave them at it, if ya get me."

"I do and I wouldn't disagree on that one." I looked about, wondering how I'd move the conversation to security. "There's a good crowd here today," I said, "for a wet day."

"Hardly anyone at all." His tone was quietly boastful. "I'll tell you now, twenty thousand in the one day wouldn't be uncommon."

"Really!"

"As true as you're lookin' at me. The buses are here from nine in the mornin' till about one. Then they're back again from around half-past two, till half-six in the evenin'. Constant. Between one and half-two they have the nose bags on."

"Twenty thousand. I'm amazed at that." I really was.

"I'd put me shirt on ten thousand today, with the weather. And then from here in, up it goes every day till we're hittin' twenty thousand. 'Tis like Croke Park on All Ireland Day."

"That must be hard work."

"I'll tell ya, there are good and bad days. Isn't that the way of every job? I'm an outdoor person, always was." He puffed and shook his head, like a horse. "I couldn't work indoors at all."

"Are you working here long?"

"Not too short of forty years. I'm local, so I'm comin' here over sixty years, man and boy."

"That's incredible. You must have seen some changes."

"The portal doesn't change." He angled his head, a smidgen to the left, and appeared to be assessing my likely level of knowledge. "You know it's a portal tomb?"

"Yes. I'm very interested in its history and its place in Irish mythology, so I know a bit about it."

He nodded, approvingly. "'Tis the people who have changed."

"I can imagine. What do you do here? What's your job?"

"I'm the caretaker," he said, with the look of a loyal sentinel.

"You're the caretaker of the portal tomb?" My curiosity was piqued.

"That's right. Well, there's two others helpin' me. I'm not on me own."

"What a fantastic job. Custodian of six thousand years of Irish heritage. The Keeper of the Portal."

"You could say that, but there's a lot here who have no idea, not a bull's notion, of what they're lookin' at. I'll tell you now. Half of them want to take pictures… on top of the capstone. Did ya ever hear the like? They have me near demented."

"No! Really?"

"As true as I'm standing here. But the best of all

was last September, a cycling group from Canada. Grown men, on a birthday bash. Wanted a picture with yer-man, the birthday fella, on his bike, on top of the capstone. On top of the feckin' thing. And he was fair thick when I said no. 'It's only a rock,' he said to me, 'I'm not going to hurt it.' And doesn't he go and get over the rope, with the bike on his shoulder."

"What did you do?" I knew he was dying to tell me.

"I'm not security here, but there was no point in me calling the Guards—they'd have to come from Ennis, and yer man would be long gone. So, I said to him, 'If you even lay a hand on these ancient stones, you might find it hard cycling home with the toe of me boot stuck up in the high hole of your arse." His delivery was deadpan.

"What happened?" I managed to say through a belly laugh.

"He didn't take the photo. And they all cycled off in their little stretchy pants."

I regained my composure with a shake of my head. But inside I was roaring with laughter as I visualised them beating a hasty retreat, in their little stretchy pants, routed by a riled Clare man. "Well done you," I said. "I've no time for that level of ignorance. It makes my blood boil when something as precious as Poulnabrone could be damaged by morons."

We chatted for a while, and it turned out he was a treasure trove of information about the site and its hinterland, most of which I didn't know. He pointed out an intriguing geological phenomenon—the shape of a human face etched by nature in the cliff about half a mile beyond the Dolmen. Many believed, according to him, that it was significant to the location of the portal. "Watching over Poulnabrone for six thousand years," he said. "Maybe he's your Keeper of the Portal."

I tried to read his expression as he spoke, to see if he was telling me something meaningful or if it was just tourist guff. But I couldn't see past his eyes because they were trying to see past mine.

"Do you believe in all the mythology about Poulnabrone?" I asked.

"Do you mean the *Sidhe*," he furrowed his forehead, "the *Tuatha Dé*?"

"Yes, I suppose. But more the stuff about it being a portal, a secret gate to another world."

"I'll tell you now, fairy folklore is very strong round-about this part of the country. And, it would depend on who I was talkin' to, if you get me."

"Yes, I understand." I sensed he liked my interest, but I was a stranger and he wasn't going to tell me any secrets, real or unreal. "How far is it to the face?"

"About forty minutes, if you went up by the hazel tree there," he said, indicating the direction with his walking stick, "at the foot of the cliff, to the left of the old white sign. Do you see it?"

"I do. Is the hazel tree associated with the fairies?"

"It would be more the hawthorn, the May tree. The

hazel is the tree of wisdom." He pondered for a moment. "I'll tell you now, if you were above that way, on top of the cliffs there, there's a fairy fort off to the right, and it has a clear view down to the Dolmen."

Fairy Fort, the voice interjected in my mind, *come Fairie Dún...*

Its words rushed uncensored from my head to my mouth... *"And captives bound with leathern thongs, shall kneel and praise you, one by one, at evening in my Western Dún."*

The caretaker looked at me peculiarly, or knowingly. "Is that from a poem?"

"Eh, yes. It's probably Yeats, but I'm not sure. It just, sort of, popped into my head."

"I wouldn't know too much about his poems, but Lady Gregory was a great help to him, above in Coole Park there. A lovely spot."

"Yes, so I hear."

I accepted the voice's interruption as you might a precocious child and considered his words. *Shall kneel and praise you. Who's you? At evening in my Western Dún.* I knew Dún was the Irish for a fort. *My western fort, my fairy fort?*

"Do you believe it belongs to the *Tuatha Dé Dannan*?" I asked, without thinking.

"Well," he said, "I'll tell you, as sure as I'm standing here now, the fairy folk, and the *Tuatha Dé Dannan*, were well believed in around these parts, and you'd have to travel a long way to find the man or woman that would move a stone or leaf or blade of grass from inside that ring fort."

"Even today?"

"Maybe they wouldn't all admit to it, but there you have it. The older people could tell you stories that you wouldn't know if they were stories or not, if you get me. About people goin' into the fort and never comin' out. Or, others sittin' under the hawthorn bush inside in the fort and ageing twenty years. And there are those that would tell you, you could lose twenty years and find your youth. All dependin' on the fairy in residence."

I listened with overt interest, partly because I wanted him to tell me about the nighttime security arrangement but also because I was enjoying the folklore, straight from the horse's mouth, so to speak.

"Lose twenty years, and find your youth. That'd be a good one." I said, thinking it was nearly twenty years since I lost Em, Finn, and my Irish spirit.

"T'would."

"Were you told these stories?"

"I was. I was for sure." He paused, and his persona became more *seanchaí* than sentinel.

"I'll tell you a story I was told, as a young lad. I had an uncle, before I was born, on my mother's side. He was above on the cliffs minding a few sheep with his young cousin, only a boy. He was twenty-five himself, that very day. A strappin' fella. But he wasn't a great man for the work, or so the story goes, and he wanted to have a snooze. Sure enough, he couldn't find a comfortable spot but doesn't he notice the grass inside in the fairy fort is long and soft and inviting. So, he tells his cousin to watch the sheep and he goes in for a sleep.

"Now, this is gospel, from the cousin's own lips. Wasn't he no more than a few minutes asleep when a beautiful lady, in all her finery, appeared from under the hawthorn. She looked about the fort and then kissed the uncle's mouth. Well, he woke up sure enough and got to his feet, with a foolish grin. Accordin' to the cousin. The next thing, she sort of dances around him and takes his hand. And then, at that very second, quick as a flash, they disappeared. Never to be seen again. My own mother told me that, about her own brother, as true as I'm standing here."

"God. That's some story. Eh, do you believe it?"

"I'm only tellin' you what she told me."

"Is it the fairy fort on top of the cliffs?"

"The very one."

"I always liked fairy folklore, especially the imagery and otherworldliness of the *Tuatha Dé Dannan*. It's all so fantastical. Part of who we are. But I wouldn't be religious about it." Strangely, I felt I should clarify my atheism. "I don't believe in any formal religion, or any belief system for that matter."

"To each their own," the caretaker said, with all the

acceptance of his ancient culture. "Tis often the blind man can see the best, if you get me."

"I do," I said automatically and wondered if there was wisdom in his simple sentence.

Its Buddha, the voice explained. *To achieve pure understanding, you must be free of views. Metaphorically blind. Only then do you have the power to enter the other shore of freedom, emancipation, and peace.*

"The people who built the portal," he explained, "were long before Christ or Jehovah or any other God we might hold today. They were of the clay, the trees, the rocks, the sea, the rivers, and the wind. Of nature herself."

I nodded enthusiastically. "I believe there are inexplicable ethereal energies in the world that we can sometimes sense, or even interact with, and that a lot of these energies have been deified in the past. Maybe like the energies when the portal was built."

His eyes held an objective look, reassessing me.

Inexplicable ethereal energies? Echoed in my thoughts. *I sound like a shithead.*

He gave me another once over and then looked to the portal. "Maybe so." A contemplative silence grew between us. "You have a lot of fine words there, educated words for sure." His eyes narrowed. "But 'tis only a small few who have the gift."

We both surveyed the portal in silence, and I

wondered if he thought I had the gift or if I was just a shithead.

"I think I'll go up the cliffs," I said, checking my watch, "and have a wander. What time do you lock up?"

"There's no lockin-up." He guffawed. "I'm either on-site or I'm not. I head off at six and one of the other lads will start at half-eight in the mornin'."

"And who takes care of the place during the night? Is there security or cameras and stuff?"

"No, nothin' like that." He looked directly into my eyes. "It has its own security, if you get me."

I was wrong-footed by what I thought was an unspoken message, and I didn't know how to respond, so I shuffled my feet and pulled a knowing face. "I'm sure..."

"If you're havin' a wander you'll need better shoes; the rocks are fierce slippy when it's wet."

"I have boots and a stick in the car," I said, starting to move away. "Listen, thanks for all the information."

"No bother. Keep an eye on the daylight. It's not a place to be after dark."

CHAPTER 13

The rocks were definitely slippy, treacherous even, and it took me a good twenty minutes to reach the white sign at the foot of the cliff which read: *No Entry.*

Who's going to catch me? I thought, as I maneuvered around the hazel tree, scaled the boundary wall, and continued toward the mysterious face etched in stone. It wasn't an easy trek; the terrain was full of brambles and briers, some of which were waist-high and concealed deep fissures in the limestone. Every leaf, branch, and blade of grass was dripping wet, but the sky was brightening, and the dark blanket cloud had given way to broken patches of sunshine.

I eventually made it to the face, drenched and bedraggled, after disappearing into the undergrowth a number of times. It was a geological phenomenon, without a doubt. Twenty or thirty feet above me, a stern male countenance loomed—carved into sheer rock, surveying the Burren's landscape for millennia. No, longer. Maybe as ancient as Ireland itself.

I gazed upon its human features and wondered about its geological, mythological, and theological significance. It had a large forehead and heavy brow over sunken eye sockets. An angular flat nose above a thick upper lip with a slightly opened mouth, and a strong square chin. Proud, somber, regal, were the words that came to mind. An ancient prince of earth and stone if ever there was one. But it was lifeless. I didn't sense anything from it other than it had been dead for a long, long time. An ancient funerary mask casting its cold eyes on an eternity of life and death. At best, a mysterious stone visage with devotional potential, now meaningless and lonely. Yet I felt obligated to linger in reverence to a god that never was, and to show respect to the ancient Irish people who most likely worshipped this geological phenomenon as a deity.

By his command these words are cut, the voice said, dramatically. *Cast a cold eye on life, on death. Horseman, pass by.*

I'm not sure that fits, I responded, with schoolboy glee. *Yeats meant that life and death are ephemeral but the caster of this cold eye is certainly not ephemeral.*

I waited for a moment but there was no response, and I passed by.

Scaling the cliff wasn't too difficult once I identified what I assumed was the goats' route. I saw they had gone a particular way many times, evident by the broken underwood and their footmarks in the muddy places. Nonetheless, with my agility firmly anchored in times past, it wasn't an effortless climb, and upon reaching the top, I was breathless but duly rewarded with a majestic view that sprawled before me.

My thoughts lazily waited for the voice to wax lyrical with some poetic quote describing the beauty of the scene. Then it struck me: *I'm the one looking at this, not the voice,* and I wondered, *should I be concerned about its prominence in my head.*

No, I thought, *it's normal for me to have an internal conversation. I've always talked to myself. The voice is just a variation. A vocal digression.*

To be honest, I wasn't really worried about it. But I knew Mary and all the other grey people might say I was delusional for traipsing across the country in pursuit of cryptic dream messages while listening to voices.

Those who are dancing, the voice said, *are thought to be insane by those who cannot hear the music.*

I laughed. *True.*

My reason told me that the grey naysayers, the delusionists, were on the outside and were deaf to the music of my thoughts. I was on the inside, where the currency of expression was emotion, and the only way certain emotions could be communicated was through poetry, forgotten wisdoms, and dreams. I didn't know enough about Jung for him to justify my aberrant behaviour but I suspected my subconscious was conjuring dreams and reciting quotes to help me reclaim my spirit and find closure with Em and Finn.

The voice was no more than a whimsical label I'd given to a particular thought process. I'd always been an avid reader, a free thinker, and there were a myriad of ideas, thoughts, and quotes of various hues lying dormant somewhere in my subconscious. The voice was simply a channel for them to be released when they seemed pertinent to my situation. Nevertheless, I was aware if I didn't stay on the right side of the sanity line, there could be serious consequences.

The view from the clifftop was spectacular, stretching for miles across low-lying treeless countryside to far-off Slieve Elva. Surprisingly, the huge landscape was dwarfed by the enormity of the sky's giant canvas of emerging blue, dashed with slow-moving dull grey clouds beneath quicker fluffy white clouds. They tumbled and raced, chasing their own shadows across the countryside.

And still, their acrobatic performance was only the background to the prima donna beams of sunshine that escaped through the ever-changing cloud breaks like celestial spotlights, illuminating neat parcels of emerald green farmland before abruptly quenching and moving to spotlight another green jewel, and another, and so on. Their palette of colours and shades was fluid, alive, mixing and jostling, blending and separating. It shouted of a higher presence, a sorcerer of ambience, whose brilliance could only be dreamed of by the clay-footed Gods of stage and screen.

My heart swelled with the beauty of my country, and I inhaled full and deep until I was lightheaded with the oneness of my place in the landscape. This was Ireland, this was me, this was who we were—me and Ireland, as one. I also noticed heavy black clouds in the distance lurking in a continuous streak of foreboding along the horizon.

There's always darkness, I thought, *you can't have light without dark.*

Heading inland, the ground was rugged and misleadingly flat, with a number of large cavernous sinkholes, forty or fifty feet in diameter. Their depths were anybody's guess, and it was a challenging hike trying to navigate around them. I wasn't complaining, though. After all, this was the unspoiled land trodden by the ancient Irish who built Poulnabrone.

These were the same skies and cloud formations at which they marvelled, the same boulders on which they sat contemplating the building of their great portal tomb, and the same exhilaration they felt as the fresh breezes swept in from the great Atlantic Ocean.

There was a natural emptiness about the place, filled with the wondrous sound of windy silence. It was awesome. I felt happy again, joyful, and I wanted to hug the landscape, to embrace its Irishness. My senses were once more overflowing with the emotions of my forebears—their struggles, their endurance, their belief, and their commitment to life. I felt that each step I took was their step. My foot was their foot, imprinting on the unspoiled, hallowed ground of Ireland.

I come from the seed of these people, the voice recited, *these people that sorrow. That have no treasure but hope, no riches laid up, but a memory of an ancient glory.*

"I am flesh of their flesh," I said aloud, finishing the quote, *"I am bone of their bone, I that have never submitted."* Pearse's defiant words took hold of me, and I roared, "Up the Republic!" in my best guttural, rabble-rousing voice. No one heard me. Not that I cared. I was all alone in nature's empty place, and its emptiness felt heavenly.

There were a few clusters of rocks and bushes dispersed across the landscape, with God knows how many sinkholes in between. But there was no obvious fairy fort, no focal destination point. I thought about forgoing my search and simply enjoying the natural beauty of the place. Then my next step put my foot firmly on the goats' path. It was hidden beneath gorse and fern, and once discovered, it mapped an intricate route across the terrain.

It will lead you by long and shadowy ways, the voice recited melodically, *where drops of dew in myriads fall, and tangled creepers every hour, blossom in some new crimson flower.*

That's beautiful, I said silently, feeling I might not always give the voice sufficient credit.

I am but a guide on your quest, it responded to my thoughts, *an eloquent flame to light your way.*

It wasn't long before I came upon a hollow that was fully encircled by an old, weathered, and partially dilapidated rock wall, about four feet high at its highest point and overgrown with tangled creepers and briers. The ringed enclosure was enhanced by a daunting swath of leggy brambles, scratchy briers, and stingy nettles. It was about twenty feet in diameter but had no entrance.

The Fairy Dún, I guessed.

In the middle, there was a patch of luxuriant grass surrounded by overgrown wildflowers, soft heathers, and a scattering of self-assured scraggy rocks covered in the finest moss and lichen. To the left of the grass patch was a large hawthorn bush with all its branches swept to one side by a lifetime of Atlantic squalls.

It sloped downwards and gave the impression that it was eavesdropping on the wind-whispering grass, which was gently wrestling with little swirling shafts of air, rustling and moving in small twisted clumps like tiny children playing.

No. It's not eavesdropping, I surmised. *It's minding, watching over its charge of little grass children.*

Above the enclosed hollow, there was a thin veil of mist, shimmering and hovering. I imagined it was a magical layer detaching the scene from my sense of time and space.

In a wild and sudden dance, the voice said, growing ever more confident in its utterances, *we mocked at time and fate and chance and, swept out of the wattled hall, we came to where the dewdrops fall.*

I reasoned it was probably no more than a circular wall, built as a marker by superstitious locals after attributing some pishoguery to its confines. Perhaps the disappearance of their lazy shepherd, who may have simply run away, drowned at sea, been murdered by his cousin, or vanished for any number of rational reasons.

But, I thought, encouraging my desire for the mystical, *it doesn't explain the unseasonal vegetation, the hovering veil, the grass children playing, the watchful bush, the time and space disparity, or the trembling excitement in my heart.*

I wanted it to be a fairy fort. To mock time and fate and chance? I wanted a bit of mental tomfoolery, a bit of *craic.* There was certainly a distinct energy about the place, and I couldn't help wondering if the wall was built to protect insiders from outsiders, or outsiders from insiders.

Or, I thought, *the gullible from their reason.*

It felt like if I entered the Fairy Fort, I'd be intruding but at the same time not unwelcome. I climbed the wall and, balanced precariously on a wobbly rock among the lanky, scratchy, stingy vegetation, I was just about to jump.

Not yet, not yet, the voice exclaimed, startling me. *I am not ready.*

I wondered why it wasn't ready. Anyway, I paused, giving it time to get ready, and took the opportunity to look around the empty countryside, half hoping to see someone who might be able to account for my last known whereabouts—should I end up with the lazy shepherd.

Captives bound with leathern thongs, the voice it said ominously, "shall kneel and praise, one by one, at evening in my Western Dún."

"Really?" I asked aloud. *Captives, bound with leathern thongs? That's what we were waiting on?*

There was no answer, and I leapt as far as I could — which wasn't far enough, as a long gangly bramble with clingy undergrowth caught my ankle. I landed awkwardly, stumbling forward onto my knees, and came to a stop at the centre of the grass patch, my ankle bound.

"Touché," I said, amused at the voice's self-fulfilling quotation.

There was a prevailing air of anticipation in the hollow, a sense that everything was holding its breath, waiting for me to turn my back before anything moved. It reminded me of the Christmas pantos when all the children would shout, "He's behind you!" as the villain snuck up behind the Prince. I looked at the hawthorn, just in case, and she appeared to be looking back at me.

She? I thought.

It was decidedly female. I didn't know how.

Why does she hide her fairy vats, the voice asked, *full of berries and the reddest stolen cherries?*

My mood was light but not light enough to get into a conversation with the voice about a bush, and I ignored its question. Indulging my bent for the fantastical had its limits.

Time for a sanity check, my reason ventured. *The hollow isn't magical; the hovering veil is no more than a trick of the light, and the other peculiarities can be attributed to the Burren being famous for its unseasonal flora and touristy folklore.*

OK. But... I can see how the place could be a wondrous source of fairytales. It has a real sense of intimacy that's in stark contrast to the wide expanse of the surrounding landscape—an unusual place of unusual energy, calm, and caring. I felt peaceful in its confines, not in a magical or ethereal way, but as though Mother Nature was cradling us.

I shall have some peace here, the voice recited contentedly, *for peace comes dropping slow, dropping from the veil of the morning to where the cricket sings; where midnight's all a glimmer, and noon a purple glow.*

It was perfect imagery, completely in keeping with my feelings.

I thought about the lazy shepherd, and for the *craic,* I decided to lie down in the luxuriant patch of grass. It was an exquisitely comfortable cushion of greenery as I lay flat on my back and watched fluffy-white clouds retreat in the wake of a quickly darkening canvas. I just lay there, unruffled by the changing sky, listening to the quiet rhythm of my breathing, feeling tranquillity reign in the hollow.

Then she sighed gently, the voice whispered. *It grows late. Music and love and sleep await where I will be when the white moon climbs, the red sun falls, and the world grows dim.*

The words wafted drowsily around me. Music and love and sleep await... the white moon climbs and the red sun falls. *Fabulous.* My eyes closed, and serenity descended on the core of my being. *Yeats,* I said in silent praise, *it is you who are gifted, a word wizard.* My thoughts drifted. *Tell me of the fairies*, I asked, *tell me about... the Fairy of the Dún.*

Through hollow lands and hilly lands, I will find out where she has gone, kiss her lips and take her hands. And walk among long dappled grass, and pluck till time and times are done, the silver apples of the moon, the golden apples of the sun.

I smiled. *Yes, that's right, the lazy shepherd kissed her lips and took her hand.*

In my left hand was a silver apple, and beneath my head a moonbeam. My lips tingled as I floated on a sea of grass, drifting... drifting... drifting into sleep and beyond. All was peace and calm until something plopped on my forehead, then on my lips, my nose. Plip plop on my hands. I was reluctant to open my eyes in case it disturbed the drowsy, dreamy drifting.

Gradually, my senses told me it was raining in the real world, and I woke to big round droplets splish-sploshing about, bending leaves and bowing blades. I immediately jumped to my feet and ran for shelter under the hawthorn just before the heavens opened with straight streams of rain, accompanied by claps of thunder that rumbled in from Slieve Elva, followed by sheets of lightning.

I love to see the lightning flash, the voice said excitedly, as if the feeling was personal to it, *across the stooping heavens, and I love to hear the thunder call to the rolling mountains.*

I didn't respond. I didn't want to.

The overhang of the bush offered an unexpected level of protection from the downpour, and I hunkered low on a perfectly dry mattress of desiccated leaves interwoven with tiny dried slips of old undergrowth. Again, I felt I was in nature's snug cradle, a comfy refuge from the outside world.

Once more the storm is howling, and half hid under this cradle-hood and coverlid, my child sleeps on.

I didn't know if it was reciting a direct quote or if it was actually addressing me. I preferred to think it was a quote. I didn't like the idea of it seeing me as its child or its charge in any way.

The rain bent inwards, split-splattering on the tips of my boots. I pulled my legs tighter, sidling closer to the heart of the genial bush. Outside, every living creature had fallen silent in awe of the downpour, and an untimely darkness permeated the air as sheets of water flayed the skin of Mother Earth.

With no idea of how long the storm would last, I threw an eye over the hawthorn's refuge, assessing its weather defences and comfort in case I had a prolonged stay. To my great surprise, there was a most beautiful red rose slightly behind my right shoulder. It was stunningly exquisite, with the weighty fullness of its blooming splendour perched defiantly atop a single stem. Each sensuously curved petal heralded its regal integrity, its godly creation, its divine purity, and incredibly, its soulful familiarity. I felt I knew this rose, and I gently took its flower in both hands to smell its scent, as you might take the face of a lover to kiss their lips.

On inhaling its intoxicating scent, the petals whispered to me in a soft feminine brogue, "This is a mischievous place. You must leave it now."

I hesitated, as I suspect any normal person would if a rose spoke to them.

"Trust me," she said, her voice full of tender concern, her leaves quivering. "Leave now!"

I crawled into the lashing rain and scrambled across the sodden ground toward the wall. All at once, an earth-trembling clap of thunder crashed directly above me and reverberated through my spine. This was straight away followed by a long, radiant sheet of lightning that illuminated the billowing black sky and cast a spectral shadow before me. It wasn't my shadow, and I stopped dead in my tracks, gulping air before turning to face its source. There was no one there. My relief, however, was fleeting, the entire hollow was in uproar. The rose had transformed into a large bush festooned with smaller blooms, growing at a phenomenal rate. Its branches were bending and twisting along the dilapidated rock wall, over the hawthorn, through the grass, and around the ankles of a beautiful female apparition who was gracefully poised in the grassy patch. She was resplendent with raven hair, black eyes, and cherry lips. Her golden gown, made of the finest silk, was held with a pearl-pale shell that wavered like a summer stream.

Bound by nature's thongs, she dropped to her knees before the majestic rose and bowed her head. "Respectfully," she said, "I kneel in your praise and humbly offer to you the deepest apology for my effrontery. In my defence, I was unaware of your presence and your interest in this soul."

The rose nodded benign acceptance and they were gone. They didn't disappear; they were just gone, as though they were never there. I stood motionless and dumbfounded, soaked to the skin with the rain cascading down my face. There was nothing for me to do but climb the wall and leave behind the drenched hollow.

"Jesus Christ," I mumbled, without looking back for fear of what I might see. *That was no fucking dream.*

No, reason agreed. *That was no dream. It was... an intense hallucination, over which you had no control—because its source was external to our consciousness.*

I was shaken. I wondered if I had crossed the sanity line or somehow strayed into a random, unrelated wavelength. It seemed to have nothing to do with Em, Finn, or my promise to Granda.

Maybe, reason said, *you found an ethereal gateway, just not the one you were looking for.*

My earlier desire for a bit of *craic* had been more than satisfied, and I seriously wondered if I was being foolhardy seeking out things beyond my normal comprehension. Supernatural things.

Cold, wet, and unnerved, I hurried in the direction of the Dolmen with the rain lashing my face, driven by gusts of squalling wind. It was a tough hike, and my waning spirit wasn't helped by several stumbles on the rocks, which were like wet glass under my feet. After what seemed like forever, the No Entry sign loomed from the greyness. *Keep going,* I told myself, peering through the dimming light and sheeting rain. *Nearly there.*

In the distance, I could make out two figures standing by the Dolmen, apparently undaunted by the thunderstorm. Their presence, however, was secondary to my growing need to get back to the car and the warmth of its heater. My cold, wet clothing had chilled me to the bone, my teeth were chattering, and despite my physical exertions, my skin was shivering.

With my head down, I trudged onward over the rain-battered land until I reached the Dolmen and paused for a moment. There was no one about—it was just me and the portal tomb. But I was too cold and wet to take advantage of the situation. I merely observed its lonely figure, drenched and dismal in nature's bleak theatre, and I thought the scene was befitting the mortal graves over which it stood.

When I turned onto the tarmacked path in the direction of the car park, a deep rumble of thunder was followed by a loud double-barrel crash with an explosive flash of sheet lightning. The lightning created a silhouette of the Dolmen, revealing two people sheltering inside. Strange and eerie as this looked, I was too cold to give it much thought and concentrated on quickening my pace towards the car.

CHAPTER 14

It was a relief to be out of the rain, but the cold had gone through me, and getting warm was the only thing on my mind. I set the car heater to full blast before changing from my wet clothes into a tracksuit and a padded golf jacket that were in the boot. A copy of the *Irish Times* and a few teen magazines were strewn on the back seat, and I quickly stuffed their warming news and gossip into my tracksuit. Once I was sufficiently insulated, I closed my eyes to sleep through the storm.

With time to dream, the voice said, *that she treads the grass, walking ghostly in the dew.*

No. I've had my fill of dreams and ghostly ladies. It's time for a few moments of peace.

It was dark when I opened my eyes again. The car was cosy, and I lay perfectly still, staring through the rain-dappled windscreen until my mind adjusted to its surroundings. I watched a handful of stars twinkling between heavy grey clouds that flew across a section of black satin sky, illuminated by a candescent moon. Humanity's blatant insignificance in the cosmos struck me as a mockery of the omnipotent Christian God, yet divinity stared back at me.

That's all very lovely, I said to myself, *but what was that in the Fairy Fort? Like, Jesus Christ, that was insane.*

Time to go home? my reason asked. *Yes, or no?*

No.

I wanted to do what I would have done twenty years ago, without hesitation: embrace the unknown. I knew the next week held little more for me than mad-cow disease with endless reams of inexplicable administrative documents. So, I decided to be brave, put the Fairy Fort behind me, and spend the night in the portal tomb. It's what me and Finn would have done.

I texted Mary and the girls: *All good here on the farm. It's been a busy day. I'm wrecked and heading to bed now. Talk to you tomorrow. I'm turning off my phone.*

I didn't want their replies to upset my mental space. I had to psyche myself up for my night in the tomb and for whatever else was at hand.

Surely some revelation is at hand, the voice sounded curt, indignant. *Surely the Second Coming is at hand.*

Stop. I don't want that poem. I'm going to be scared enough lying in a cold, dark tomb, trying to conjure my ancient spirit. I have no idea what to even expect.

The Second Coming!

No. I told you. Stop.

It ignored me and continued reciting one of Yeats' most ominous poems. *A vast image out of Spiritus Mundi troubles my sight: somewhere in the sands of the desert. A shape with a lion's body and the head of a man, a gaze blank and pitiless as the sun, is moving its slow thighs, while all about it reel shadows of the indignant desert birds.*

OK! That's enough. I demand that you stop. Surely, I can decide what's in my head.

Then reason cautioned me: *maybe it needs to be said. Maybe he knows something we don't.*

Oh, for God's sake. OK. But I'm not happy with it. The voice is a visitor who has overstayed its welcome.

The darkness drops again, the voice said defiantly, *but now I know that twenty centuries of stony sleep were vexed to nightmare by a rocking cradle. And what rough beast, its hour come round at last, slouches towards Bethlehem to be born?*

I took a deep breath. This was all I needed in my head. Yeats believed the world was on the threshold of an apocalyptic revelation, that a great ancient beast, the antichrist, would be woken from its 2,000 years of stony sleep. The world was on the cusp of the second millennium, and his words rampaged through my mind: *vexed to nightmare by a rocking cradle, blank and pitiless darkness, and from the stones crawled the beast.*

The beast? The Devil?

Panic gripped me, and a slew of questions followed. *Am I the rocking cradle? Am I the conduit to awaken the beast? Is this a warning? Is Yeats warning me? Have I been lured like a patsy to use my ancient spirit to unleash a new order of horrible violence, anarchy, and blood?*

My mind was slipping into a dark, uncertain place. I got out of the car, and the sharp fresh air instantly assailed my lungs. It surged through the deep recesses of my mind, upending thoughts and anxieties, while the mere openness of the night rounded the jagged heights of my angst. I squared my shoulders and breathed in and out, deeply, ten times. After a few repetitions, I walked about the empty car park, focusing on coordinating my steps with my breathing. An easy rhythm took over, and my thoughts gave way to the present moment.

Let's do this, I said to myself, still frightened.

First things first, my reason cautioned: *you don't believe in God, not in any conventional sense of good and evil, so you can't believe in the Devil?*

I can't or I don't?

Can't will do for now.

Okay. But I'm able to say, I don't. I don't believe in the Devil.

Good. You think Yeats is a genius of word imagery, a word wizard.

Yes, definitely.

But you never had any time for his prophecies, his gyre, his philosophies, elitism, and all that stuff.

No, that's right. I see where you're going.

So, Spiritus Mundi, the beast, the apocalyptic second coming, the pitiless eyes, the rocking cradle, all of it, are no more than words. Fabulous word wizardry.

Yes, I know. It just took me by surprise, and I panicked.

Well, are you content to follow to its source, the voice interrupted impatiently, *every event in action or in thought?*

Yes. I'll see it through to its source.

I got a torch from the car boot and set off in search of my ancient spirit, taking the same path I walked earlier with the ignorant tourists. This time, when I turned the corner, I was stopped in my tracks by the separateness of the Dolmen. It stood aloof on its stony stage, the unabashed protagonist, commanding the light from the sky's heavenly lantern. This was the great portal tomb that my soul had longed to see.

My stomach fluttered with a mix of awe and anxiety. Stillness permeated the air, the calm after the storm, and the closer I got to the Dolmen, the more nervous I became. The path doubled back on itself as if intentionally slowing my progress. Impatient, I cut across its meander until I stood in front of the portal's entrance, facing 6,000-year-old souls, and hopefully, an ancient ethereal gateway. I peered into the bowels of Ireland's prehistoric past, more nervous than ever.

The spiritual gravity of the site had overcome my practical atheism. Its centre was dark, but then it gave way to dim moonlight emanating from the rear aperture.

"Off you go. Good luck," I heard Mr Flynn say.

I was reluctant to enter and felt the need to step back and walk its circumference, just in case there was something too unexpected, too otherworldly, something demonic. I'd like to say that I prowled around this sleeping megalith contemplating my next move, but in reality, I skulked. I imagined it was awake and watching me, like a predator ready to pounce. Like Yeats's sphinx, treacherous and merciless, flanking the entrance to another world. I stopped close to its mouth and again looked inside. My legs were actually trembling.

Many times, the voice said, adding to my unease, *we live and die between our two eternities, that of race and that of soul. And ancient Ireland knew it all.*

The quote had never seemed more prophetic, and the words filled my head to bursting. I didn't want to die between my two eternities. I wondered if it meant my soul was inside the tomb and my race outside?

My heart was thumping. I moved closer, but I couldn't bring myself to step inside. It felt like a huge step, a leap into the unknown. At the very least, an intrusion into the dwelling place of the ancient dead.

Come near, come near, the voice lured, irritatingly, *no more blinded by man's fate.*

I stepped inside, and within seconds my heightened emotions were immersed in serenity as my anxieties sank gently into what I can best describe as tranquillity. The roof was lower than I remembered, and I had to kneel on the uneven stony ground to edge further towards the tomb's centre. I looked back through the Dolmen's ancient frame. The outside world shimmered, moonlit and otherworldly—as if from another time.

An incredibly deep sense of self-awareness came over me. I felt I was at the far end of six thousand years of unadulterated time, never more hidden from the constraints of society or more external to my own consciousness. It was like I was looking out from a surreal place, from deep within the expanse of existence, onto a vast eternal canvas.

Imagine, reason said, *you're looking through the exact same door, from the exact same interior, with the exact same view, of the exact same heavens, as the first people who built and prayed there.*

I know. Jesus Christ! I feel so privileged, yet insignificant, and hugely underqualified to conjure an ethereal gateway.

I lit my torch, and its beam of artificial yellow invaded the eternal dim dark of the tomb, probably not dissimilar to the glow from naked flames thousands of years before. The inside was unfamiliar to me, and it seemed an age since my childhood visit. Intuitively, I stroked the stones with the outside of my fingers as a gesture of reacquaintance, and I was disappointed not to see Granda's funeral or to sense that someone, or something, was standing behind me. With great anticipation, I looked over each shoulder, only to find a memory of me swiveling on my heels. I was struck by how small I must have been.

Don't get bothered, I told myself. *Clear your mind and call upon your ancient Irish spirit.*

I quenched the torch and cleared my thoughts and anxieties.

"I call upon my ancient Irish spirit," I said, hardly able to speak with my trembling voice.

There was no response.

I refocused and tried again with a more resolute tone. "I'm seeking my ancient Irish spirit. If you can hear me, please let me know."

There was no answer, no energy, just enormous stillness.

I wondered, *should I ask the actual people buried in the tomb for help.*

"Souls of Poulnabrone," I said, "help me make contact with my ancient Irish spirit."

Ask them directly.

"Spirits of the Poulnabrone dead, make contact." This felt very eerie. After all, these were real dead people, and I stiffened with the possibility of something touching me, coming from the ground beneath me.

Nothing happened.

"I am the grandson of Michael O'Brien, the Irish warrior of 1916. Ancient spirit, he told me you called his name."

There was no response, no sense of contact, ethereal or tangible. I opened my eyes. The ancientness of the place was beyond reproach, so I wondered if I was doing the conjuring wrong.

Maybe lie flat on the ground, I thought, *it might be more appropriate, given that it's a tomb.*

I lay on the ground, closed my eyes, and tried again, with doubt already skirting my hopes.

"Ancient Irish spirit, ancient spirits of the Irish, I offer you my..."

No! Reason shouted. *No... you're not offering anything. Your life and your soul and your heart and your mind are yours.*

"Forget that one, ancient spirit," Reason said aloud. We're not offering anything like that".

OK. You're right. I don't believe the Jonesy stuff but let's not test it here and now. Eh, I'll try that one again, ancient spirit. "I just want to talk to you. Please. I'm sorry I lost you. I want you to wake up."

It is with regret I say, the voice said. *Freedom now so seldom wakes,* the voice said with great disappointment, *the only throb it gives is when some foolish heart it breaks to show that it still lives.*

You mean I'm the fool. The broken-hearted fool. "So be it," I said, crouched in what was now a profoundly empty space.

So sleeps the pride of former days, the voice explained apologetically, *so glory's thrill is o'er. And hearts that once beat high for praise, can feel its pulse no more.*

I understand. I do. It's my regret too. I'm sorry I can't feel the pulse. I'm sorry, Em. I'm sorry, Granda. Finn. Ancient spirit.

Feelings of inadequacy weighed down on me, and I didn't know what else to do but exit the tomb.

Before I left, the voice reprimanded my ancient spirit; *Conchobar Mac Cárthaigh called to you from far and near, to bring your crown from out the deeps of time and it is my grief that his call you couldn't hear.*

It's okay, I said silently. *It's not your fault he couldn't hear me. I called to him, but he couldn't hear me. I couldn't feel the pulse. I thought I would, but I didn't.*

I left the portal and walked carefully over darkened fissures of limestone to sit on a rock and gather my thoughts. No sooner had my arse touched the rock than a male voice spoke from the darkness. "You were blocking the energy." I nearly jumped out of my skin with fright and dropped the torch, breaking it into three pieces. "I'm sorry," the external voice said, caringly, "we didn't mean to frighten you."

I looked about with faux bravado. "Where are

you?" The moon was hiding behind a dense white cloud, and the immediate area was dark.

"We are here." I followed the voice to within about six feet of where I was standing. The moon reappeared, and two smiling faces, male and female, emerged from the darkness into its silver beam. I could only see their faces; the rest of them was enveloped in black, like a Beckett stage set.

"Forgive me," he said, "I thought you would like to know; you were blocking the energy."

"OK. Who, eh, what do you mean? Who are you?"

"We are travellers," the female said, assuming a natural authority. "You were blocking the energy, in the portal."

"Blocking the energy in the portal?" I repeated, trying to give myself time to work out what was happening.

"Yes," the male said. "It's a portal, through which energies move."

"We saw you, earlier, in the rain," the female said.

"Oh. Were you the two in the Dolmen, I mean the portal?"

"Yes," they answered in harmony, and the male continued. "For many years now, the energies only come when there is a sky eruption."

"Some directly before it," the female said, "but mostly during it."

My eyes adjusted to their distance, and I could see they were both in a hunkered position, wearing long black rain cloaks with hoods that covered them from head to toe.

"A sky eruption?" I asked.

"He meant to say a thunder and lightning storm. Do you mind if I ask why you are here?"

The male cleared his throat. "We were watching you in the portal, but we were unsure as to what you were doing."

"Eh, it's hard to say," I said, feeling light-headed. My body was sweating and extremely cold at the same time. I must have wobbled because the male stood and grabbed my arm, easing me to a sitting position on the rock.

She moved closer and put her hand on my forehead. "You may have a fever. You looked exceptionally wet and cold when we saw you earlier."

"You might be right," I said. "I'm feeling very cold."

From under her cloak, she produced a crystal hipflask of clear liquid. "You should take a drink of this. It will fight your fever and heat your bones."

I considered her offer and remembered my Granny saying, "Never take sweets from strangers." She smiled, recognising my reluctance, and with a knowing glint, pulled the ornate stopper from the flask. She then twirled it between her thumb and forefinger until it refracted the moon's beam, and multiple tiny rainbows danced on her slender hand.

"It is *poitín*," she explained, putting the flask to her pouted lips and sipping its contents. Once again, the crystal caught the moonlight and fired fabulous colours around her cloaked head. "It is from the mountains of Slieve Bloom, with some additional herbs. It will calm your fever." She proffered it again, and her button nose twitched, like a rabbit.

She was over twenty years of age and under forty, but it was difficult to be more precise because I could only see her face. Her skin was smooth, freckled, and oatmeal in colour, exuding a healthy natural aura. But her hauntingly dark eyes were her standout feature, dominating the shadows beneath her hood like deep aquatic pools watching curiously from a mysterious cave.

"I haven't had *poitín* in years, not since I was in college," I said, taking the bottle and putting it to my lips. It was unusually sweet and slipped smoothly, deceptively, down my throat like warm honey. Then, without warning, on reaching my stomach, it burst into intense heat and for a moment took my breath away. They both watched me, waiting for my reaction.

"Wow! That's some *poitín*," I managed to say after a sharp intake of air.

"Do you feel it warming your bones?"

"Yes, like a fire."

"You need to drink three times," he said, "to calm your fever." He had a touch of a foreign accent, and his complexion was darker than hers, tanned and rugged with heavy stubble on a dimpled chin that sat beneath a wide mouth and crooked nose. His eyes were dark brown and set back beneath thick dark eyebrows, which would have given him an intimidating look if it wasn't for the warmth of his smile.

The female noticed I was wondering why he was encouraging me to drink more. "Three," she explained, "is a thing of mythology. Three is a powerful number. But you only have to sip it, if you wish."

"Okay," I said, and took more than a sip. It wasn't like any *poitín* I had before, and its wallop was nearly instant. Smooth and silky in my throat with glowing embers in my belly, it radiated through my veins until molten blood heated every achingly cold muscle in my shivering body. I raised my eyebrows, and like a seasoned wino, offered him his turn on the bottle. Mini rainbows circled my hand, leaping from my forearm with melting hues of gold, amber, and blue, piercing the deep shadows with their soft light.

He gestured with an open palm and genial smile for me to drink again. Which I did, willingly. It was delicious. The inner glow expanded from my veins and muscles and shot fire bolts through my bones. Up and down my spine, through my arms and legs, my fingers and toes, and, finally, my skull, until its marrow was scorched with heat. Within seconds, the fever was burned out, the awful cold was gone, and my body felt warm and snug.

"Are you feeling better?" she asked politely.

"Yes, much better, thanks. That's great *poitín*." I offered her the flask to be mannerly, but I would have preferred if we had one each.

She took it and sipped, delicately, twice, before putting the flask beneath her cloak. "It is the power of three that can shake bad from good... or good from bad."

I felt great, warm, and exuberant. "It definitely blew the cold from me. I feel wonderful, nice and warm."

"We are pleased," they said together.

"What's your name?" I asked the female.

"Biróg."

"I am Faebar," the male said. "It is my Irish name. I am originally from España."

"I see," I said, smiling and nodding more than I normally would. "They are both great names. I'm Conor. Thanks for the *poitín*. I was definitely catching a chill."

"You are most welcome," Faebar said.

"What was it you were doing in the portal?" Her voice had a lilting Kerry brogue. "We grew overly curious watching you."

I gave a little laugh to cover my embarrassment. "You must have thought I was mad."

"No," he said, reassuringly. "We did not understand what you were doing, but we sensed it was important to you."

I moved off the rock, for no obvious reason, and sat cross-legged on the flat ground as if at a campfire. They followed and created a small circle around the absent fire. Their faces and hands, which were still all I could see, had become unusually bright, gleaming, and a fantastical perspective warped my vision.

What was in the poitín? I asked. My lips, however, didn't move.

"Are you unwell?" I heard Faebar say, but the words were coming from Biróg's mouth as her face billowed down from a white cloud of transparent silk like the Muriel Levy portrait.

What was in the poitín? I asked again, my mind swirling about the transparent cloud.

"I don't know the exact ingredients," Biróg answered beside me. She sounded unconcerned, and it felt like time had been clipped, edited. "It's an old cure. For warding off colds and flu. Are you unwell? You passed out for a moment."

"Really? I don't remember."

"You called upon an ancient spirit. I think that is what you said." She looked at Faebar for confirmation.

"Yes, they were your words. Ancient spirit."

"I'm sorry. My mind has been doing and saying strange things over the past while. I hope I didn't frighten you."

"Spirits are seldom frightening," Biróg said softly. She leaned closer, and I could see the reflection of the silver moon resting in her dark, dark eyes. "Is your mind troubled? Is that why you were in the portal?" Before I could answer, she shot a questioning glance at Faebar, and he returned a reassuring look. "I know it is not my place to ask. But we are concerned you may be troubled by an energy from the portal."

I guffawed. "No, my trouble, as you put it, started well before today. But it's a long story, which funnily enough, does start here." Jonesy's possession crossed my mind, and I wondered if that was the type of energy she was talking about.

"Short stories are seldom interesting," she said, with a faraway glint of encouragement. The moonlight caught the curve of her cheek, and I wasn't sure if she was speaking to me—or someone I couldn't see.

Strangely, I felt like unburdening myself. It was probably the *poitín*. I wanted to tell them, to tell her, about the loss and disappointment that was in my heart. "Are you sure? I don't want to delay you."

"We are here for you. Our time is not valued."

I told them everything: about the schoolboy in the Dolmen, my Granda, my love of Ireland, losing Em, losing Finn, losing my spirit, the voice, my Portugal dream, the lady in the Western *Dún*, and the emptiness of the portal.

They listened quietly, respectfully nodding as I spoke, intermittently looking at each other in recognition of some finer point. There was no attempt to solve my situation; they simply listened. On reaching the end of my tale, I tightened my lips and raised my eyebrows. "And that's what I was doing in the portal."

Faebar looked to Biróg before speaking. "It makes perfect sense."

"Yes," she said, with a cold, knowing smile. "We are immensely pleased that you shared your story with us. Very pleased indeed. Now that we understand, we can continue on our way."

"OK," I said, frustrated at the quickly changing situation. "Who are you?"

"We travel the land of Ireland, in all of its dimensions," Faebar said, "and we stay close to the stones and the trees. Our preferred walking is in the dim light, during dusk and dawn."

"Before we depart," Biróg said, "let me address your story." She paused, as an actor might before delivering a closing. "Your soul is valued. But you will not find your ethereal gateway here."

"What?" I asked, surprised at her summation.

"This is not to say it cannot be found," Faebar advised, "only that it is not here."

"The Lady in the *Dún*," Biróg whispered, as if someone might be listening, "has many names; the folklore often calls her *An Cailleach Dubh*."

"My soul is valued. Valued by who?" I asked, with

more skepticism than I felt.

She shrugged her shoulders. “I cannot say. It is your words I have interpreted.”

“You spoke of the Western *Dún*,” Faebar said. “We do not know *Dún An Cailleach Dubh* as the Western *Dún*. The Western *Dún* is *Dún Dúchathair*, on Inis Mór. It is, and always will be, the fort at the end of the mortal world, the most western refuge.”

“The last ruling *Dún* of the *Fir Bolg*,” she added, “after their defeat by the deceitful *Tuatha Dé*, at *Maighe Tuireadh*. Have you heard of the *Fir Bolg*?”

“I read about them in *Leabhar Gabála*,” I said, “and the Battles of Moytura.”

She gave me a long meaningful look. “There is a powerful energy in *Dún Dúchathair*. I think you should go there.”

They stood in unison. “We have to leave you,” Faebar said, bringing matters to a swift close.

“Yes, we must be on our way,” Biróg said, taking the crystal flask from beneath her cloak. “There are six swallows left. You should take them, three, and three, and then sit as you were, on the rock.”

I stood and took the flask, protesting slightly about the generosity of her gift. “Are you sure? It’s a beautiful flask.”

“Certainly, take it. It was meant for you. I have ...” She paused, then smiled—clearly choosing not to finish the sentence. “You will find the ethereal if you should travel to *Dún Dúchathair*. It may be a long road from here, but there you will be found. I know it."

I will be found. I pondered the thought. *What does she mean by that—I will be found?* "OK," I said. "Thank you for your help—and your gift."

They pulled their deep hoods forward to the point where I could barely see their faces, and within seconds of walking away, they were lost to the dark.

I looked around me, wanting to share my experience. *"What was that all about?"* I wanted to say to someone, and we'd shake our heads, bewildered. But I was alone, and in the wake of my experience in the *Dún*, I wondered if they were even real.

Check the poitín flask, I thought, rapping the flask with my knuckles. It was real. I put it to my mouth to make doubly sure and was satisfied by the sweet fiery taste on my tongue. I took the mandatory three drinks and they hit me like a depth charge, sinking gently and slowly until they reached the bottom with an awesome explosion that engulfed my stomach and set fire to my chest and groin. Shards of self-belief shot through my crumbling ego, and I held the crystal aloft, momentarily entrapping the moonbeam before it burst from the bottle in a myriad of hues. A sense of freedom washed over me, untying me from the burdens of my grey life and releasing me to a blissful world full of colour.

"Fuck them all!" I shouted, defiantly, at no one in particular. Followed by a more introspective, "Fuck them all."

I was drunk, and I finished off the *poitín* in three more unequivocal swallows before returning to the rock as directed by Biróg. I sat, not unlike Padraic O'Connaire on his rock in Eyre Square, one hand on my knee, the other gripping my lapel. Unlike him, however, I wasn't in contemplation. I was giddy and eagerly awaited what might happen next. The air was moist with a sense of surreal levity and I nearly giggled.

Suddenly, I couldn't feel my legs and slid off the rock, landing on my arse like a rag doll, sitting with my legs straight in front of me. "Not to worry," I slurred. Next, my arms went. I couldn't lift them. "Well now." I tried again. "Nope." My head grew too heavy for my neck and sloped forward onto my chest, but I managed to right it for a few seconds, then it was gone again.

You could try to get up, reason said.

I'd fall over and split our head. Our head! That's funny.

Or, you could wait it out. Unless you're having a stroke.

"Havin' a struck... a strock..."

Try again.

"A strr... I don't car."

It seemed my thought process was untouched by the *poitín*. I could think, but I couldn't talk. In fact, I was experiencing intense clarity of my senses to the point where everything in my line of view, which wasn't much given the malfunction in my neck, was magnified to minute detail. I could see the spines of individual blades of grass as if under a microscope, stretching and bending to their pin-point tips. A woodlouse halted its route, and throwing its fourteen legs into reverse, maneuvered its armored-plated shell to examine a rotted apple with its long spindly antennae. I could hear a slight breeze whisper in the unseasonably bare branches of an ash tree a few hundred meters away.

A mouse scurried in the grass beyond the Dolmen. An owl hooted in the far-off distance. It was all magnificent, and I was happy to wait for my body to reengage with my brain. Then, without warning, I lurched to one side and keeled over, hitting the ground with a thud. My eye line was now at ground level, and I was looking across the flat limestone to the massive portal tomb on its stony stage. Everything was grey, every shade of grey from light to dark, but I was completely content to lie there discerning the different shades, as drool dripped from my paralyzed mouth.

A vixen, wearing a sleek coat of shiny auburn fur with a gleaming milky-white chest, walked straight towards me from the direction of the Dolmen and stopped about two feet from my face. Her disproportionately large ears gave the impression of extreme alertness, and her deeply inquisitive, glassy, auburn eyes, with rims of black around their lids, made her look intelligent and intensely interested in my predicament. The clarity of every detail was extreme, and as she nudged closer, her shimmering wet nose at the end of her long snout, winged by perfectly groomed jet-black whiskers, captivated me. I was mesmerised by the moist sensory organ that was exploring my space with delicate twitches and sniffs until she yawned, and I could see her breath vaporize in the damp air like fairy droplets. Its scented warmth touched my face, and I realised the canine potential of her razor-sharp teeth.

"Shoo," I managed to slur. She was startled but didn't lose her composure and sauntered away, swooshing my face with her big bushy, white-tipped tail.

My levity drained quickly, and the extent of my stupor made me realize *I was poisoned.* With this my eyes closed; my heart slowed to a near stop. My mind grew numb and cold. I was at death's door—not the ethereal gate—as my soul loosened from my body."

Immense darkness was creeping over my brain when the vixen returned, touched my nose with hers and released an unearthly scream that jolted me awake. All my limbs began working again, and my mind seemed sharp as a tack. I was like a computer rebooting.

She smiled – I don't know how, but she smiled at me, as if amused at my fright—and then disappeared into the night.

I got to my feet and walked, unsteadily, to the Dolmen before sitting on my calves in front of its entrance.

This is not a menacing place, I thought, as I gazed into Ireland's prehistoric past. *Nor is it the place of my ancient Irish spirit, or my imagined ethereal gate.*

I became exceptionally tired, exhausted, as my brief reboot plunged into an extreme energy crash and I needed to lie down. I stretched my hands out in front of me across the flat wet stone until my forehead touched the ground, inadvertently kowtowing.

"What now?" I mumbled, bone tired.

Go to Dún Dúchathair, a female voice whispered from deep inside the empty portal.

CHAPTER 15

The stench of rank body odour filled my nostrils as I squinted against the blinding morning sun pouring through the small window of the cottage. I couldn't remember how I got there other than some hazy, sketchy images of the roadway from Poulnabrone. A repulsive smell of rancid semen from a filthy blanket curled my mouth and nearly made me vomit. I didn't move. I couldn't move. I was too ill. Too weak. I was breathing rapidly. My mouth tasted of sick. My eyeballs were throbbing. My body shivered in cold sweat, and I thought my heart might burst, beating like a racing piston as my brain swelled with pounding pressure.

The smell proved too much and I retched, heaving bile from the pit of my empty stomach into my mouth. I tried to spit it out but failed and swallowed the slimy secretion. Panting, I retched and heaved, but there was nothing to expel other than black-green bile. I retched and heaved again, and again until I was exhausted and passed out on the putrid bed.

Deep in my comatose brain a repetitive, dull sound reverberated through my approaching unconsciousness, incoherent words reawakening the throbbing pain. It grew closer, the throbbing grew stronger. *Stop,* I thought. *I'm too sick.*

"Cabhair liom," they said. *"Cabhair liom."*

I didn't understand.

"Cabhair liom."

The unintelligible words grated on my shattered nerves, until I slowly realised they were a cry for help, in Irish.

"Cabhair liom." Help me.

I opened my eyes, hoping the words would stop, only to be confronted by a huge disgusting cockroach on my pillow. It scurried over the dried vomit and under the blanket. With horror, I realised my skin was crawling and I jumped out of bed, as a multitude of cockroaches swarmed over my body. Cursing, shouting and writhing, I swept them off as quickly as I could. On hitting the ground, they hurried in a crawly pitter-patter over the floorboards to a corner of the room. There were hundreds of them, teeming around a dirty, smelly crack at the base of a mildewed wall.

"Cabhair liom," a young voice implored. This time the words came from behind me. I turned abruptly and saw an unkempt girl standing in the far corner by the open door. She was about nine years of age, with a dirty face, matted black hair and snotty nose.

Before I could adjust to what was happening, a huge hulk of a man rushed through the door and towered over her. He was wearing a deep green uniform with dark buttons down the front of his tunic and a polished wooden baton hanging from a waist belt. His hands were shovel-like, and he forcefully gripped the girl's slender wrist. "Gotcha."

I was stunned and, although disbelieving, I wondered if he had caught a burglar in my room. I waited for him to explain what was happening, but he ignored my presence and grabbed the waif by the hair. He then violently gripped her between the legs with his other hand and lifted her from the floor. A perverse sneer consumed his face, and he looked me directly in the eyes, as he violently groped her. She screamed, and he groped. She screamed, and I stood there—caught in the glare of his bloodshot eyes, paralyzed with disbelief. They moved towards the door, and I instinctively lunged across the bed, wrapping my arms around her tiny waist. Thankfully, he didn't struggle because I could barely stand with weakness. He calmly spat in my face then released her and walked out the door. I fell backward onto the bed and held the waif as if my life depended on it. When I was sure the man had gone, I loosened my hold and she got to her feet, frightened, as was I.

"Are you OK?" She looked at my lips but gave no answer. "Are you all right?"

"Níl an Béarla agam," she said, in a raspy voice followed by a congested cough that amplified the phlegm gurgling in her chest.

My mind was frozen, and we looked at each other, not knowing what to do.

She was completely emaciated, nothing but skin and bone. Her eyes were drained of life. Her feet, shoeless and filthy. Her clothing, dirty and threadbare. Her matted hair chopped about her scrawny neck.

"It's okay. *Tá tú sábháilte,"* I managed to say, looking around for a make-do weapon, almost hoping the man would return.

She squeezed my finger and searched my soul with hauntingly tormented eyes before struggling to say, "Dank you." I was dumbfounded. Then, she turned on her heels and ran out the door faster than a hare. I immediately ran after her, but she was nowhere to be seen, nor was the uniformed man. I was confused and terribly sick.

She must have been a hallucination, reason said.

Jesus! She felt so frighteningly real. I could feel her tiny body in my arms.

Regardless of who or what she is, let's get out of here. Now.

I mustered any strength I had left and went back into the cottage for my things. The smell was gone from the bedroom and there was no sign of the cockroaches, not even the dirty crack at the base of the wall. I hastily packed my bag and headed for the front door, but I was pulled to a halt by the sight of the rocking chair. It had long grey hair partially covering a withered and bruised face. At the end of its armrests were spindly frail hands with curling fingernails, and at its foot was a sleeping Irish wolfhound.

"Be careful," the chair croaked, "if you stare long enough into the abyss, it will stare back into you."

The hound changed into Spiritus Mundi, a demonic human head with salivating jaws on a lion's body and a blank pitiless stare. I panicked and ran out of the house straight into a lake of blood, waist-deep. Beyond me cows were drowning, bellowing and screeching, soaked and matted with blood. Their eyes, wild with terror. The uniformed man watched me from the bank and, dropping his pants, defecated into a human skull. He laughed hideously as emaciated, naked toddlers crawled from the ditch and began eating his excrement. Another vile-looking man with crown and sceptre emerged from behind a gnarled tree before tearing a howling toddler limb from limb. He then feasted on its torso as the blood ran down the sleeve of his bejewelled gown and dripped, dripped, dripped, into the ghastly lake.

Revolted and terrified I hid my face in my hands, but I couldn't shield the high-pitched squeal of the child being devoured.

Please stop, I begged. *Please.*

It's the drugged poitín, reason shouted over the squealing. *Ignore it. It's a bad trip. Ignore it. It's a bad trip.*

Over and over, reason shouted the words in my head, until it became a chant. *Ignore it. It's a bad trip. Ignore it. It's a bad trip.*

Eventually, I risked opening my eyes and was

more than relieved to see the countryside back to normal. But I was shattered with sickness and slumped onto all fours, puking up globules of greenish-black bile. My mind grew dim and dizzy, my surroundings vaporous. I crawled to the car, retching and puking twice more. The door handle seemed unreachable. I struggled to my knees. Retched. Climbed in, and lost consciousness.

The discomfort of the handbrake sticking into my ribs woke me. I had no idea where I was. My body was emptied of energy. My brain was burning like fire. I moved from the handbrake and leaned against the door with my face pressed onto the cool glass. Gradually, the realization of my situation came into focus and I wiped the slobber from my open mouth.

What now? Reason asked.

I don't know. My head is fucking melting.

The voice made its presence known before speaking, unsure of what its reception might be.

I groaned. *Jesus, no. I don't want to hear from you.*

Your heart hath sealed its fountains, it chanced saying, *to the things of time, and they shall be opened no more.*

When I first heard those lines, I was in Stephen's Green with Em. The sun was shining, the ducks were quacking, and the world was colourful. I remembered her asking me, "Did you ever hear of Margaret Fuller?"

"No," I said.

"Right! What sort of education system do we have? I only came across her last week. Pure brilliant! Mid-nineteenth-century feminist, writer and poet, and a lesbian to boot. Listen, you'll love this."

She read the poem *Meditations*, and she was right, I loved it. It was a far cry from Yeats, but I was taken by its sentiment and honesty. It helped that I was in love with Em.

If the fountains to the things of time are sealed, reason asked, repeating the voice's sentiments, *is it over? Can we go home?*

Con, Emily said, picking up the recitation. *The voice of the eternal is calling you to feel his other worlds; to feel that if you could deserve a home, you still might find it in other spheres. And he bade you not despair.*

"Jesus! Emily!?" *Oh, Em, where are you? I can't find the gateway. I'm in such a hole here, such a black hole. Are you telling me not to despair because the eternal is calling me? You think I should try again, to go to the other sphere.*

Wait a minute, reason said, alarmed. *We should go home. You're too sick.*

It's Emily. I have to try again.

So, we're not going home?

No. It was Em. You heard her. The eternal is calling me to the other sphere.

What does that mean? Where do we go?

To Dún Dúchathair. I have to.

And what about the real world? Your family? Your job?

They're not expecting me back for a few days. They think I'm with Donal. I'll text them.

Emily interrupted; *If you don't go, you'll regret it.*

Wait! Reason demanded. *Emily can't be in this conversation. If she's in our internal conversation, the door is open to all comers. That's when the shit hits the fan. You might as well sign us into the Gorman now.*

OK. You're right. You can't be in our internal conversation, Em. But I'm going to Dún Dúchathair.

My mood was foul, my body was barely functioning, and I couldn't get away from the horror cottage quick enough. After about fifteen minutes on the road to the Inis Mor Ferry, I stopped for petrol at a small service station, with a grocery area and a coffee machine. After paying by card for the petrol, I realised I didn't have any coins for the coffee machine, so I asked the man behind the counter for change. He was a hail-fellow-well-met type, barrel-chested, stocky, mid-fifties. "Not a problem," he said cheerily. Opened the till and placed the coins on the counter. "Were you doing a bit of hiking?"

"Yeah."

"It's a lovely spot for it all right."

I nodded, unable to even crack a smile. The poison was coursing back with a vengeance, and I thought I might vomit.

"You know," he said, with a toothy begorrah smile, "the Burren has been compared to the lunar surface, and it's often been said; 'There's not wood enough to hang a man, nor water enough to drown him, nor clay to bury him.'"

Without warning or thought, I exploded. "God forgive you! Do you know who said that?"

Shocked by my reaction, he stepped back from the counter. "Bord Failte?"

"Well, if they did, shame on them. It was first said by the murderer Edmund Ludlow, one of Cromwell's generals, when he wasn't fifteen minutes march from this very spot, with his boot on the throat of one of your ancestors. Mother to your bloodline." The words came from my mouth, but they were new to me. I was hearing them for the first time. "Her only crime was that she was a Catholic. He cut her stomach open and spilled her intestines onto the ground, having already done the same to three of her children, in front of her eyes. Leaving them on the road to die in agony. Shame on you for using the words of that English butcher."

Ashen-faced he said, "I'm sorry. I didn't know. I didn't mean to offend you."

"Offend me! Offend me? It's you, you're offending. Your integrity. Your humanity. Your heritage. You. Not me."

"I'm sorry." I could see he thought I was deranged and that I needed to be placated. "With God as me witness, I'll never say those words again." His tone was nervous and conciliatory. "We'll shake hands. Eh, and the coffee is on me."

"I wouldn't drink your filthy coffee," I said, flinging the coins across the floor. "I'd prefer to cut my throat. Shame on you. Shame." I stormed out the door, incandescent with rage.

For Christ's sake! Reason shouted. *What the fuck are you doing!?*

I don't know. I don't know.

Jesus Christ!

Stop! I feel crap. I'm still really ill. Those fuckers.

You better go back and apologize.

Yeah, of course.

When the man saw me re-entering the shop, he took a sweeping brush and held it as you might hold a rifle and bayonet at the ready.

I put my hands up in surrender and placed them together, beseeching. "I'm so sorry. Please forgive me. I'm so, so sorry for that outburst." I could see his relief with my apology, but he didn't lower the brush. "I haven't been well. My nerves are at me. But I don't know what came over me. I'm really sorry. Did I break anything? I'll pay for anything I damaged."

He lowered his brush and appeared to empathize with my admission that 'my nerves are at me.' "No damage done."

"Really, I'm so sorry."

"Nothing broken. We'll leave it at that."

"Thanks," I said, and turned for the door.

"I won't be saying it again," he ventured, re-inhabiting his gombeen persona. "Unless I spit before and after."

"OK," I said, with an all-purpose agreeable expression. "Sorry again."

Back on the road, I pulled into the first stopping area I came upon. I couldn't believe what had happened. The shocking eruption of rage left me reeling.

How did you know that about Ludlow? Reason asked.

From history. From reading.

Yes, I know that. But the bit about his family being murdered. I didn't know that. How does that work? How can you know something, and I don't?

I don't know. I don't know how I know it. I just do. And I don't understand how only part of me knows it.

This is starting to get very serious, reason said. *It all sounds a bit schizo. And what was that about not being well with your nerves. Who said that?*

I said it. I thought it needed to be said. To explain my outburst to the man. It worked, didn't it?

Yes, it worked. But I didn't know you were going to say it. Are we having trouble with our nerves?

No, I don't think so.

I think we should go home. It's all getting too psychotic. I think you're losing it. You could have hit that gombeen. Tell me you know you could have hit him.

Yes, I know. Yes, I know it's nuts. Yes, I know it's bordering on the psychotic. But we have to go to Dún Dúchathair. I can't turn back now."

Bordering on! This is full-blown psychosis. Fairies and roses. Blackouts and aggression. Babies being torn apart. Did those fuckers last night even exist? Where was the flask this morning? I didn't see it unless you're now able to hide things from me.

Stop. This is getting crazy. There is only you and me. Heart and mind. We are two sides of the same transparent thought process, mental construct, whatever we want to call it. I know I'm way out on a limb and I know the hallucinations are insane, but I was drugged. The other stuff, the other imagery is from my dream world. I know it's not real. The gombeen man is because I'm fall-down sick. Vicky and George were because they were so fuckin condescendingly English.

What about the Rose and the lady in the Dún?

I don't know. But that doesn't mean I'm mad. There could be hundreds of explanations that we don't know or understand.

Like?

Eh, like Einstein, Hawking, and hundreds of other physicists who think the multiverse could be real.

Parallel time, alternate dimensions—whatever you want to call it. I'm not saying that's the answer. I'm just saying... maybe there are explanations that don't involve me having a breakdown.

You're comparing yourself to two of the greatest minds of the 20th Century?

No. I'm saying let's be open to other possibilities. We are in this together—as one—and we can't be arguing.

I'm not arguing. We just have to be sure we're on solid ground.

I agree. One hundred percent. Now, are we done with this little chat? Are we going, as one, to Dún Dúchathair?

Yes, of course, as one. But we have to remember that you are walking on very thin psychotic ice. If it breaks, we're straight into the loony bin. So, if I pull you back, you have to come with me.

OK.

I flicked through the tourist guidebook before starting the car; *Dún Dúchathair, translates to English as Black Fort. It is an ancient stone fort on the wild western coast of Inis Mór, an island off the west coast of Ireland. Perched on the edge of 100-meter vertical cliffs, it was built by the Fir Bolg, one of the original tribes of Ireland. They constructed it after their defeat at the Battle of Moytura by the forces of the Tuatha Dé Danann, around 1500 BC. Over the subsequent 3,500 years, much of the fort has eroded. However, a large defensive wall, 6 meters high and 5 meters wide, still protects a rocky promontory that stretches into the churning waters of the Atlantic Ocean. Inside the Dún, the walled remains of the Fir Bolg's prehistoric dwellings offer succor in the ancient antiphonal music of the ocean. Dún Dúchathair is a hidden gem, a place of timeless, stark beauty and untold pagan secrets.*

CHAPTER 16

Most of the ferry passengers remained on deck, eager to experience the vast Atlantic Ocean while I found a quiet corner in the lounge to curl up on a seat and sleep. Thankfully, there were no dreams, nightmares, cold sweats, or puking, just peaceful disengagement from my dystopian thoughts.

"Last stop! Last stop now. Ellis Island! Last stop!"

Ellis Island? What!? I opened my eyes to find a crew member standing in the aisle ushering people off the boat. He was black. He looked American. *"Inis Mor?"* I enquired loudly.

"You missed it. Last stop now. Ellis Island."

"What!?"

He started to laugh. "Yeah, yeah, Kilronan, *Inis Mor."* Then he shared the joke with another crew member. "Ellis Island." They both chuckled, it was obviously not the first time they had played this prank.

"I had you goin' for a minute," he said, with a full youthful smile. His accent was West-of-Ireland with a hint of African. Probably Irish-born to African parents.

"Yeah. I was in America for a second."

He turned to the other crew member. "I had him. He was in America." They chuckled again and moved along the aisle, continuing their ferry-clearing duties.

My forced good humour didn't last long and I was quickly back in Ireland in search of the ethereal gateway, the other shore, and my ancient spirit. I wondered was the ferry symbolic.

The Greeks made a big thing about ferries, I said to myself.

I'm not a big fan of Greek mythology. Charon was the ferryman. Right?

Right.

So, is our black Irishman a modern version of Charon? Is Inis Mor, Hades? Is it literally the other shore?

Well, if it is, let's hope we docked at Elysium.

Really? You're calling on our knowledge of the Marvel comics.

That's about the sum of our Greek mythological knowledge, unless the voice wants to enlighten us with some hidden gem.

The voice responded. *Despondently you come. Holding tight your dreams. To Hades. Charon's doubleted shadow. Takes you cross dark waters.*

OK. That sounds ominous.

You did ask.

Thankfully, the awful hangover, bad trip, was lifting. I disembarked and followed signs to a small tourist office where I booked a B & B that was in the vicinity of *Dún Dúchathair*. The girl behind the counter said the accommodation was about a twenty-minute walk outside the village, "along a quiet road with lovely views overlooking the bay." Another time, I'd probably have been in rapture about the scenery, but not this time. Physically, my body was making a spirited recovery. However, mentally and emotionally, I was down at heart and still reeling from the nightmare and hallucinations. A dark cloud hovered over me, and I could have very easily cried.

Is this all nonsense? I asked the roadway as I trod its uneven surface. *If it wasn't for Mrs Mulcahy I'd be back in work with the mad cows. Maybe, I should go home.*

I think we should, reason said. *The ice is too thin and the cavern beneath too deep.*

There is an inner thing in every man, the voice interjected, *do you know this thing, my friend?*

What is wrong with you? I said. *Am I not depressed enough? Do you really think now is the right time to start quoting Bobby Sands at me?*

It persisted. *Do you know these words, my friend?*

Yes, I know these words.

Then let him speak to you. Say his words. Enough of doubting yourself.

A breeze skimmed across the stone walls.

I don't want to say his words.

Maybe he wants you to.

Why would he want me to?

He too was in a room without a flame. He too was called. Say his words.

I stopped and looked about the rugged countryside. *Has Bobby Sands ever been here,* I wondered? It seemed like a place a republican poet like Sands would have connected with or perhaps dreamed about, as he lay dying in his prison cell.

You have to, reason said, *as if I would be slighting the legacy of Bobby Sands, and Finn, if I didn't.*

I know.

It was a powerful poem. A reflection on his resilience, resistance, and his enduring Irish spirit. It had made me cry numerous times in the past and I knew it would plunge me back into the heartbreak of 1981. I remembered Finn bringing a bustling hall to stoney silence with his recitation during Sands' hunger strike, leaving many in tears. Now, I looked out to sea, steeled my spine, and recited the words.

There's an inner thing in every man,
Do you know this thing, my friend?
It has withstood the blows of a million years,
And will do so to the end.
It was born when time did not exist,
And it grew up out of life,
It cut down evil's strangling vines,
Like a slashing searing knife.
It lit fires when fires were not,
And burnt the mind of man,
Tempering leaden hearts to steel,
From the time that time began.
It lies in the hearts of heroes dead,
It screams in tyrants' eyes,
It has reached the peak of mountains high,
It comes streaking 'cross the skies.
It lights the dark of this prison cell,
It thunders forth its might,
It is the undauntable thought, my friend,
That thought that says, I'm right.

I took a deep breath and gathered myself. My mind rooted in the last line. I imagined him skeletal, on the cusp of death — steeled by the thought that said, *I'm right.*

Do you know this inner thing? The voice demanded.

Yes.

He too was called. Take strength from his dying thought. That thought that says, I'm right.

I guess we're not going home, reason said.

I guess not.

I stood for a moment, filled with the eternity of his words, and my heart spilled with empathy.

It wasn't long before the B&B came into sight, a sturdy two-story slated house with a nondescript rear extension that stretched the house into a bland *Bord Fáilte* aspiration. Built by the letter from America, then ruined by grants in search of the tourist dollar.

On the front door was a sellotaped A4 laminated sign with an arrow directing me to the side of the house where there was another door with another sign; *Tar Isteach* / Come In. This door didn't have a bell or knocker, and I rapped on its glass panel with my knuckles before entering an inauspicious square porch.

"Hello!" I ventured.

There was an overflowing coat rack, a pair of muddied Wellington boots, two umbrellas, a dog's bowl, and a plastic bucket. Also, what appeared to be a dead crow in the corner, behind the bucket. The internal door to the main dwelling was ajar and I could hear a woman in the next room speaking Irish. Effortless vocabulary and lyrical colloquial pronunciation. I guessed she was on the phone and had I understood what she was saying I might have been more confident about interrupting her.

"Tir gan teanga," the voice said, *"tir gan anam."*

"Hello!" I tried again.

The woman peered from behind the internal door; she was sharp faced with grey hair swept into a bun and had the look of someone who was tired of tourists. *"Fáilte isteach,"* she said. "Welcome. *Fan nóiméad*. I'll be with you in a minute."

I really wanted to say something to her in Irish, but I felt awkward. My vocabulary was too basic compared to her native flourish. "No rush, take your time."

She ended the call and beckoned me into the breakfast room where we stood among six partially set tables and a sideboard with untidied cutlery. On the walls were three Paul Henry prints that had seen better days. Nonetheless, they depicted a serene and picturesque West of Ireland, cosy thatched cottages against a backdrop of soft billowing white clouds in a vast blue sky.

"Is it Conor?" Her manner was rehearsed but not unfriendly.

"Yes, I booked at the office in Kilronan."

"You made good time."

"I was glad of the walk after the ferry."

She moved toward another door, and I followed her trim frame into a small reception area which was the hallway of the original house, behind the front door.

"I'm sorry about the phone. I've no time for that meself, people too busy to take their head out of their phones."

"Ná habair é." I said, confidently. "I'm sorry for interrupting you."

"Twas a neighbour I was talkin' to," she said, with a quiver of anxiety in her voice. "He heard *An Bhean Sí* last night and he's worried who she might be comin' for."

A Banshee! I thought, mockingly. But I said nothing and gave a noncommittal half-nod.

"She's been about the past couple of weeks and has taken two souls from above Cloonfert."

"The Banshee?"

My disbelief hung between us, and she considered her reply. "There's the stories in the city, to frighten the children, and then there's the truth of life and death. She only follows certain Gaelic families and Paidín, my neighbour, has heard her many a time through his life. He's an O'Brien, and not a man for the idle word."

"Does he think he's going to die?" I asked inquisitively before I could temper the question's insensitivity.

"He doesn't know. It could be him or someone close to him. Or someone in the locality. She doesn't come for visitors, only islanders, and only certain families at that."

"That's good to know," I said, quickly realizing I might sound patronizing.

"There's no need to worry, 'tis an island thing. What's your family name?"

"McCarthy."

She hesitated. "That's an old Gaelic name to be sure. But there are no McCarthys in the locality and Paidín is an O'Brien. Do you have family on the island?"

"No. Not that I know of." I didn't tell her that Granda was an O'Brien.

"Well sure," she said, before giving me the once-over, "there's no fear of ya." I could see her formulating her question: *no fishing gear, no hiking gear, just one small haversack*. "What brings you to the island?"

"To visit *Dún Dúchathair*."

Her jaw dropped. "Why so?"

"You look surprised. I thought it was a famous

place."

"Oh, 'tis," she said, now visibly unsure of me. "There's been sorrow there."

"A death?"

She blessed herself. "God between us and all harm. The truth of the Devil travels far."

"Sorry. I didn't mean to..."

"Twas a young woman, Molly O'Brien. Took her life above on the cliffs, not three weeks ago. *Labhair an fhírinne agus beidh anam slán."*

"I'm sorry to hear that. *Ar dheis Dé go raibh a hanam."*

She blessed herself. *"Go ndéana Dia trócaire ar a hanam."*

There was a pause, then she proffered two keys dangling from a block of wood. "You'll be wanting your key." Her tone turned brisk, almost rehearsed, and I sensed she had retreated behind her practiced B&B script, regretting that she had shared local sorrow with a tourist. "Second room on the left, at the top of the stairs. The big key is for your room; the small one is for the front door. You can come and go as you please. No overnight guests. Breakfast is between 8.30 and 10."

"I'm very sorry if I intruded on your grief," I said, touching her arm. "I didn't mean to."

Her eyes softened. "'Tis me that's sorry. *An Bhean*

Sí is a thing of the island, and the families here. Nair a thing to do with visitors. I shouldn't have mentioned her. 'Tis that you were beside me when I was on the phone to Paidín. I wasn't expecting the news and me head kept talkin' after I hung up the phone. Molly, the cratur, was his granddaughter. God rest her soul."

"I'm sorry."

"Put it out of your head. You're a visitor. Pay no heed to talk of *An Bhean Sí*. I'll see you tomorrow at breakfast. Please God."

The bedroom was in keeping with the house, drab. Certainly not a place to while away an afternoon. I was still tired from the poisoned *poitín* and considered resting on the less-than-inviting bed, but hunger pangs got the better of me. I decided to head into the village for something to eat.

I'd prefer if we went home, reason said. *The woman in the Dún, the demon RIC man and the grotesque King were bad enough. But now it's banshees and real people committing real suicide.*

I can't. You know I can't. I've come too far. Dún Dúchathair is only a mile or two over the hill.

Can you hear what you're saying? We've come 'too' far. When someone goes 'too' far, it's time for them to go back.

I have to. I started to cry. *Ah, fuck it. What was in that poxy poitín! Jesus Christ! I'm still shattered.*

All right. Stop crying. We'll go to Dún Dúchathair.

But I wouldn't get my hopes up, if I were you.

You are me.

Very funny. You know what I mean.

Kilronan had numerous places to eat, including one called, The Bar. I liked the bluntness of the name and sat at an outside table away from any fuss or possibility of meeting another Liz and George.

The waiter approached with the menu. "Can I get you a drink, while you decide?"

"I'll just have water thanks. And I'll order now, save you a trip."

"It's not as if I have something else to do." His face was cherub-like, bright, and happy. "Take your time."

I looked at the large logo on the menu. "It's a good name, The Bar. No messin' about."

"It used to be called The American Bar because, long before my time, some of the emigrant ships on route from Galway to New York used to stop at Kilronan. To pick up the islanders who had congregated here for their American Wake."

"Human cargo."

"My grandmother remembers it."

"You're from here?"

"My father. But we're livin' years in Galway city. I'm at Uni there. I come out to work during the summer."

"What are you studying?"

"Physics."

"Good man. That's a far cry from human cargo."

"Well, I might be going to the next parish yet. America."

"With the smartness of your brains. Not the sweat of your brow."

He laughed. "Well, I wouldn't be flyin' me flag yet. There's many a slip between the cup and the lip."

I was going to say, is that a law of physics? But I had exhausted my chattiness, and instead, I just ordered. "A pint of water. Cream of mushroom soup with homemade brown bread and the salted butter."

After my food, I sat for a while looking down on the harbour and thought about the sadness of the emigrants who probably sat in the very same place waiting for their ship to dock. Leaving Ireland forever. It must have been heartbreaking for them.

On the way back to the B&B, my body was recovering, but my mind was subdued and my eyeline hardly rose above the tarmac until I came upon an old sign for *Dún Dúchathair*. It was pointing up a twisty overgrown boreen that disappeared into a labyrinth of rock walls and rockier fields. The scene dripped with ancient peace and tranquillity. It wasn't the route I had planned to take, but its forgotten look appealed to me, and I turned into its path, with the emigrants still on my mind. There was an untouched sense about the location and I imagined a group of young men and women traipsing down the hillside to get the boat to New York. Some carried their meagre possessions wrapped in rags, others had nothing but the clothes they stood in. A young woman, no more than a teenager, withdrew from the group and stood by the wall. "We'll part here," she said, to a gaunt-looking young man. "'Tis the spot we first met."

He pulled off his cloth cap and took her hand, "I'll send for ya, and Seamus Og."

"Don't forget us. Stay…" She bit her lip fighting back the tears.

He kissed her hand. "Never, Brigid. Me heart's pure destroyed leavin' ye. As soon as I earn your passage, we'll be together again, we'll…," his words drowned in grief and he buried his face in his cap.

"Stay strong for us, Tighe. May every blessin' go with ya and God speed till we're standing beside ya in New York."

"Please God… God bless and protect ye both," he said, his lip quivering. *"Slán go fóill."* He then rejoined the group as they turned onto the road for Kilronan and New York, not a pair of shoes among them.

Sobbing, Brigid climbed the rock wall and took off across the fields.

I stood and watched until the last remnants of the scene faded and the peaceful tranquillity of the place was left drowning in their sadness. The breeze lifted and the field regained itself.

It was hard for me to fathom how they coped, leaving the natural solitude of the island to live in the concrete chaos of New York. A stone-grey concrete jungle, screeching and howling with humanity. I was reminded of Yeats' *Lake Isle of Innisfree. They must arise and go now, for always night and day they hear lake water lapping with low sounds by the shore, while they stand on the roadway, or on the pavements grey, they hear it in the deep heart's core.*

What a mournful journey it must have been, I thought. Turfed out of their homes onto the grey concrete pavements of New York, always longing in their deep heart's core for the cultural essence of their ancient homeland.

The longest journey is the journey inwards, the voice said, as if oblivious to my emotions. *Of him who has chosen his destiny, who has started upon his quest for the source of his being.*

I'm talking about them, I snapped, irritated. *Not my quest to find the source of my being. I'm talking about the poor emigrants.*

It means, reasoned said, *you have to look inside yourself if you are going to find an answer to your search.*

I know what he means. I don't care what he means. He's an idiot, babbling in cryptic quotations. I heard myself refer to the voice as *he,* like a separate person. It registered—but it didn't settle.

Calm down. Take a deep breath.

I know. I'm just not in form for him.

The voice challenged my anger. *The principles for which you give your life are so sacred that you now walk to your death in the most calm and collected manner. You meet death for Ireland's cause.*

Jesus! He's making that up, I said. *Just to freak me out.*

No, reason said. *It's eh… paraphrasing Mac Diarmada's last words before his execution.*

Oh. Did I know that?

You must have. But it's an odd thing for it to say.

I huffed. He's an odd thing, full stop.

Does the voice know something I don't? Have you some hare-brained notion of self-sacrifice for Ireland, to enter the gateway?

No, of course not. You know what I know.

Is the voice telling us what Finn warned us about in the dream. That a dark spirit means to harm us, wants our soul?

No. Jesus! You're meant to be the rational part of me. Get a grip. Finn's stuff was a dream. We're… on an explorative cultural and spiritual trip to an ancient fort. Touching base with our cultural and historic past, so to speak.

A tourist jaunt?

Yes, exactly. A tourist jaunt. Anyway, the voice is your friend, not mine. I think he's an idiot, trying to sound intelligent. One original thought is worth a thousand mindless quotations. I've lost my tolerance for affected self-inflated idiots.

Stupid is as stupid does. The voice retorted.

Fuck off!

Don't let it annoy you. We're on thin psychiatric ice already.

To be clear, I said to reason. *You know the voice doesn't actually exist as an independent thinker? It's only the conduit for stuff being released from our subconscious. A leakage of shit that we already know. Stuff that we've read, seen, or heard at some point in our life and then stored in our head.*

Well, I'm not sure that's true. Sometimes he says stuff that we have zero recollection of.

I stopped to consider the thought, and it was only then I realised the distance I'd travelled from the old sign. It was a steady incline and the view behind me stretched as far as the sea, over poor countryside that was disconcertingly absent of trees. Not a single tree, not even a decent-sized bush, just a patchwork of rock walls that enclosed rocky fields with a few small buildings dotted about. A scene probably unchanged in over a hundred years.

There would have been a lot more houses, reason said, *and people in the fields, tending to their tiny holdings.*

Yeah, I suppose so. Maybe the odd donkey and cart, stacked with turf from the mainland, walking unhurried along the boreen. Led by hardy men with knitted caps, baggy tweed trousers, and cable knit sweaters. There'd be other men too, with muscular arms hanging from a spade or scythe propped across their toughened shoulders, chatting, as they strolled home. Elderly women in black shawls and red skirts would be leaning on the half-door of their white-washed thatched cottages, smoking clay pipes, while the younger women were indoors preparing a skillet of spuds for the arrival of their men from the fields.

In reality, reason said, *it would have been more Michael Davitt than Paul Henry. Behind those walls were malnourished children with rickets and scurvy and lice and worms, and behind the half-doors were decrepit men and women ailing with consumption or pneumonia or other poverty sicknesses. Laying on infested straw mattresses, waiting on the Banshee to call. The men returning from the impoverished fields weren't chatting about football or the currach races or the crossroads dance. Their chat was about more serious matters; fair rent, fixity of tenure, free sale, the English dumping cheap woolen goods on the Irish market, the welfare of their emigrant children who they'd never see again. Or the premature death of those who stayed behind.*

It felt as though there were centuries of sadness and endurance hidden in plain view behind the stone walls. An endurance that was derived from the islanders' ancient belief in themselves, a belief in their seminal place of kinship. As I neared the end of the boreen I wondered if the ancient Irish spirit might actually live in the endurance of the islanders, in their sadness.

CHAPTER 17

On reaching the brow of the hill, the boreen ended in a cul-de-sac and my eyes were lifted over the rock wall by the unexpected appearance of the enormous Atlantic Ocean. There was no gate in the wall and no obvious way of crossing to the other side, which had a strikingly different landscape. Rows of large flat stones ran to a cliff edge before plunging into a timeless border between land and sea. The flat stones were divided by thousands of right-angled fissures running up and down, left and right—like giant neolithic paving. It was bleak and barren terrain and it made the path I had travelled look positively fertile.

I was immediately taken by the spirituality of the vista beyond the wall. It was an incongruous place, as though inhabited by something that couldn't be seen with the naked eye—teeming with real-world emptiness and otherworldly fullness. I imagined the wall was a frontier to a realm without dimension, an all-encompassing place of unknown emotions. Where the ethereal ran hand in hand with the tangible flat grey stones to the edge of Ireland, the edge of Europe, the very edge of human civilisation.

My heart fluttered with excitement at the

expectation of entering this timeless landscape. I was slow, however, to forge ahead because I wanted to respect its obvious solemnity and stillness. Pausing for a moment, I listened to the quietness of the breeze that rolled in from the Atlantic. In the distance, I could hear the muffled sound of waves pounding the unseen cliff base – an endless conflict between ancient land and sea. It made me think of the ethereal energies that might be at work on the other side of the wall. There was something other beyond the wall, something irresistible, and it was drawing me to a place where Jesus Christ had no footprint.

Don't let your imagination run wild, reason cautioned. *You have to stay real. Remember, it's only this morning that you were tripping out of your head.*

Yes, OK. I know, stay real.

I mounted the wall, and my jacket ballooned in an unexpected gust of wind that made me steady my legs for fear of being hurled back to whence I came. When the wind settled, I took advantage of my elevated viewing point. Behind me was a quilt of neatly divided fields leading to a harbour with a ferry to more neatly planned fields. Beyond that was a motorway to neatly compartmentalised lives. Then a garden path to my neatly presented home, and my fading existence disappearing into my neatly grey world. In front of me was the unknown. A great unknown, perhaps. Another world, maybe. The place of the ethereal gateway to my old self, hopefully.

After I jumped from the wall, the only discernible

difference when I landed was its height. I could no longer see where I came from.

It's a wall, my reason said, *what did you expect, Alice in Wonderland?*

The formidable ruins of *Dún Dúchathair*, however, were visible about a mile to my left. Silhouetted against a vivid horizon, it appeared to be hovering above the cliff coastline, creating a mystical allure befitting a Disney fairytale. In between me and it lay a flat expanse of Neolithic paving, littered with enough cracks and fissures to break every ankle in an advancing army.

A great defensive location. I thought. *Finn would have loved this. Pity we didn't include Inis Mor on our hikes.*

The place seemed alive with mythological wonder, as each whisper of the wind carried echoes of ancient tales. It was spine-tingling.

When I reached the Dún, its walls rose from the ancient paving to a height far greater than I had imagined. It was detached from its hinterland like a great dam built to hold back something lost in time, and although its natural grey harmonised with the surrounding geology, its architecture was starkly human. Thousands and thousands of chiselled stones had been crafted and painstakingly positioned to create a sheer face of landward impregnability. Seaward, the Dún jutted into the wild ocean, protected by huge vertical cliffs on its other three sides. The overall fortification, only part of the original structure, still smacked of a physical and cultural last stand.

I was in no doubt, if the *Tuatha Dé Dannan* had tried to breach these defences, they would have needed more than mortal slingshot and arrow.

I got an eerie feeling. Like there were other energies close by. *Maybe Tuatha Dé Dannan?* I jibed, half-heartedly.

We should go back, reason said.

Stop, would you? I'm joking. We're here now. Let's keep going.

Finn warned you, remember? He said there are dark forces that want your soul. Want to harm you. I think they're here.

Jesus, come on. It was a dream! I know what Finn would do if he was here. He'd be scaling the wall.

To the left of the wall was an ad hoc entrance that teetered perilously close to the cliff edge, with a petrifying drop to the sea below. Surprisingly, it was the only way in or out of the Dún and I guessed there must have been an original grand entrance that had collapsed into the sea after millennia of wave erosion. I passed, cautiously, along the entrance path.

Steady, reason said.

I stepped carefully, but my thoughts were giddy—imagining a slip.

This frivolity shall not bring an end, the voice said,

unimpressed with my childishness. *For I perceive the path to death lies here.*

"Jesus Christ!" I muttered. *Stop with the fucking idiotic quotes.*

We should go back, reason said, again.

Stop. We're not going back to our dull grey life. That's it. Look how far we've come. There is nothing grey about the past couple of days. No grey. Not since Mrs. Mulcahy. She changed everything. We're on the path to our old self, to reengage with our ancient spirit. To find Em and Finn.

I'm not sure, reason said. *But you're the boss. Be it on your head. Which, of course, is my head.*

Stop with the nonsense. The voice is bad enough.

Once inside, the continuous thrum of the ocean struck me with all its elemental wildness, something that wasn't apparent outside the Dún. Also striking was the reality of its isolation, dominated by the huge vertical cliffs that stretched along the coast on either side with powerful waves crashing and bashing their base. It felt different from the outside—less spine-tingling, more subdued.

The interior layout was divided into two by a small wall, creating a type of grassy courtyard behind the main defensive wall. This wall was nearly as thick as it was high, with three buttress terraces connected by ancient steps, allowing quick access to repel would be attackers. At the foot of the wall were several curved, unroofed, cell-like structures.

Wow, I thought, *probably the last dwelling places of the Fir Bolg as the Tuatha Dé bombarded the Dún with their magical arsenal.*

I was about to investigate the dwellings, but my eye was drawn to a white boulder in the centre of the grassy courtyard – every other rock and stone in the *Dún* was slate grey.

Maybe a podium? Used to address the inhabitants?

Or, reason teased, *maybe an enchanted rock hurled by the Tuatha Dé.*

I sat on the white boulder, admiring the 3,000-year-old fortification, and realised the inside of the *Dún* had captured my thoughts, not my emotions. I was historically sympathetic to the *Fir Bolg* and the great sense of achievement they must have had in their architecture and craftsmanship. But it was a surprisingly vacuous place, with all feelings of spirituality outside its walls. Then, in contradiction to my thoughts, a stony cold sentiment crept upon me and I began to view this empty forgotten place as a reflection of my inner self. Desolate loneliness seeped through my bones, and before I could consider my feelings, a man emerged from one of the ancient cell dwellings.

To say I was startled would be an understatement.

He was in everyday clothing, a dishevelled figure with dark, hollowed eyes that stared at me with an unsettling gaze, as if peering from times past.

A rigid smile lingered on his desiccated lips,

hinting at some shared memory. "You don't remember me, do you?"

"Eh, I don't think so," I managed to say. "Sorry."

"Not to worry, Connor, or should I call you Macker?"

"What?" I was dumbfounded. "Eh, how do you know me?

"I said!" he shouted, "what should I fuckin' call you?"

I automatically assessed his frail physique. He didn't strike me as a physical threat. I was cautious, nonetheless, and readied myself for a possible attack, even though he kept his distance.

"You can call me whatever you want,' I said, the hair standing on the back of my neck. "I don't care."

"You will. Mark my words, Macker. You will.

Who the fuck is this looney? I thought, utterly spooked.

"Emily and Finn are gone forever," he said. "There is only you. You lonely miserable shit."

"Who the fuck are you?" My flight instinct had turned to fight.

"Can't you guess?" He said in a sickly child's voice and moved closer. "Don't tell me you forgot your old pals from Saint Aidan's."

I tightened my fists. "What? Who are you?"

"C'mon. You nearly have it."

"Jonesy?"

"Bingo."

"He's dead." I scoured the *Dún* with my eyes for hidden accomplices to a sick joke. "This isn't fucking funny. If you think this is a joke, it's not."

"It's no joke, Macker. You never liked my jokes, did you?"

"If *Biróg* and *Faebar* put you up to this. It's not fucking funny. If you don't stop now, you'll get a smack in the head."

He kept his distance but showed no fear. "You were always an aggressive cunt. Always a fuckin' bully. Remember, you punched me in the face for having a bit of fun. You made my nose bleed." He put his hand to his nose and then looked at it, as if checking for blood. "You picked on me just because you were bigger. You never punched Mulligan."

"This is fuckin' crazy." I turned to leave, but I was disorientated, and I couldn't see where the exit was.

"Oh, it's not that easy, Macker. We have to have a chat, a catch-up."

"I don't want a catch-up."

"I know what you want. You want to punch me again. Be the bully that you've always pretended you weren't."

"I don't. I won't touch you."

"I fuckin' know you won't. Because underneath it all, you're a fuckin' coward."

"This is not why you are here," a deep, angry growl said. It came from Jonesy's face, now distorted—like some demonic energy had surfaced from within him.

"Jesus," I whispered, the ominous growl sapping all of my aggression. My legs nearly went. "Why am I here?" I asked cautiously. "I'm sorry if I bullied you." It was time to appease whatever Jonesy was and get out of there. "I didn't mean to. I'm sorry for what happened to you, Jonesy."

"Silence," he growled, less menacingly. "We have juicier concerns, than my loyal little spy, Jonesy. Juicier confessions to be made. Juicier offerings to be sacrificed."

"I don't understand what you're saying. I want to go. This is fucking nuts!"

"Unfortunately, for you," the growl now sounded reasonable, "sanity and horror can be cosy bedfellows. This is your day of reckoning, Conor. This is acute reality."

"I don't understand. What do you want from me?"

"Now, you're getting the picture. What do I want from you? Or, what do I have that you want?"

"You don't have anything I want."

It must be a flashback, I thought, without conviction. *Tell it to go away.*

It's a flashback, I recited silently. *Go away. It's a flashback. Go away.*

"No, Conor, it is not, as you say, a flashback. You can chant all you want. I'll still be here. My *poitín*, peddling disciples at Poulnabrone did guide you to me, but alas, this is not a drug-induced flashback. Ironically, I would not have known about your presence if it were not for *An Cailleach Dubh*." He snorted a laugh. "An unlucky escape for you, because here you are, with me. *Ó ghrása na Cailleach go greim an deamhain*."

"I don't know how you're doing this. I don't know why you want to frighten me."

Be forceful. Show authority.

"But top fucking marks. You've frightened me. OK. That's enough. Where the fuck is the exit?"

The demon-growl started to laugh; it was heartfelt and sinister. "I was told you wanted to pass through the ethereal gateway. Was I misled?"

"I know it's you Faebar, Biróg." I was clutching at straws. "You're the only ones I told my story to. It's not fucking funny anymore."

"Macker and Finn," Jonesy said, reinhabiting his body "The big men of Saint Aidan's. Let me tell you, Finn's not so fuckin' big now, squealing and squirming like a bitch."

"Jonesy, listen to me. I'm sorry. I didn't mean to bully you. But you're right, I was a bully. I didn't punch

Mulligan because he would have beaten me in a fight. I'm sorry I hit you. I really am."

"Too late, too late, is the cry. The man with the thumbscrews has just passed by. If you listen, you might hear Finn squeal."

"Please Jonesy, stop."

"Squirmy, squirmy. I haven't even started."

"Finn is dead," I said emphatically, hoping fact might penetrate madness and bring the insane travesty to a close.

"His body might be dead, but I'm delighted to tell you his soul is not. *Anima non discessit,* as your classics scholar might say."

"I don't know what you want."

"I want to see you squirm, and grovel in pain like the pathetic shit that you are. I want to hurt you."

"Why!?" I pleaded. "Why?"

He giggled excitedly, mockingly. "Why? Why? Because. Because. Oh, this is music to my ears. I can't wait for you to hear good old Finn squeal."

"If you really have Finn. Let me talk to him?"

"Hah, you are the last person Finn wants to talk to. A fuckin' informer. It's because of you he's destined to everlasting torture."

"What? No, you're wrong. That's wrong. This whole thing must be a huge mistake. I would never inform on him."

"You're a fuckin' traitor. A traitor to Ireland. A traitor to your Irish spirit. A traitor to your Granda. And, most of all, a traitor to your Blood Brother. You're fuckin' scum."

"That's not true, Jonesy. You've got that wrong."

"I fuckin' know. I saw you. I saw you in the bar. In Dundalk. With the SAS. I saw you selling out your best friend for a few whiskies." His voice spat. His lips curled. His eyes burned. He stabbed the air with a pointed finger. "I fuckin' saw you. You were always jealous of Finn. He had the courage you never had. He was the Republican you never were. He fought and died for Ireland. You sat on your hands mouthin out of yer arse."

"No. I never informed." I went to grab him but missed. "You're a lying little bastard."

He sneered. "Ah, here's the real Macker. The fuckin bully. Let me refresh your memory. It was Sunday, the 2nd of August, the day Kieran Doherty died on hunger strike, the day after Kevin Lynch had died. Republicans were reeling, traumatised. But you were slobbering in your drink, crying over your poxy posh girlfriend. Flannery's Bar. Dundalk. Remember?"

I remembered Flannery's Bar and the two hunger strike deaths, but I didn't answer.

"I said, do you fuckin' remember!"

"Yes."

"Good. Do you remember your two English

drinking buddies?"

I remembered drinking with two English fellas and snippets of drunken laughter.

"C'mon. Don't be shy. Do you remember?"

"Yes."

"Did you wonder why they were happy to buy drink for an inarticulate slobbering Irish drunk?"

"They were tourists."

"Stop the fuckin' lights! Stop the fuckin' self-deception. I know, and you know, they weren't tourists. Did they look like fuckin' tourists?... Did they look like fuckin' tourists?"

"No."

"No. They looked like fuckin' SAS commandos."

"I didn't tell them anything. I know I didn't."

"Ah now, Bubbles. I think you know you did. Let me help you remember your way through that drunken haze. You and the two English fellas, down the back of Flannery's. They thought you were so funny. The more offensive you were about their Queen and her 'floppy-eared idiot son' the more drink they wanted to buy you. You were funnier than Billy Connolly. Do you remember?"

"Yes. But..."

He held up his hand. "I have the floor. So, you're back in Flannery's. August 2nd, 1981. It's early evening. You've been drinking all day. Don't mind the fella at the end of the bar, that's just me. The English fella with the blonde hair, pretending to be drunk, says; 'Thatcher hates the Irish. She doesn't care how many prisoners starve to death. She'd be happy to see another famine here. I think... she's going to crush the IRA. The hunger strike is the end of them. They're finished.' And, you said. Do you remember?"

"No."

"I think you do. You said, with all the jealousy of a drunk, bragging about his courageous friend, you said, 'I know the IRA, and I can tell you; the IRA is far from finished. There's big things happening in the States. Big fuckin' things.'"

"To which your genial English commando said. 'Like what?'

"And, you said, ringing every fuckin' security bell from Dundalk to Whitehall, 'Surface-to-air missiles.' Holy fuck! 'Surface-to-air missiles. Even the Queen got shivers down her spine because that would have been a game changer. Do you remember telling your English buddies about the surface-to-air missiles?"

"No."

"Are you sure?"

"No." Finn had told me about trying to source surface-to-air missiles. "Even if I did. Even if they were SAS. I never said anything about Finn."

"Ah, but you did. In your drunken self-pity you spilled the beans like any common traitor, any common informer. Remember, they laughed at you. They laughed at Macker, Mr Tough-Guy-Macker. They laughed at you, the stereotypical Irish drunk scrounging whiskey from the English table.

"'Surface-to-air missiles!'" They laughed. "'How the fuck would you know that.'"

"And you said?... C'mon, what did you say?"

"I don't remember."

"And you said, with great drunken indignation, 'Because my best friend Finn Mulcahy is fucking buying them.'

"To which blondie said, 'Wow! We didn't know you were so well-connected. I hope we didn't offend you saying the IRA are finished.'"

"Proudly vindicated, you sat back like a member of the IRA's Army Council, while they licked your imposter IRA arse and ordered another round of drinks.

"'I know you probably can't say,' the quieter Brit said, 'but is he buying them in Chicago?' To which you slurred, 'Boston,' effectively signing Finn's death warrant."

"I don't remember any of that," I said, doubting myself and aghast at the possible scenario.

"Tell yourself lies," Jonesy said insidiously. "Or don't remember it. I don't care. I remember it, because I was there. I saw you give up your blood brother. I saw you bring shame on the spirit of your grandfather and death on the Mulcahy family."

"If that's true, what happened. How did...? What happened to Finn?"

"It didn't take long for the betrayal to travel from your lips to Finn's head – the English military are so fuckin efficient. Your SAS buddies, straight away, reported your information to their Captain, and it then shot up along the chain of command. Military, to MI5. MI5, to MI6. MI6 verified what Finn was up to then paid a member of the Whitey Bulger gang to assassinate him."

"I can't believe that."

"You can't believe it, or you don't want to believe it?"

"I don't want to."

"Let me put it this way, could it be true, that you informed on Finn when you were stupid drunk? Is it a possibility?"

"I don't remember."

"That's not what I asked. Could it be true? Is it possible?

I opened my mouth to say, *No. That's not possible.* But the words wouldn't form. "Yes."

"Bingo. Confession number one." He swaggered triumphantly in a small circle. "But I don't want you to get all the glory. It was, after all, me who set you up with your SAS buddies."

"Poor Finn." *I'm sorry, Finn.* My stomach turned—repulsed by the idea of me betraying him. *I don't remember it, but I can't say it didn't happen. I'm sorry. I remember the bar, the two English fellas, but not much else. I remember bragging about my friend in the IRA. I'm sorry Finn. I'm sorry.*

"Yes, poor Finn. And now we have his soul for all eternity to torture and degrade."

"What? What do you mean? He never did anything to you."

"You're right. He didn't. But hurting him hurts you, and I want to hurt you. We've been waiting on this day for eighteen years."

"Please don't hurt him. Why are you doing this?" My voice cracked. I wanted to cry for help— but I had no one. No god. No man. "If it's a game to frighten me, you've won. I'm terrified."

"It's no game, Macker. It's deathly serious. Today is your day of reckoning. And guess what?" He made a heinous sniggering noise. "I have another juicy surprise for you. Can you guess who else we have here? Can you guess the other soul we have to torture, humiliate and demean forever and always. Yes, of course you can. It's little sexy Emily and her little incestuous foetus. I have to tell you; she's finding it very difficult here. It's just as well she's a great fuck because she's bleedin' deranged. The anguish and pain in her head is off the poxy' charts. It's fuckin' severe, really. She's just writhing and screaming with the pain of betrayal and loss. All the fuckin' time. Fuckin' constant."

My throat closed. A scream blocked. I couldn't swallow. "Stop! Just fucking stop! Please. Please stop."

"So, you don't want to know her last thoughts, as the blood flowed from sexy Em's wrists?"

"No. Stop, please. I'm begging you."

"Thankfully, Macker, I can't. I work for a higher power. As did my ancestors. You're not the only one with lineage. I think you might have heard of Henry Jones, head of Cromwell's Intelligence. He was my twelve times Great-grandfather. It was Granpa Henry who developed the twin themes of irredeemable Irish barbarism and universal Catholic guilt against God. Happy days."

"What do you want from me? Please don't hurt Em." I lunged at him, but he managed to stay just inches out of my grasp. Smirking.

"Now, now, Macker. There's that temper again. Tut-tut."

"She has nothing to do with Saint Aidan's, or school, or whatever the fuck this is about. She is an innocent. She wouldn't hurt anyone. Please—don't hurt her. I beg you. I beg you. Please. Please don't hurt her."

"You're missing the point here. I enjoy hurting her because I know it hurts you. You'll get to see me hurting her later. I'm looking forward to that." He rubbed his hands gleefully. "But I'm running ahead of myself. Do you want to know Emily's last thoughts before her veins dripped the last drop of life into her pool of congealing blood?"

"No. I'm not playing your sick fucking game."

"Let me explain. The longer I'm here teasing you, the longer I'm not torturing your soul mates. So, do you want to know Emily's last mortal thoughts?"

"Yes."

"Great. I'm happy to say, you're not going to enjoy this. The reason why dear little Em committed suicide was because she couldn't bear the pain in her heart. The pain of your betrayal. You were the only light in her darkness, and you betrayed her."

"I didn't betray her."

"You are such a fuckin' hypocrite, going around like a heartbroken puppy. Oh, poor me, I lost Em, the love of my life. When all the fuckin' time it was you who killed her. It was your betrayal that left her nowhere to turn. No escape but death. Granted," he sniggered, "she didn't know she was escaping to a fate worse than death.".

"That's wrong. You've made a mistake. This is a mistake. I loved Em with all my heart and soul."

"Then why did you betray her to Mummy?"

"What? I don't know what you... I didn't."

"Oh, yes you did. I heard you. How do you think she

got your phone number? Who do you think suggested the £1,000?"

"I don't understand."

"I don't remember. I don't understand. All very convenient, Macker. All very fuckin' convenient. You have a wonderful gift – you can tell yourself anything. Let's start with, did Mummy phone you? Just a simple yes or no."

"Yes."

"And you agreed with Mummy that Uncle Reggie, father of Emily's rapist, would pay for her abortion. Would send you, first class, all expenses paid, to London with her. To make sure she didn't back out."

"I didn't agree to anything."

"Did you disagree? Did you protest? Well, did you!? Yes, or no?"

"No."

"Fuckin' right you didn't. Mummy sweet-talked you. Told you how you'd be welcome in the big house 'once this dreadful mess is cleaned up.' Told you how you could attend the summer garden party and eat fuckin' cucumber sandwiches with the gentry."

"It wasn't like that."

"I fuckin' heard it. I was on the fuckin' phone. Poor working-class Macker always yearned to rub shoulders with the aristocracy, and here was Mummy offering you afternoon tea with the Vicar. All you had to do was take Jeremy's money."

"You can say what you want, it wasn't like that."

"Did you tell her that Jeremy raped Em? Well, did you? Yes, or no?"

"No. It wasn't up to..."

"No, you didn't. Did you say, I don't want a penny of your filthy money. I'll look after Emily myself?"

"No."

"No, you didn't. You left Emily at the mercy of her rapist. What did you do? You did what Macker always does, you unleashed your macho aggression and beat the shite out of old Jeremy. No empathy in that for little raped Emily. No thought of how it might impact on her. Just, me, me, me. It's always about Macker. Me, myself, and I."

"I can't remember about the SAS, but I know it wasn't like that with Em."

"You can tell yourself what you want to hear. I'll tell you what Em, raped and pregnant, heard from Mummy only hours before she sliced her wrists. I quote, verbatim:

'I can't change your sexual deviance, Emily; that is for God to do. I have been made aware that you have seduced boys and young men like a succubus since you were a child. It has broken your father's heart to know he has raised a harlot. I will not let you bring further shame on him with the fruits of your sinfulness. I have spoken to Conor, and he agrees you must have an

abortion, as soon as possible. Uncle Reggie will pay for everything and he'll pay Conor £1,000 to go to London with you. He knows an excellent man in Harley Street, he'll give Conor the details.'"

"No. I didn't agree to any of it. It wasn't like that. That's not how it was."

"Your agreement was inferred by your cowardly, greedy silence. Fuckin' hell, you're such a fuckin' narcissist. Be a fuckin' real man. Stand up and take the blame."

I looked down. My fists were clenched—not in anger, but restraint. Trying to stop my mind from buckling.

"Do you think Mummy could have said that to Emily?"

"Yes."

"Based on your conversation with her?"

"Yes."

"Bingo! Job done. Confession number two."

"Can I talk to her?" I heard myself ask, in some hellish insane hope. Barely believing my words.

"She wouldn't hear you over her deranged squeals. I told you a white lie earlier. I'm not the only torturer. It's constant. You'll know that soon enough."

"Thank you, Conor," the growly voice said, in a softer, rounder tone than before, "for admitting your culpability in the deaths of your two soulmates. It is a pleasure to have you before me at last. I was told you disappeared after their deaths. Your light was lost, and Jonesy was unable to find you. You are a slippery one. *An Cailleach Dubh* had you in her grasp but for that disgusting, despicable *Onóraigh* creature."

"I'm sorry. I don't understand. *Onóraigh* creature?"

"You don't have to understand. We've met before, you and I."

"Can you help me? Please." All I had left was to throw myself at his mercy. "There's been a terrible mistake. Jonesy made a mistake. I didn't mean to bully him. He says he has the souls of Em and Finn. They did nothing wrong. Em didn't even know Jonesy..."

"Silence. It is of no relevance. As I was saying, we met by chance in Poulnabrone when you were a child. Your lineage glowed with such youthful innocence that I instantly wanted your soul. I nearly had it, if not for that self-righteous, loathsome sow. You slipped from my grasp. But all was not lost; I acquired the soul of Jonesy, a descendant of an old acquaintance. He was eager to track you, and I was content to wait for the right moment. Alas, that loathsome, sanctimonious *striapach* kept appearing, interfering. So, my cruel, resourceful Jonesy persuaded me to take your soulmates as bait. He even tried to titillate me with their torture, a type of consolation revenge. Unfortunately, their torture is no consolation for me. Jonesy, however, derives endless pleasure from inflicting unspeakable pain on them."

"I don't understand any of this, it's beyond insanity..."

"Insanity? Nay. It is beyond your elusive ethereal gateway. You have found what you sought, but it is not as you envisaged."

"You are obviously a powerful, entity..."

"Let me stop you. Flattery will not please or vex me. Do not waste our time with it. What is the question you want to ask?"

"What do you want from me?"

"Yes, that is the question. And my answer is simple: I want your soul. But it must be freely given."

"You can have my soul," I said without hesitation. "If you release Em and Finn." Strangely, sacrificing my soul emboldened my spirit. A locked door creaked ajar and a cold draught from my old self raised the hairs on my neck.

"How noble of you. Jonesy's little plan has come to fruition. You must understand, I cannot restore them to life."

"Can you release their souls to a place of eternal peace?"

"Yes. But your resolve unsettles me." He looked about the Dún with a single beaming eye in his forehead, his two normal eyes now sealed. "Your soul has been weighed, and well valued. However, either it has been undervalued or there is something afoot. Jonesy, are you certain there are no other energies in the Dún?"

"Certain, my Lord. Your Guard has told me so."

"It seems I will enjoy your soul more than I imagined."

"Will you release them to eternal peace?"

"I will."

"Can I trust you?"

"I am Lord *Balor* of the Exalted *Fomorians.* I rule by the integrity of my intent. It is not a matter of trust; it is a matter of preserving the fundamentals of my rule. They will be released to eternal peace." He leaned in, neck jutting, head low—like a predator tasting the air before the pounce. "First, you must say a few words, 'I, *Conchobar Mac Cárthaigh,* give my soul in self-sacrifice to Lord *Balor* of the Exalted *Fomorians.*'"

I stood straight and squared my shoulders. I didn't want to let him see I was terrified. "I, Conchobar Mac Cárthaigh, give my soul in self-sacrifice to Lord *Balor* of the Exalted *Fomorians.*"

"Excellent," he said, wiping drool from the side of his mouth.

"Are you going to torture me?"

"I have no desire to hurt you. I have no desire to protect you from hurt. Jonesy may crave your suffering, but he is irrelevant now—he has already overindulged his cruel appetites tormenting your soulmates.

"What are you going to do with my soul?"

"I'm going to nurture it, fatten it, and then I'm going to eat it."

Somehow, I didn't care. "Will it be painful?"

"For you? Very. However, until the feasting, you will be treated like the fatted calf from your holy book."

"How long will it take?"

"I'm intrigued by your curiosity. Every question increases your value and flavour. I will want to savour you, prolong the gratification, and slowly distil your energy. A long time."

"Do you promise they will be released?"

"There is no need to promise. They are already gone."

"Do I just stand here? Is someone going to kill me?"

"No. For your soul to be sweet, you must take your own life."

"How?" I was nearly impatient to end the insanity.

"Walk twenty strides to the right from where you stand. There, you will find *Lia Sóis*, the ancient stone of solace jutting out over the cliff. You simply close your eyes and take your last few steps along the stone, the same steps that many hundreds have taken before you.

"Once upon the stone, all the turmoil and noise in your head will be replaced with tranquillity and silence. You will have complete peace of mind on your final short journey to the sea below."

I walked to the stone, a flat slab of weathered limestone, jutting like a high-diving board into the void—three feet wide, six long, and precariously balanced.

"Step onto the stone."

I stepped onto the end of the stone.

"See the awesome, hypnotic power of the churning waves beneath. You don't have to be afraid, just edge a little further."

My heart was in my mouth, my mind spinning, and I was transfixed by a repellent attraction to the gigantic precipice with the swirling waves 300 feet below. I sidled along the stone to slightly beyond the cliff's edge. There was nothing but air between the stone and the churning, swirling waves, three hundred feet below, writhing with anger, furiously pounding the cliff's base with savage blows. The booming sound of their power, caught in battered caves, seemed to vibrate through the stone. My heart was beating furiously, but my mind had stopped spinning.

"See past the turmoil," *Balor* said. "Hear the majestic rhythm of the waves."

He was right. It wasn't a battle – it was a dance. The waves were swirling and twirling, lifting their turquoise gowns from the dark waters and swooshing their full white petticoats as they executed balletic spins and pivots before throwing themselves high above the swell and crashing against the rigid rocks in glorious eruptions of self-sacrifice. Then they selflessly disappeared from centre stage allowing the next wave to perform its final act of life, jeté-ing high in the air with all the grace and courage of a Bolshoi principal.

The wind picked up, and straight in front of my eyes a seagull was riding the air currents, hovering and gliding with natural elegance. My heart grew quiet, my mind peaceful and my soul became one with the rhythmic dance of the sea. I heard the brazen door of hell move on its hinges, the blood ran cold in my veins, and I took the penultimate step to the tip of the stone. It nearly tilted into the abyss and my life swayed in the balance.

"Lean into the wind," *Balor* instructed, "and the stone will tilt. You will fall effortlessly into comforting peace and nurture. Lean forward, let the stone tilt in your favour."

I leaned into the wind, goading it to take me. The stone began to tilt. My feelings of guilt and betrayal were enormous. I readied my soul for its fate – to be fattened, savoured, and slowly eaten by *Balor*, a malign ancient Irish spirit.

The wind dropped. "Come with me, Conor," a female voice said from behind. "This is not your destiny."

Startled, I steadied myself on the tip of the stone

and turned. Before me was a hooded figure dressed head-to-toe in a black cloak, standing on the opposite end of the stone.

Balor was silent. Jonesy stood, motionless as a statue. Everything seemed trapped in an unnatural stillness where time itself had ceased to move.

Two ivory-white hands appeared from the cloak. They had intricately woven gold rings on each finger, and her forearms were adorned with thick gold bands engraved with silver spirals. Slowly, elegantly, she raised her hands and swept back the hood. The inside glowed emerald green, creating a halo of light that shaded her face and reflected on an interlaced gold band about her forehead.

"Am I dead?" I asked.

"You are not."

"Are you here for my soul?"

"I am not."

"Are you an angel?"

"I am not." She stretched out her left arm. Its white skin radiated against the black velvet-like cloak. "Take my hand. Come?"

"Are you from beyond the ethereal gate?"

"In a manner of speaking."

"Are you real?"

"I am real. Come, time is pressing, take my hand."

I looked at her open palm. It was without blemish.

I then looked at the waves below. They were no longer dancing but smashing and crashing with monstrous anger. It was like a cauldron of malevolent creatures enraged that my soul had not slipped into their demonic depths.

I reached for her hand. As soon as our fingers touched a tingle ran up my arm, down my spine and through my body.

She gripped my hand firmly and led me off the stone.

"Who are you?" I asked, pulling, half-heartedly, against the force of her will.

"There will be time for words later," she said, without looking back. "We must go quickly."

"Where are you taking me?"

She pivoted and put a finger to shushed lips. "We must leave this place without delay. You should have heeded Finn's warning."

Her face was serenely beautiful, like a Greek sculpture, and her skin like the finest porcelain. I only got a fleeting glimpse before she tightened her grip and quickly turned away. "Come," she said. "Do not let go of my hand."

"No!" *Balor* roared, incandescent with rage, as though he had only just recognised a great deception. "You deceitful whore! *Striapach!* You have broken the Treaty. I will not stand for it. You will pay! You will pay!

CHAPTER 18

Outside the walls of the Dún, her pace lessened, and we followed a narrow path through the fissures until it ended abruptly at one of the island's ubiquitous rock walls. Standing side by side, she loosened her grip, and as our fingers slipped apart, I immediately felt the loss of her touch. As if aware of our close proximity, she stepped back, gathering her cloak over sculpted shoulders. Beneath, seamless black fabric clung to a svelte body—shaped not by labour, but by ethereal design. Her bare arms were pale and statued. My gaze lingered, overcome by her presence.

You're going to get caught ogling her, I thought, quickly averting my eyes altogether.

"We are now safe," she said. "What words did you wish to ask?" Tongue-tied, I raised my eyebrows and pretended to consider her question.

"Conceivably," she said, not waiting for a reply, "you need warmth before answers. Your teeth are chattering."

"No, I'm OK." Unlike the previous night, I was sure about not taking warming substances from strange strangers. "Who are you?"

"Saving you from the water and losing you to the air would be an act of folly." She squinted, ever so slightly, and her porcelain skin creased at the corners of her sky-blue eyes. "Speaking metaphorically."

I think she thought she had made a joke and I smiled.

"Please, put this around you," she said, sweeping auburn curls from her face while offering me a cloak, identical to her own, draped over her outstretched arm. "It will keep you warm."

I wanted to say, *where did that come from?* Instead, I said, "Thank you."

Her face seemed familiar, like an actor or personality who was lodged in my subconscious. "You saved my life."

"It was my duty. No—that is incorrect. It was my pleasure. My words are clumsy, but they will improve."

"OK. But who are you?"

"My name is *Onóraigh*." Her accent was unusual, Connacht with a Scandinavian overtone, wrapped in aristocratic authority.

"*Onóraigh?* Are you the one Jonesy's demon was shouting about?"

She tightened her lips, her eyes sparkling with apparent satisfaction. "Yes. Your cloak—please, put it on."

It was lighter than silk, and when I placed it around my shoulders, I couldn't believe its warmth. Mystified, I had to ask again. "Who are you? Where do you come from?"

She inclined her head, and with fox-like curiosity watched my eyes. "I come from a place beyond the western twilight." She smiled. "Beyond your ethereal gateway. I am the daughter of *Fírinne,* the one we call Truth, and direct descendant of *Beatha,* a giver of Life. It is with sincerity that I reveal myself to you. I am, what you might call, a Princess of the *Tuatha Dé Dannan,* which means the tribe of the Goddess Dannan."

Her eyes twinkled with knowing and she turned the palm of her right hand skyward, whereupon there was a clap of thunder with a lightning bolt that flashed above our heads.

"I am not of human origin." Her eyes were now complex, fathomless. "We have met before."

"Where?"

"For the first time, in the portal of Poulnabrone."

"Last night? Were you with *Faebar and Biróg*?"

"I was not." She smiled fondly, giving a hint of some past meeting, but I couldn't grasp the link.

"I don't remember."

"When you were a child. Your friends were calling your name. You touched my spiritual being with the outside of your fingers. It was I who touched your lips and opened your breath."

"I don't understand. You were the silver light in the Dolmen?"

"We can take many forms, but our fundamental being is a form of ethereal energy that is not normally perceptible to humans. Unless we wish it."

"I don't understand. Wait… I do. I remember your eyes. You were the skinhead girl. Red Hugh's friend. McDonald's."

"That is correct. But we do not always manifest in human form, nor are we gender specific. We can take any form. I was also the rose bush who chastened *An Cailleach Dubh*, and the fox who nudged you from stupor. We have met many times. Would you prefer I took another form?"

"No." She was stunningly beautiful. But I didn't have the nerve to say it.

"How you look is not the problem."

"Good. I find human females interesting beings."

"Are you another delusion, like *An Cailleach Dubh*, that's my problem?"

"I am not an illusion, delusion, or dream."

"Would you go away and let me be, if I asked you?"

"This is not a course I wish to take until your mind is settled. Do you know of the *Tuatha Dé Dannan*?"

"I know mythology says they were one of the early tribes of Ireland and had magical powers."

She said nothing, and I assumed she wanted me to continue.

"Eh, I know they defeated the *Fir Bolg* tribe, and the magical *Fomorians* were their enemy."

"What do you know of *Balor*?"

"I know he was the evil *Fomorian* leader. I know someone with the same name, nearly got me to jump off a cliff." I looked into her eyes for affirmation but could only see twinkling sapphires of curiosity and it made me lose my train of thought. "Eh, am I right?"

"You are not incorrect, nor are you correct, for it is human mythology." Her cheeks dimpled and I think there was a flicker of mockery about her lips. "It is sufficient knowledge for the moment."

"Do I amuse you?" I wasn't in the mood to be the butt of her humour, regardless of her origin.

"Yes."

This wasn't the answer I expected. "Well, I don't appreciate it. Someone, or something, has just frightened the life out of me, persuaded me to commit suicide, and convinced me that I am responsible for the death of my two closest friends."

"Let me explain. From the day we first met, I have prized our association. You are not a usual human being and I have at times wondered how it would be if we met in conversation. Today, my changing of form needed to be abrupt and with sudden transformation comes a delay in the calibration of human emotions, such as humour. I am with pleasure that we are conversing and this is my amusement, that is to say, I am enthused to speak with you. However, let me assure you, you are not responsible for the deaths of Emily and Finn."

"You know their names?"

"I know your life."

"No. This can't be. I can't just go from one insanity to another. I need to know. Have I gone fucking mad?"

"You have not. You have crossed in and out of a neutral space between different dimensions. Your comprehension is challenged, but your sanity is intact."

Again, this was not the answer I expected. "Eh, I don't know how to respond."

"I did not ask you a question."

Her face was so earnest, all I could do was smile.

"It is satisfying to see your heart lighten," she said, "and hopefully, it is indicative that your inclination to dwell with the sea creatures has waned."

My lips pressed tightly to stop an amused grin, and I nodded. "It has."

"Are you hungry? Tired?"

"Yes. Both." I was exhausted.

"Let us rest by a fire and roast a salmon."

She gathered a pile of rocks and from her hand

dropped a ball of fire. Within seconds, the rocks glowed red with heat and flame. Beside the fire was a large salmon.

"Please," she said, "sit. Your cloak will cushion the ground."

I did as she suggested and it was like sitting on a luxurious mattress. "You do magic?"

"If a dog can hear what you cannot, is it magic? An adult can lift a weight that a child cannot, is it magic? A horse can sense what you cannot, is it magic? We can do things you cannot. I can tell you truthfully, magic is in the mind of the beholder."

"I'll need to think about that one. May I ask you questions?"

"You may. The night is upon us and it is best if we settle here. All being well, there will be sufficient time for your questions before sleep steals your thoughts."

"What about Em and Finn? Are they safe?"

"They are safe. Rest assured. I delayed my intervention until I saw them pass to eternal peace."

I gave a heavy sigh, tension draining from me. *Thank God. Jesus, thank God.*

Oh my God, reason whispered, trembling. *That's brilliant. Best news ever. You did well. You stood up. You were counted. Finn would have been proud of you.*

"Thank you," I said to *Onóraigh*. Tears rising in my eyes. "Thank you. Jonesy had me believing that I betrayed them."

"Their deaths were instigated by Jonesy alone, partly to please *Balor*, and partly to vent his animosity towards you. There was no betrayal."

"Are you sure I didn't betray them? I couldn't live with that."

"I am certain of it. Jonesy is a malign and devious soul, a discontent, working at the behest of a powerful demon-lord capable of making you believe that black is white or up is down. Your honour and integrity remain unblemished; you were wholly unentangled and blameless in the deaths of Finn and Emily. Be at peace—it is not a matter that should trouble you. They are at peace because you offered to sacrifice your soul in exchange. They know it. *Balor* knows it. The Grand Council knows it. This cannot be undone. Be at peace."

"Thank God. I couldn't... You have saved us all. Are you a God?"

"I am not. Though I have been worshipped in earlier human times."

"My mind is racing. I want to ask you every question all at once."

"That would be unproductive. There is no hurry."

"Who were we hurrying from, running from?"

"*Balor*, a *Fomorian* Lord. Let me explain, I exist in one of Ireland's parallel dimensions, within which lie multiple realms. Human mythology has named the three principal realms as those of the *Tuatha Dé*, the

Fomorians, and the *Discontent Human Souls,* like Jonesy.

Each realm is fluid and has porous borders but we try not to stray beyond our reach as our realms do not coexist in harmony and any breach of territorial sovereignty could initiate serious consequences. The *Fir Bolg* were once powerful. Now they hold little sway—except that they fall under *Fomorian* protection. The human organic dimension, your dimension, also has a porous border and we can each enter your realm with impunity. There are three-times-three recognised crossing points between our dimensions, one of which is Poulnabrone, where we had our first moment of mutual awareness."

"And *Dún Dúchathair*?"

"No. You were lured to *Dún Dúchathair*. It is part of the *Fir Bolg* realm and under the protection of the *Fomorians*. It is a place the *Tuatha Dé* have agreed not to enter. The *Fomorians* are formidable adversaries, they utilize the destructive powers of nature and are the personification of chaos, darkness, death, blight, and drought. Thankfully, they are not sophisticated and it is with this weakness we arm ourselves against their might."

"Why did you enter the *Dún,* if it is not allowed?"

Her eyes blinked slowly. "The why, begins with *An Cailleach Dubh*. She is *Fomorian* and chooses to live between realms. A vulnerable choice—yet ideal for her favourite vice, catching human souls. A depraved practice not covered by legal covenant. Consequently, I was within my rights to subdue her. However, the display of my energies created a ripple through the dimensions and *Balor* became aware of your presence."

"Why does he want my soul so badly?"

"You are *meascán-ghéineas*."

"What?"

"Mixed lineage. Hybrid. The genes of Dannan rest in your soul."

"Eh... can you explain that?"

"Certainly. Your twelve-times great-grandfather, *Donough Mac Cárthaigh*, a great Irish leader, is the product of a Human-Dannan union. Hence, your soul is highly valued by *Balor*. It would be a great prize for him."

"You're kidding me?"

"I am not. It is what your grandfather O'Brien and Red Hugh saw in your face."

"Are they eh...?"

"*Meascán-ghéineas?* No. Your Grandfather O'Brien was human. It was his Irish warrior heart that recognised the uniqueness of your soul. Red Hugh is of the *Tuatha Dé*, —a visionary, a negotiator, by your measure."

"Jesus," I said, trying to take in the incredibility of it all.

"No." She gave a broad smile. "He is of a different mixed lineage."

I laughed heartily at her unexpected humour. "Very funny. It explains a lot about Red Hugh. Is he well?"

She grinned, pleased with my laughter. "I am thankfully adjusting to my human persona. They are well."

"Was my father, eh, a *meascán-ghéineas*?"

"Yes. All of your line, male and female, for twelve human generations."

"Did he know?"

"I cannot say. I have no knowledge of it. It was serendipity that brought us together in the Poulnabrone portal. Otherwise, who knows your fate?"

"*Balor's* dinner?"

"It is a possibility, not a certainty."

"Does the... eh... Dannan part of my lineage, explain my dreams and openness to otherworldly things?"

"Possibly, not necessarily. However, you are likely susceptible to unintentional crossings of dimensions."

"Why does Jonesy hate me? I hit him once, when we were children, maybe twice. But he was the bully. At least, I think he was."

"He was a malevolent child with a black heart. His

hatred for you is rooted in the lineage of his soul. In your year 1642, *Donough Mac Cárthaigh* humiliated and outwitted Henry Jones in the eyes of his idol and master, Oliver Cromwell. Enraged, Jones swore eternal revenge on *Donough Mac Cárthaigh* and his entire bloodline. It was ill-fated that you and Jonesy came to the attention of *Balor* at the same time."

"I can't believe that such an answer actually makes sense. Can you tell me about the *Tuatha Dé Dannan*?"

"Certainly. To adopt your words, 'it is a long story.' However, I will start with the fundamentals. There is no life cycle in our realm. There is no birth or death, but an evolving of one ancestral energy. I am my origin and will be my end. Our concept of time is not linear and yet there are marked stages in the evolution of our ancestral line, such as *Beatha, Fírinne,* and *Onóraigh*. Life, Truth, and Honour. Also, something that intrigues humans; gender does not exist. Consequently, I am not a princess in the human meaning of the word. I am the single descendant, within a long chain of single descendants, in a highly esteemed ancestral line."

She's not female? I thought, confused and disappointed.

"And here I am," I said, feeling the need to be avant-garde but sounding decidedly flippant. "Mentally, emotionally, and spiritually lost, talking to a nonbinary energy of the *Tuatha Dé Dannan*."

"What is nonbinary?"

I wasn't really sure. "Not gender specific."

Her eyebrows furrowed. "I have manifested as a gender-specific human female."

"Maybe I should have said gender-fluid."

"Your no-gender description is immaterial to me." Her words were tetchy, and her tone dangerously wounded.

"I hope I haven't upset you."

She straightened her back and, poised to stand, an enormous cloud billowed around her. Her eyes dilated to saucers of stormy sky. "Rest assured, I am of the Tuatha Dé. And be I binary, nonbinary, fluid, or ethereal—I am diminished by none."

"Eh," I stammered, taken aback, "I don't doubt it for a second. I think maybe..."

"Humans are consumed by their own limited perceptions of sexuality and gender and yet, besides the physical attributes, gender fluidity is determined by your socially constructed roles, behaviours, and activities. The rigidity of your gendered society is deeply ingrained with religiously thwarted perceptions dictated by supposedly celibate narrow-minded elderly males."

Jesus Christ. Say something quick.

"I think you might have misinterpreted my words. I agree with everything you've said. I didn't mean to diminish you, in any way. Eh, I suppose, I'm self-conscious of my human inadequacies, my failures, and

I think I wanted to appear… sapient. To impress you."

"Sapient?"

"Intelligent. I don't want you to see me as limited or coming from a single subjective view. I'm in awe of your strength and confidence and the femininity of your female manifestation. The working of your mind is intimidating, and you are the most beautiful being I've ever seen. So, if I've upset you, forgive me. If I haven't, let's put this conversation behind us. My approach to life is live and let live, regardless of gender, religion, ethnicity, or origin, provided the vulnerable are not harmed."

"It is an admirable approach, and you have correctly highlighted my misinterpretation, which was likely due to my unfiltered human emotions. I suspect there may be an additional dynamic, a sensitivity, to our seminal connection that I have not encountered before. You touch me emotionally. Let us put my misinterpretation behind us."

"Yes, let's do that," I said, greatly relieved.

I touch her emotionally. The words bounced around my head like a rubber ball. *Jesus Christ. I touch her emotionally. What does that mean?*

"You have another question?" she said.

Tell her that she touches you emotionally too, reason teased. *That you're completely smitten.*

"Eh," I said, "are we safe here? *Balor* sounded very angry. Our fire must be visible for miles."

Coward.

"We are safe. The Covenant of Peace and War forbids other dimensional hostilities in the Human Realm." Her tummy made a rumbling sound and she lifted her eyebrows with surprise. "Is it acceptable that we momentarily suspend our discourse? My human appetite for organic sustenance has awakened?"

"Yes, of course. I'm hungry too."

The salmon was delicious, washed down with honey-sweetened spring water. We continued chatting and I learned she had manifested in a form that she believed would be "endearing to my perceptions."

Tell her it's very endearing.

"I used to dream about meeting the people of Dannan," I said, "when I was a child, mostly."

"The timing of our meeting is unfortunate, yet the outcome is pleasing."

"Yes. Very." We smiled and I felt our auras touched in harmony. But the comfort of the cloak and the heat of the fire was stealing my thoughts. "Is it OK if I sleep for a while?"

"It is. May your thoughts flow from the mountain to the meandering river and the still lake beyond."

"Is that a Tuatha De Dannan saying?"

"It is. A prayerful wish."

When I awoke the fire was at my back and I was facing a landscape more static than a picture, there were huge stars in a crystal-clear sky looking almost near enough to touch. I couldn't see the moon, but it must have been behind me because everywhere was immersed in soothing spectral light. My mood was light, as though I had morphed with nature's serenity. Yet, I was contemplative, and fully aware that this was not a normal place for me to be.

Are you alright? Reason asked.

Yes.

So, what happens now?

I don't know. I'm half afraid to turn around, in case she's really there.

Or in case she's not there.

Yeah, both.

Are we going home?

I don't feel like moving. I'm nice and warm. I don't want to think about yesterday, about Em and Finn. It's too sad. Or about trying to commit suicide. Or... the insanity of Jonesy and Balor.

All right, don't think about it. You've been through the mill and probably need a rest.

Is she real?

It felt like she was.

Do you think she's still there?

I don't know.

I turned onto my other side and at once felt the warmth of the undiminished fire on my face. She was still there, eyes closed, looking aristocratically complacent in an aura of self-assurance.

"Have you finished your sleep?" she asked. Her tone was soft and warm but her eyes remained closed and not a single muscle twitched in her motionless body.

"Yes. The cloak is really comfortable. My thoughts less so."

In one slow effortless move she sat upright, crossed her legs, and let the cloak fall from her shoulders before tying her luxuriant hair in a tight ponytail. This gave me a chance to study her heavenly face of porcelain skin, her straight regal nose, and her exuberant eyes. All life was in her eyes. They overflowed with experiences I couldn't begin to imagine.

She noticed me watching her and smiled, slowly, until her face radiated with affection. "It has been said in your world, 'that a troubled mind can know no rest'. We need not tarry. The sun shall be up presently, I can quench the fire and we can wander to the rain pool. It is a generous place for peace of mind."

"I like it here. Can we stay a while longer?"

"Certainly."

"Eh... I have a problem."

"Can I help you solve it?"

"I guess. My problem is that I don't know if you're real, or if I've gone completely mad. If I've gone mad, I'd prefer to keep my psychosis here, to myself. Do you understand?"

"I understand. You need not believe in my existence." Her eyes looked away from me. "When your mind becomes more settled, I will depart your company."

"No, that's not what I mean. I've offended you. I mean… I must believe you're real, I'm talking to you. I suppose I'm afraid to admit that I believe you are real."

"You have not offended me. Thankfully, my sensitivities are not so fragile. Even if you had, the offence would emanate and dwell in my own expectations. Requiring no apology from you."

"OK. Eh, that sounds a bit Buddhist?"

"I don't know Buddhist. Is it a God?"

"Eh, sort of… a religion."

"Human religion and psychosis are not dissimilar. They have no basis in your reality. Yet one is sanity and the other is not. Insanity is a perception, a subjective point of view and there are as many points of view as there are humans. Yet, as a species, you crave the pretence of conformity, outside of which is madness. It is one of the human things that baffle us."

"I'm sorry, but I'm not really up to a philosophical discussion at the moment. Assuming you are real, why are you...? How were you at the school dance? Are you my guardian angel or protector?"

"I am not. When first we met in Poulnabrone there was a seminal connection between our two energies and while this type of connection is not unheard of, neither is it commonplace. It means when your energy is going to cease, my energy is alerted and I am drawn to counter the cessation."

"Do you mean if I'm going to die you appear and save me?"

"Only when death is not your destiny."

"Who alerts you?"

"Intuition."

"Do you know my destiny?"

"I do not. I am alerted if your pending demise is not your given destiny."

"My given destiny? Are you not just interfering in my destiny? If I had died at the dance or jumped off the cliff surely that would be my destiny."

"You have free will, you can overrule your given destiny and I will not try to alter your free will, provided it is grounded in your own stable thought process. You did not wish to die at the dance, nor did you wish to die in *Dún An Cailleach Dubh*, and it is my sense that you did not wish to die on the cliff. However, if after the settling of your mind you wished to throw your person from the cliff, I would say goodbye to you and mourn your loss."

“I’m not going to jump off the cliff and thank you for saving me all those times.”

She stood unexpectedly, with the ease and grace of an ethereal deity. “It pleases me to hear your aversion to the cliff. Saving you is my great pleasure and given destiny.”

I joined her, standing less gracefully. “What is my given destiny?”

“I do not know. You have found your light, your Irish spirit. You have made peace with your soulmates. Your mind is settled. The future is yours.”

She placed her hand on my shoulder, and with a lump in my throat I realised it was the beginning of our farewell. My mind quickly adjusted to the future. “It seems crazy,” I said, “that I’m thinking of my future in the real world, the human realm. I have to book the ferry, collect my car, sort my divorce!”

“There is a ferry to the mainland in three hours.”

Three hours!

There’s so much left to say, to ask.

Suddenly, I was shy. “Eh, I can’t thank you enough, for everything.”

She nodded her acceptance, stoically.

“Will you come to the ferry with me?”

“I will not. For we also feel sadness.” She took my hand in a formal shake. “Goodbye, Con.”

“Will you visit me?” I felt the situation was getting

away, ending too quickly. “Eh, not only when I’m going to die.”

“Certainly. It would be another great pleasure for me.”

“Really?!”

“Yes. I needed you to ask. We are slow to offer that which should be asked for.”

“Jesus Christ, I thought I was being dumped. OK. So, will you please come to visit me?”

“On one condition.”

“What?”

She smiled radiantly. “That you also visit me, on the shore of freedom, emancipation, and peace.”

“Really?!” Is that possible?”

“Certainly. Dannan genes rest in your soul.”

The End

IRISH GLOSSARY

(In order of appearance in text.)

Maith an buachaill. English: Good boy.

Bígí ciúin. English: Be quiet.

A haon, a do, a tri. English: One, two, three.

A ceathair, a cúig, a sé, a seacht, a hocht, a naoi, a deich. English: Four, five, six, seven, eight, nine, ten.

Begi cúramach. English: Be careful.

Lámha suas. English: Hands up.

Buachaillí. English: Boys.

Anois! Go tapaidh! English: Now! Quickly!

Ciúnas. English: Quiet.

Uimhir a hocht. English: Number eight.

Tir gan teanga, tír gan anam. English: A country without a language is a country without a soul.

Fine Gaelers. English: Supporters of the Fine Gael political party who supported the division of Ireland in 1922.

Sinn Féin. English: A republican political party who

never agreed to the division of Ireland.

Ógra Shinn Féin. English: The youth wing of Sinn Féin.

Craic. English: Fun, banter and laughter.

Ar dheis dé go raibh a hanam dílis. English: May her faithful soul rest at the right hand of God.

Ceart go leor. English: Alright.

Óglaigh na hÉireann. English: Volunteers of Ireland / Irish Republican Army, IRA.

Réidh! English: Ready!

Eirígí! English: Raise! (weapons).

Seasaigí! English: Stand!

Cuir! English: Fire!

Cath Fionntrá. English: Battle of Ventry.

Tuatha Dé Dannan / Tuatha Dé. English: People of the Goddess Dannan / God people.

Emain Macha. English: Navan Fort.

Maith an fear. English: Good man.

Éirinn go Brách. English: Ireland forever.

Is fearr cairde ná ór. English: Friends are better than gold.

Leabhar Gabhála. English: The Book of Invasions.

Fomorians, Nemedians, Fir Bolg, Tuatha Dé, and Milesians. English: Names of mythological Irish tribes.

Céad Míle Fáilte. English: A hundred thousand welcomes / traditional welcome.

Poitín. English: alcoholic drink / illicitly distilled for over 300 years until 1997.

Cailleach Dubh. English: Black hag / dark witch.

Dún. English: Fort.

Dún Dúchathair. English: Black Fort / fort of the black stoned city.

Maighe Tuireadh. English: Moytura, place of two definitive mythological battles.

Cabhair liom. English: Help me.

Níl an Béarla agam. English: I don't have the English.

Tá tú sábháilte. English: You are safe.

Bord Fáilte. English: Tourist board / welcoming board.

Tar Isteach. English: Come In.

Fáilte isteach English: Welcome in / Come in.

Fan nóiméad. English: Wait a moment.

Ná habair é. English: Don't mention it.

An Bhean Sí. English: The Banshee / fairy woman.

Labhair an fhírinne agus beidh anam slán. English: Speak the truth, and the soul will be safe.

Go ndéana Dia trócaire ar a hanam. English: May God have mercy on her soul.

Slán go fóill. English: Goodbye for now.

Ó ghrása na Cailleach go greim an deamhain. English: From the caress of the hag to the grip of the demon.

Lia Sóis. English: Stone of Solace.

Striapach. English: Whore.

Beatha. English: Life.

Fírinne. English: Truth.

Onóraigh. English: Honour.

Meascán-ghéineas. English: Genetic-mix / hybrid.

ABOUT THE AUTHOR

Frank, a native of Dublin, Ireland, comes from a proud working-class background. Holding degrees in History, Economics, and Business from Trinity College Dublin and Dublin City University, his deep love for Ireland is woven into both his life and work. Growing up in Dublin during the 30 years of the *Troubles* in Northern Ireland profoundly shaped his views on liberty, equality, and fraternity, as well as his outlook on romance and love. Frank is happily married and a proud father.

www.ingramcontent.com/pod-product-compliance
Ingram Content Group UK Ltd.
Pitfield, Milton Keynes, MK11 3LW, UK
UKHW020149191125
465164UK00005B/98

9 781919 247007